Every woman goes throug
Just not... th

SUDDENLY PSYCHIC

Robin Brannon was a normal wife, mom, and antique-shop owner until a brush with death turned her day-to-day life upside down. Now she and her two best friends are seeing things that belong in a fantasy novel. Ghosts. Visions. Omens of doom. Nothing that belongs in the peaceful mountain town they call home.

Added to that, Robin's marriage is on the rocks, her grandmother's health is failing, her mother is driving away the customers at her shop, her teenage daughter refuses to get her driver's license, and her left knee aches every darn morning.

Robin doesn't have the time, energy, or knees to unearth the secrets buried at the bottom of Glimmer Lake, but fate doesn't seem to care. Some secrets are just *dying* to be exposed.

Suddenly Psychic is stand-alone paranormal women's fiction and the first book in the Glimmer Lake series by *USA Today* best seller, Elizabeth Hunter, author of the Elemental Mysteries.

Elizabeth Hunter actually makes me look forward to growing older, especially if comes with these awesomely fun psychic perks. Her new paranormal women's fiction series is a truly fun, entertaining read!

— MICHELLE M. PILLOW, NEW YORK TIMES AND USA TODAY BESTSELLING AUTHOR OF THE WARLOCKS MACGREGOR SERIES

Elizabeth Hunter's books are delicious and addicting, like the best kind of chocolate. She hooked me from the first page, and her stories just keep getting better and better. Paranormal romance fans won't want to miss this exciting author!

— THEA HARRISON, NYT BESTSELLING AUTHOR OF THE ELDER RACES SERIES

This book made me laugh...it was pure and real and I wanted to be a part of what these ladies were doing so badly!!

— THIS LITERARY LIFE

Refreshing. That is the word the came into my mind over and over again while reading this book.

— MAEGS IN WONDERLAND

I think I've become Suddenly Psychic after reading this book, as I just KNOW I am going to love the Glimmer Lake series.

— KIMBERLY, GOODREADS REVIEWER

To all the rockstars out there
Laughing at the years,
Taking all our vitamins, and
Showing the world how it's done,
This one is for you.

SUDDENLY PSYCHIC

GLIMMER LAKE BOOK ONE

ELIZABETH HUNTER

Suddenly Psychic
Copyright © 2019
Elizabeth Hunter
ISBN: 978-1-941674-51-2

Cover: Damonza
Content Editor: Amy Cissell, Cissell Ink
Line Editor: Anne Victory
Proofreader: Linda, Victory Editing

Recurve Press LLC
PO Box 4034
Visalia, California 93278
USA

CHAPTER 1

*R*obin Brannon woke up three minutes before her alarm. In the sleepy, drifting moments before the alarm forced her to life, a persistent question shoved itself into her mind.

Is this the rest of my life?

The question had been haunting her since her forty-fifth birthday earlier that year.

Is this my life?

Really? This? Every day until I die?

She stretched her right arm across the bed, but Mark was already gone.

The alarm went off, and she quickly tapped her phone screen to get rid of the noise. Her daughter, Emma, had reset the alarm to the La's "There She Goes" a few weeks before because it was "so retro."

Whatever. The song made her happy, but she'd never admit it to Emma. She swung her legs over the side of the bed and extended up and over, bending down to stretch her back and spread her toes on the warm, honey-toned wood that filled their house in the Sierra Nevada Mountains.

Empty bed.

Soon to be empty house.

Emma would be gone the following fall, and then it would just be Robin and Mark.

Mark's whereabouts weren't a mystery. Not much was a mystery when you'd been married for twenty-three years. He'd be down in his basement office, working online at his job in San Francisco. Though the city was hundreds of miles away, Mark had been telecommuting in one form or another since their kids were young.

Robin pulled her hair into a quick bun, then threw on a pair of leggings and a sports bra before stepping into her favorite running shoes and lacing them tightly.

These days telecommuting was common, but when she'd first told her parents that they'd be moving back to her home-town in the mountains because Mark could work from home, the idea had been revolutionary.

Does this mean they're going to fire him?

How will he go to meetings?

Is this because of Y2K?

She bounced on her toes to warm up. The physical thera-pist had outlawed running, but Robin still needed the outdoors. Power walking with a knee brace would have to take the place of five-mile runs.

She paused in the upstairs hallway to make sure she heard Emma getting ready. She passed Austin's empty room and wondered if he'd scheduled morning classes for the semester.

Not your problem, Robin.

She unlocked the front door, stretched a little in the driveway, then started walking down the hill, breathing in the cold Sierra Nevada air.

It filled her up. Lifted her. The mountain air was such an essential part of her she sometimes felt like she couldn't breathe when she was at lower elevations.

She thought about headphones, but that morning she was craving silence. Unfortunately, silence made her mind drift.

Am I a bad mother for not following up on Austin's schedule?

Austin was at the state university near Mark's parents in Chico, and Robin was legally allowed to no longer care if he ate a balanced breakfast. Or scheduled his classes sensibly. Or slept through his alarm.

Do I care if I'm a bad mother?

She was probably still supposed to care about all that on a maternal level, but getting Austin out of the house had been such a relief she couldn't bring herself to feel guilty.

Robin had needed a break.

She loved her son—she *really* did—but he was *work*. He always had been. She'd almost passed on having kid two because kid one was such a pain in the butt.

Thank God she didn't, because Emma was night-and-day different from her brother. Robin had sent Austin off to college with a wave and a happy heart. When Emma left next year, it might break her. It would just be Robin and Mark, married for twenty-three years, parents of two successful kids, and...

What? What else were they? A software programmer and the owner of an antique shop?

Is this the rest of my life?

Really? This? Every day until I die?

Her legs were pumping and her lungs started to burn.

So did her eyes.

What the hell is wrong with you, Robin?

She dashed the tears from her eyes. She wasn't a crier. She was famously immune to crying. She hadn't cried during *Steel Magnolias*. *Beaches* made her roll her eyes. She was forbidden from watching chick flicks with her two best friends for that very reason.

Robin needed to get out of her head. She reached for the phone in the pocket of her leggings and realized a notification had popped onto the screen at seven a.m.

Monica Velasquez 45th Birthday—All Day

"Shit!" How had she forgotten it was Monica's birthday? Monica had lost her husband to a heart attack six months before, and this would be her first birthday without Gilbert making her Queen for the Day.

She tapped on her phone icon and went to her favorites list, touching the top contact.

It rang and Val picked up seconds later, clearing her throat before she spoke. "Why are you calling so early?"

"You remember Monica's birthday is today?"

"Yeah, of course. We're going out tonight, remember?"

"Was that in the group text?"

"No, stupid. We're surprising her, remember? Her son's taking her out for lunch today. The rest of the kids are coming up this Saturday for dinner, and I texted you three days ago that we needed to take her out tonight."

"I didn't text you back?"

Val sniffed. "Are you out walking?"

"Of course I am." Robin turned the corner, waving at her

neighbor as he moved the trash cans out to the curb. "Are you still in bed?"

"The boys can make their own breakfast. I was up late reading." Val must have taken the phone away from her mouth because the next words were muffled. "Jackson! Andy! Are you getting dressed?"

Robin couldn't hear anything, but she assumed Val's two boys had answered in the affirmative because her friend came back on the line.

"Anyway, you probably thought about texting me and then forgot. Don't pretend you have anything more important than this. We're taking her out. We absolutely have to take her out tonight."

"Of course we're taking her out." Robin made a quick decision as she turned back toward the house. "I'll even drive so you and Monica can have all the wine, okay?"

"Sounds good to me." Val sighed deeply. "Fuck congenital heart defects."

"I know." Robin's heart ached every time she thought about Monica's husband. "Damn, I miss Gil."

If there was a dream husband who embodied all rom-com boyfriends, it had been Gilbert Velasquez. Movie star handsome, Gil had been a fireman with the state. He was a certified hero who had medals and got choked up when he thanked his wife in speeches.

Robin would have been jealous of Monica and Gil's marriage, but she was too damn happy Monica had such an amazing husband. He'd been a stellar dad and an amazing friend too.

"Okay, when do we want to pick her up?" Robin blinked hard. "Seven?"

"Yeah, that works. I already checked with Jake. He told her he's cooking a special dinner for her tonight, so she doesn't have any other plans."

"We need to remember to text her happy birthday though. Remember when Mark surprised me for my thirtieth?"

Val started laughing. "You were so pissed."

"I thought all my friends had completely forgotten about me on my birthday, Val. Of course I was pissed."

"Mark's the one who told us—"

"I know. I remember. Let's just make sure we call Monica, okay?" She finished her regular circuit and saw her house peeking through the trees. "Talk to you later."

"See ya."

Robin was panting when she reached the kitchen door on the side of the house. She opened it and immediately yelled, "Emma?"

"In the kitchen, Mom."

Robin walked through the mudroom and hung her sweatshirt on one of the pegs in the wall. "You almost ready?"

Emma was sitting at the counter, eating a bowl of cereal and staring at her phone with a smile on her face. She glanced up. "Yeah."

"Anything going on today?"

"Not much." She slid her phone into her backpack. "I have a group project for physics though. Can I go to the library with everyone after school?"

"Who's in the group?"

Emma narrowed her eyes. "Uh... Heather Bix. Jordan Havers. Some guy named Christian who I don't really know. I was going to ride with Heather though."

"She a good driver?"

"Mom, it's like five minutes to drive to the library."

Robin pursed her lips. "This wouldn't be an issue if you'd just get your license."

Emma sighed deeply. "I will. This year. Before I go to college, I promise."

Robin glanced at her daughter's cereal bowl and back-pack. Then the clock. "Clean up. We should go."

She heard Mark on the stairs. Her husband walked through the door and straight to their daughter.

"Morning, sweetie. Did you say you have a physics project?"

"It's nothing big." She lifted her cheek and her father kissed it. "Like a 'Physics in the News' project. It's not even an experiment or anything. We just need to make a poster."

Robin stared at Mark. He was nearly six foot, which she liked because she was almost five foot ten. He was slim and still had a runner's build even if he was starting to get a bit of a belly. They'd met on the track team in college, and she'd fallen in love with his humor, his persistence, and his kind smile. Plus she couldn't lie, the sex was *really* good.

And twenty-three years later, she woke up every morning alone in bed.

Mark hadn't even looked at her. He hadn't said good morning. Hadn't even glanced her direction.

Am I a ghost in my own house?

He grabbed the handle of the coffeepot and refilled his mug. Then he kissed the top of Emma's head and said, "Have a good day, honey."

Robin watched him disappear down the stairs.

Really? This? Every day until I die?

She didn't have time to think about it. She grabbed her keys and nodded toward the door. "Time to go."

———

SHE GRABBED a coffee at Val's café after she dropped Emma off at school; then she headed to Glimmer Lake Curios, the antique shop she'd taken over from her mother.

Robin had gone to school to be an artist. She'd never intended to follow in her mother's footsteps, but her mother had run the shop successfully in the quirky lake town for decades. Both of Robin's kids were in school when Grace was ready to retire, and the timing made sense, so Robin became the proprietor of a store that sold everything from antique desks to glass art to decorative horseshoes.

She told herself that working at the shop would give her more time to work on her own art, but she never did.

Robin pulled into the parking lot and parked her trusty Subaru in the space nearest the log house her parents had meticulously restored. As a child, she'd lived in the upstairs until her father, Philip, could afford a newer house in one of the developments on the edge of town.

Now the upstairs and downstairs were filled to the brim with carefully curated antiques, designer accents, and local artists' wares.

Cabin chic, not cabin kitsch.

Glimmer Lake was a year-round vacation town. In the summer, the cool waters of the lake attracted swimmers, boaters, and anglers from the valleys at the base of the Sierra Nevada. They came to escape the baking summers in the lowlands and to enjoy the crisp air. In the winter, heavy snow made the lake town a destination for skiers, sledders, and those looking for the rare white Christmas in California.

It was four hours from San Francisco and only a little bit farther from Los Angeles. The town that occupied the banks of Glimmer Lake had replaced the old logging and mining town of Grimmer, which had been flooded in the 1940s to create a reservoir that could serve the thirsty population boom in Southern California.

It had been Robin's grandfather who suggested changing the name to the much more pleasant Glimmer Lake. Grimmer now lay under 120 feet of water, a ghost town looking up at happy vacationers and locals alike.

Robin walked up the steps of her store to the wide porch and swept off the scattered debris of pine needles and bark the wind had blown in, then she unlocked the door and flipped the OPEN sign over. She wouldn't get a visitor for at least an hour because people on vacation slept in.

Which was fine. Robin liked quiet mornings, and she really needed caffeine.

She set her coffee on the counter and pulled out her phone, then touched the second number on her favorites list and waited for the line to ring.

"Hello?"

"Happy birthday to you. Happy birthday to you," Robin sang. "Happy birthday, dear wonderful-woman-who-is-like-a-sister-to-me." She took a breath. "Happy birthday to you!"

Monica was laughing by the time she finished. "Thank you. You must have had your coffee."

"Drinking it right now, my friend."

"How's your knee?"

"Eh." Robin flexed it. "It's fine. The same."

9

"Are you taking the apple cider vinegar?"

"I don't think it really does anything, Monica."

"No, you just have to keep taking it." She heard her friend moving through her kitchen. "I'm telling you, it helps."

"I'll keep taking it." Robin nearly asked what Monica was wearing to go out that night until she remembered it was a surprise. "So, I hear Jake is making a special dinner for you tonight."

"That boy is so sweet," Monica said. "I know he's between apartments right now—"

You mean between girlfriends who let him freeload.

"—but he is so helpful around the house. He cooks. He changed the oil in my car yesterday. He's such a good boy."

He's a spoiled boy. "He loves his mama. He better." Jake did love his mama. He also probably felt guilty that he'd been freeloading, but working at the marina didn't pay that much, and Jake seemed incapable of moving more than a few miles from his childhood home.

"Well, I hope you enjoy your dinner." Robin needed to change the subject or she was going to end up spilling about their girls' night out. "I'm going to give you that dresser for your birthday, by the way."

"It's a nine-hundred-dollar dresser, Robin. Don't even think about it."

"It's been sitting in that corner for over two years. It's practically taken root. I don't want it anymore, and you love it." She heard the bell ring over the door and the creak of old hinges. "I'll call Jake to come pick it up. Bye-gotta-go." She blew a kiss into the phone and ended the call.

"Hello?" She walked out from behind the counter. "Can I help you?"

She walked to the door of the shop, but there was no one there. Maybe whoever it was had peeked in and left? Robin looked out to the parking lot and saw no new cars. No pedestrians.

She frowned. "Weird."

Robin shrugged and walked back to the counter. It was hardly the first time the door had blown open and hit the bell. It happened pretty regularly.

"Because old houses, that's why." She logged on to her computer and checked her online sales page and her retailer accounts. She sold as much via the internet these days as she did in the store, but since her family already owned the building and the furniture needed to be kept somewhere, it made sense to keep the shop even with the extra overhead. After all, if the shop wasn't open, what would Robin do to pass the time?

She responded to an email from Emma's guidance counselor.

She texted her mom about visiting her grandma Helen that afternoon.

At noon she forgot to eat lunch while she was helping a couple from Marin County choose between two dining tables for their vacation home. She grabbed a granola bar after they left.

By two, she locked up the shop so she could go visit Grandma Helen.

This is my life.

Robin climbed in her trusty Subaru to drive the five miles to Russell House, the enormous family home that overlooked Glimmer Lake.

This.

This is my life.

"Whoo!" Val was cackling in the back seat. "I knew we were going to surprise you!"

Monica was beaming. "I wondered why Jake was so insistent that I dress up for dinner. I was actually a little irritated with him. I'd already taken off my bra."

"Truth," Val said. "I'm glad you decided to put your knockers back in the boulder holder, because we are taking you out. There will be wine. There will be dancing. I'm going to make Robin sing karaoke at the lodge."

"Uh..." Robin navigated a sharp turn leading up to the dam. "I don't think that will be happening, but I'll be sure to gather video evidence of you two. Emma can post it on YouTube for me."

Big Creek Lodge was mostly for tourists, but they did have Thursday-night karaoke and half-price drinks, perfect for both the vacationer and the celebrating local. The only downside was the road leading up to the lodge, which was narrow, twisted, and had almost zero lights. Robin absolutely hated driving it at night.

As long as there are no drunk tourists coming down the hill, we'll be fine.

Robin listened with a smile on her face while Val and Monica chatted about their day. Val had recently shaved one side of her short hair and dyed it green. Her makeup was ruthlessly cool, and her fitted halter top showed off numerous tattoos. Monica, on the other hand, was in a dress. Monica loved wearing dresses. And lace. And ruffles. Anything soft and feminine. Her short, curvy figure looked amazing in wrap dresses, and she had a closet that took up half her bedroom.

Robin... well, she'd thrown on a pair of black pants and a leopard-print top that Val had forced on her last spring. She also had a pair of sensible shoes and a large purse. She didn't need to carry a large purse anymore; she just couldn't seem to break the habit.

Why am I always the uncoolest friend?

Val and Monica were approaching their midforties with style and attitude and way better wardrobes. They had plans and adventures mapped out. Monica was taking her daughter to Spain for the summer. Val had been approached by an investor to expand her café.

And Robin sold antique dining sets to rich couples from the Bay Area.

She had slipped out of the house without anyone even noticing. Mark and Emma had cooked dinner without her and were engrossed in a new TV series they were bingeing. They hadn't even noticed Robin saying goodbye.

A squirrel ran in front of the road and Robin tapped the brakes, certain it was too late to miss the little creature. Luckily, she didn't feel a thunk. She was a careful driver, but this road freaked her out.

Val and Monica had started singing. The lyrics to "Always Be My Baby" filled the car, and Robin glanced in the rearview mirror when Val hit a particularly painful high note.

"Robin!" Monica yelled next to her.

She glanced back at the road to see a massive white deer frozen in the middle of the road.

Her heart stopped.

Robin swerved in the darkness, letting out a single hard breath when she realized she'd avoided the deer. Then her stomach dropped when she realized there was nothing.

No deer.

No road.

Nothing but the darkness and the moon over the water.

Val screamed a second before the car nosedived into the dark water of Glimmer Lake and everything went black.

CHAPTER 2

She woke to the feeling of cold all around her. Crying and a low thunk like the sound of Mark chopping wood in the backyard.

"Robin!"

"She's not waking up."

Why was she wet? When her eyes finally blinked open, she thought she'd fallen in snow. It was white and wet.

"Robin, wake up!"

She looked to the side and nothing made sense. Val was next to Monica, but she had her feet in the air.

"Did I fall?"

Monica's face was red and wet.

Wet. Everything was wet.

It came back in a horrid rush. The deer. The road. Flying into the darkness and the crash of water around her. The white was the air bag that had exploded in her face. The wet was the car, filling quickly with water.

"Oh my God. Oh my God."

Val had crawled from the back to the front seat, bracing

herself in the middle as she thrust her legs up toward the windshield, trying to break it open.

"The doors won't open." Val kicked at the window. "I tried the windows, and they don't work either."

"Are you sure?"

"Of course I'm sure!"

The car was sealed shut. Robin tried opening the door, but the pressure of the water was too great. The window lever did nothing. They were completely immersed. She could feel them moving downhill as Val kept kicking. They'd hit the bottom of the lake and were slowly but surely rolling toward the deepest part where Grimmer Canyon had once cut through the mountains.

A scream had worked its way up from her chest and stopped in her throat as Val slapped her. "Robin!"

"Why did you slap me?"

"We cannot panic. You have to help me. What do you have in your car? We need to break the window."

Monica was crumpled against the far door, weeping and holding her arm. Her head was bleeding. "I can't feel my arm."

"The windshield scraper," Robin yelled. "Monica, get the scraper in the glove compartment. It has a pointy thing that will break the glass."

Monica moaned, "I can't feel my arm."

Val stopped kicking the windshield and reached for the glove compartment as Robin unclipped her safety belt. She needed to be able to move. As Val opened the glove box, more water poured in, making all the napkins, papers, and various receipts Robin had stuffed in there float by them and into the back seat.

The water was up to her waist.

"There's no scraper," Val said.

"It's in there."

"There's no scraper, Robin!"

"It has to be in there!"

"Maybe Mark took it out!"

"Why would he do that? It's my scraper!"

"Fuck if I know, but it's not there! Stop yelling at me!"

Monica started pounding on the car window, screaming and crying. Her hand was bloody, but none of the glass was cracked. It was all perfectly, securely sealed.

That was her Subaru. Not one single leak in the snow or rain. Ever.

Focus, Robin!

Focus.

"Okay." Robin fought back the nausea that threatened her. "Okay. We can do this. When the water fills the car, the pressure will be equalized and we'll be able to open the doors. We can swim out. We're all good swimmers."

Val started to breathe faster. "We're going deeper."

"How deep is the lake?" Monica asked, wiping her eyes. "How deep does it go?"

"I don't know," Robin said. "I can't remember. But we're all good swimmers."

She should know this. Her family had lived in Grimmer before the dam was built. She should know these things. The water pouring in was cold. So very cold. Robin knew she had to keep calm, but it might have been the hardest thing she'd ever done.

I need to live.

I need to be there for Emma and Austin.

I need to live.

Something hit the bottom of the car, making water pour in faster.

"We're stopped!" Val said. "I think we're stopped."

"It's getting higher," Monica said. "Oh my God, we're going to die."

"We're not going to die!" Robin said. "We're going to stay calm, take deep breaths while the air is in here." She started pulling at her clothes. "Take your clothes off. It'll be colder, but we don't want them to weigh us down. Monica, take off that dress."

Val didn't return to the back seat, but they all managed to remove most of their clothing. It was freezing cold, and they were sitting in their bras and panties while the car slowly filled up with water.

At least we're not moving anymore.

Robin's teeth started to chatter as the water reached her neck.

"I wanted to kill myself." Monica's voice was shaking. "I thought about taking sleeping pills after Gil died because I couldn't imagine my life without him. I thought about the future, and there was just... nothing. There was nothing without him." Her voice caught. "But I don't want to die. My kids need me."

"*We* need you," Robin said. "And we're not going to die." She grabbed shaky breaths and coughed out some water. "Monica, try your door."

Monica tried, but she couldn't budge it. "Nothing yet."

A feeling of dread began to overtake Robin. It was cold. Really cold. Her knee began to ache. She could talk a big game, but none of them swam regularly anymore. Monica did

Zumba at the community center twice a week, and Val was a biking nut. Robin couldn't even run anymore. How were they supposed to swim to the top of the lake and all the way to shore?

She looked into the black water that surrounded them and imagined them driving into the ghost town that lay at the bed of the lake. Her old Subaru drifting to the bottom and rolling silently down Main Street while the fish picked at their bones.

"I love you guys so much," Val blurted. She started to sniff. "Don't tell my kids, but I think I love you two more than anyone. I really hate most people. I kind of wish Monica and I were lesbians so we could marry each other, but I really don't know if I'd like lesbian sex, and also I think I'm still kind of in love with my ex, even though I hate him. But the sex was really good and I miss that. And I think I'm turning into my mother because I am so judgmental now, and I really hate that."

"You're not your mom, Val."

Monica laughed, sniffling at the same time. "I'd marry you if I was a lesbian." She wiped her eyes. "Actually, I wouldn't because I cannot handle how much you let laundry pile up on your sofa. That would drive me crazy."

"Oh shit." Val's shoulders convulsed. "My boys."

"Stop crying." Robin blinked back tears. "We need to be calm." The water was at her chin. "We need to be calm and focus on breathing. As soon as the water gets high enough, we're getting out of here."

"We are not going to die," Val said. "Fuck this lake. We are not going to die."

"We're not going to die." Monica tilted her chin up.

"We're not going to die."

Robin stared into the black depths of Glimmer Lake. "I don't think anyone would even notice if I died."

"What?"

"Robin, don't be ridiculous."

"I hate my life," she whispered. "I'm a zombie. I do the same thing every day. And I hate all of it. I'm nothing. Mark doesn't look at me anymore. The kids don't care. No one looks at me other than you two." The press of water against her chest forced the words out. "I hate my life, but I'm too scared to do anything to change it. That's the saddest part of all."

They were pressed against the top of the car, and if they were going to make it out, the door needed to open now.

"I'm going to try it now," she said. "As soon as I get it open, the water is going to rush in. We ready?"

Val and Monica were both crying, but they nodded.

"I love you guys." Robin nodded. "Really. I love you both so much."

She ducked under the water and reached for the handle. She tugged at it and pushed three times before she realized it was still locked. She grabbed the tip of the lock and yanked, but nothing happened. She yanked again.

Nothing. The smooth plastic only slid between her fingers.

No. She pounded on the window. NO!

She pushed up and grabbed more air before she went under again.

There. She managed to get the lock up, but when she went to open the door, it still wouldn't budge.

A quiet tapping on the window.

Robin looked up and her eyes went wide.

There was a man by the car, a dark-haired man with pale skin. He lifted a rock and pointed it at the window.

Robin didn't even think, she nodded and pushed away from the glass.

With a muffled crack, the car window broke into pieces. She and the man cleared the glass and he reached for her hand.

Robin shook her head, her lungs burning as she grabbed Val and tugged.

The man pulled hard and they were rising.

She could see the full moon rippling above the surface of the water.

Her lungs were burning.

No.

No!

She choked and the water rushed in. The taste of the lake weeds was the last thing she remembered before bright lights flashed behind her eyes.

HER THROAT BURNED, but she was breathing.

Robin opened her eyes and coughed water from her lungs. She rolled onto her side, and hands held her back, dragged the hair from her mouth and eyes.

"She's breathing! This one is breathing!"

She heard Val crying somewhere. She was crying and yelling.

"Monica?" she rasped. Where was Monica?

"Don't try to sit up." Someone shoved her back down.

"Stay on your side. Keep coughing. They're bringing oxygen for your friend."

"My friend?"

In the glaring white lights, she saw the silhouette of someone doing CPR over a body lying on the lake bank.

"Monica?"

"Just keep still."

"Where is he?" Robin looked around, but she didn't recognize anyone. No, wait, she did. The woman talking to her was Jackie Parker, who worked at the hospital. No, not the hospital. EMT.

Someone started coughing, and Robin heard someone throw up. A cheer went up from the person doing CPR.

"She's breathing! She's breathing! Where's that oxygen?"

Someone shoved a mask in her face, and Robin tried to push it away but she couldn't. Someone else was wrapping what looked like tin foil around her. No, not tin foil. An emergency blanket.

"Where's Val?" She lifted the mask. "Where's Val and Monica?"

"You're all safe now." Jackie was grinning. "Holy shit, Robin, I cannot believe you guys survived that. Your car must be fifty feet underwater."

Fifty feet? Who'd managed to swim down fifty feet? Had they seen the lights? Did they see the crash?

She pushed the mask away again. "There was a man. He broke the window."

Jackie frowned. "What?"

"There was a man who was by the car. He broke the window."

"Sweetie, you're imagining things. A tourist from the

lodge saw your car go in. Thank God. He waded out and helped you guys to shore."

Blinking, Robin looked around and saw a blond man standing near an ambulance, wrapped in another emergency blanket. He didn't look wet. He wasn't the man who'd rescued them.

"No," she said. "There was someone else. Is he all right?"

"Just keep calm." Jackie pulled the blanket around Robin more tightly and unfolded a thicker woolen blanket beside her. "Here. Roll over on this if you want. Good thinking taking your clothes off for swimming, but we gotta get you warm."

Robin rolled onto the woolen blanket and felt the immediate relief of her skin against something soft instead of the cutting stones on the shore. "No, there was a man with us. He got the window open."

"He was in the car with you?"

"No, he was swimming..." Robin blinked. Had she imagined it? Would anyone have been able to swim down that far? She couldn't have imagined it. He'd broken the window. He'd rescued them. Without that man, they'd all be dead.

"It's a flat-out miracle you're all alive, I'll tell you that much." Jackie helped Robin sit up. "I'm gonna get you another blanket, okay?"

Robin spotted Val, who was up and walking around. She was trying to get rid of the young EMT trailing her with an oxygen bottle.

"Will someone please call my mother?" Val said. "Just shut up about me and call my mom so I can talk to my kids. And don't touch me!"

Monica wasn't talking, but Robin could see her. She was

pale and her eyes were staring into the distance. She was nodding and shaking her head as they asked questions, but she held an oxygen mask to her face like it was a security blanket.

And Robin... felt fine. Her chest hurt, but other than that, she felt fine. Her knee wasn't even hurting.

Nothing about this made sense. They were near the lake, and Robin's car was underwater. They'd managed to swim to shore—

No, they hadn't managed. She hadn't been able to get the door open. There had been someone there. A man had broken the car window with a rock and pulled her out. She'd pulled Val. Val must have pulled Monica.

But she was looking around, and their rescuer was nowhere to be found. Had a Good Samaritan actually swam down to her car, rescued all three of them, and then disappeared?

There were too many lights and sirens and people. She couldn't think straight.

"Robin?"

Was that Mark?

"Robin!"

A pair of arms gripped her and held her close.

That felt odd. And nice.

"I thought I'd lost you." His voice was shaky. "They called and said your car went in the lake." He pressed his cheek to the top of her head. "I thought I lost you. Oh my God, I thought I'd lost you."

She patted his arm. "I'm here." Over Mark's shoulder, Robin's eyes were drawn to the edge of the forest. There was a flicker of movement. Was it an animal?

24

SUDDENLY PSYCHIC

"There was a white deer," she said. "I've never seen one of those before. I can't believe I swerved. That was so stupid."

"Shhhh." Mark kissed the top of her head. "You're safe. You're safe."

He was rocking her back and forth. Robin couldn't take her eyes off the trees. There was something there. Something important. She was halfway expecting the stranger with the dark hair to walk out of the woods, but he was nowhere. No one even mentioned the man who'd rescued them.

"You need more blankets," Mark said, rubbing her arms up and down. He pulled off his flannel and wrapped it around her. "You've got to be freezing. They need to take you to the hospital. They're taking you to the hospital, right?"

"I feel fine." Robin lay with her head on Mark's shoulder, watching in silence as a young girl—maybe twelve or thirteen—stepped out from the edge of the trees. No one seemed to notice her but Robin.

"Honey, you nearly drowned. The police said they had to do CPR. You need to go to the hospital."

That sounded absolutely horrible. "I just want to go home."

The girl was wearing an old-fashioned white nightgown. She stepped forward, her eyes locked on Robin; then she stopped and looked around. Her head tilted to the side as if she'd heard something in the distance. She looked back at Robin, put a finger to her lips in a "hush" gesture, then disappeared into the trees.

Huh.

Of all the weird things that'd happened, that might have been the weirdest.

CHAPTER 3

*E*mma's face was as white as the sheets covering the hospital bed. "Mom, I am so sorry."

Robin had to talk around the oxygen mask covering her face. She was too exhausted to be angry. "Baby, you had no idea my car was going to go in the lake. It's not your fault."

Her daughter sniffed. "It's been months and I completely forgot I loaned that scraper to Lauren. It was when we had that sleepover last winter and there was snow on her windshield and we were late for school and I grabbed it out of your car and—"

"Emma." She gripped her daughter's hand. "Not your fault. And I'm fine. Val and Monica are fine. We survived and we're going to be okay."

The tears didn't stop, but Robin's words seemed to set Emma at ease. She nodded and laid her head on Robin's hospital bed. "Where's Dad?"

"I'm not sure." She was exhausted, and all she wanted to do was sleep, but she didn't want to leave Emma alone. Mark had picked Emma up and driven her into Bridger City where

Robin, Monica, and Val were being held overnight for observation. Her parents were on the way. At Robin's request, no one had told Grandma Helen.

She'd been battered by tests and all sorts of medical terms she couldn't keep straight.

Blood oxygen levels.

Anoxia.

Hypothermia.

Brain hypoxia.

Post-traumatic stress syndrome.

She knew what the last one meant, but she was having problems keeping everything straight in her mind.

Someone had saved them.

No, there was no one there.

There was a girl at the lakeside.

The EMTs never saw her.

Someone was in the water with them.

No, it was just them and the blond tourist when emergency vehicles arrived. The car was under fifty feet of water. They had escaped from the car and floated to the surface. Val and Robin had already been breathing when they were found. Monica had to be resuscitated, but she was talking and that was good.

But someone had saved them. Robin knew she hadn't imagined it. There was a man. He had dark hair and a square jaw. He looked vaguely familiar, like maybe he was a weekender who came up to the lake fairly often. Not a local, but someone familiar.

Someone tapped on the door. It was a nurse.

"How you feeling?"

Robin blinked. "Tired."

27

"You should sleep." The nurse looked pointedly at Emma. "Is your dad around, honey?"

"I think he said he was talking to someone about insurance or something. I'm not sure."

Robin was never more grateful for Mark's insurance. His company had great coverage, which they'd found out when Austin had nearly taken out his knee playing football.

"Austin." Robin looked at Emma. "Did Dad call Austin?"

Emma nodded. "Dad told him to stay put for now. He told him not to miss class. Austin is really upset; he's been texting me."

"I should call him. Do you know where my phone is?" Robin never went anywhere without her phone.

Emma frowned. "It's in the lake, Mom."

"Oh. Right." Shit. She hated getting new phones.

"Did you back up to the cloud? You know Dad is always reminding us—"

"Yes, I'm backed up. I'll be fine."

She had insurance on the phone. And the car. And great health insurance. At least she didn't have to worry about going bankrupt on top of almost drowning.

Thinking about the accident brought back a rush of memories. Val, Monica, and she had been in the car. Robin had thought they were going to die. They'd all thought they were going to die.

I wanted to kill myself. I thought about the future and there was just... nothing.

Don't tell my kids, but I think I love you two more than anyone.

I don't think anyone would even notice if I died.

The punch of memories made her close her eyes in

shame. What had she been thinking? How could she have said that to Monica and Val? Her life was so much easier compared to both of them. She wasn't a single parent. She wasn't a widow.

She had good insurance and a steady business and a faithful husband and kids who were mostly fine. Did it matter if she felt invisible sometimes? Did it matter that Mark had lost interest in her?

Her husband pushed the door open, and Robin saw the lines marking his forehead. He scanned the room and his eyes immediately went to Emma.

"Emma, you're not still crying about the scraper." He looked as exhausted as Robin felt.

Emma burst into tears again and Mark turned to Robin.

Seriously? his eyes said.

She rolled her own. *I know.*

Mark walked over, brushed Robin's hair back from her forehead, and kissed it. "I don't want to leave you alone."

"No." Robin pulled the mask away from her face. "It's fine. Take her home. Mom and Dad are going to be here pretty soon. I think I'll be able to go home in the morning, and all I want to do is sleep."

"I called Austin and filled him in—"

"Emma told me."

"But I told him to stay put. He'll probably call in the morning."

"I'm surprised he didn't immediately start driving home. Having your mom in the hospital has got to be an excused absence, even in college." No one laughed at her feeble attempt at a joke.

Mark sighed. "You know, he's getting better. He's taking

this year a lot more seriously than last. Can you cut him some slack?"

"I was just..." She shook her head. "Can we fight about this when I'm not so tired?"

"Fine." He stepped away. "Let's not fight about it at all, okay? I'm tired of fighting about it."

Emma had stopped crying and was slumped in her chair, tuning out her parents like she always did when the subject of her big brother came up.

Focus, Robin.

She rearranged her pillows. "Can you guys check on Val and Monica before you leave? I can't get anyone to tell me anything."

"Sure. I'll see if anyone is in the waiting room. Maybe harass them a little." Mark swallowed hard. "I wish Gil were here."

She nodded. "Yeah. Me too."

"Do you want your mom to drive you back once you're discharged?"

"Please don't do that to me."

"I'll see you in the morning then." Mark kissed her forehead again, letting his lips linger on her forehead. "Are you sure you're okay with me leaving?"

"I promise I am."

"Okay."

Emma gave her an awkward side hug, but it was difficult when Robin was hooked up to monitors and IVs. She felt completely fine except that she couldn't remember everything that happened, things were all a little muddled, and she was exhausted.

Come to think of it, that could describe most days in her life lately, so maybe she should just go home.

Mark and Emma left the room with the television tuned to HGTV at low volume, but Robin felt like she'd only closed her eyes for a minute before she opened them. Someone else was in the room. A nurse stood at the foot of her bed, perusing her chart with pursed lips.

"Hey." Robin blinked her eyes, but she couldn't seem to clear the sleep from them. Everything was kind of hazy and half the lights were shut off. "Did they put something in my IV to help me sleep?"

The nurse looked up. "I don't think so. You're a lucky lady, that's for sure."

Robin smiled. The older woman was wearing the exact same uniform Robin remembered from when she'd been a child getting her tonsils out. A smart white cap perched on her head, and her crisp collar was neat at her throat. Her uniform read D. Hawkins.

"I didn't know nurses even wore those anymore." The older woman had probably worn the same uniform since she'd been a student nurse. Funny that they let her keep the hat. Robin was used to seeing nurses in scrubs.

"Wear what, honey?" The nurse kept looking through her chart. "Looks like they're keeping you off the big painkillers for the moment. You having any headache? Body aches?"

"Body aches. Some headache, but just like I get when I'm really tired." She touched her face. "Is my face bruised? I hit the airbag in the car pretty hard."

"The what?" The nurse frowned. "You're scheduled for a few more tests, but I want to check on these. I think Dr.

McMurty might have written something down wrong." She smiled. "That man. His handwriting is just awful."

Robin frowned. "Doctor who? I think my doctor is named Patel."

"Patel?" The nurse's eyes went wide. "Never heard that one before."

"Really?" Patel was a pretty common last name.

She patted Robin's foot. "There're so many doctors in and out of this hospital, I can hardly keep track. He must be new."

"It's a she." Robin was confused. How did the nurse not remember the nice young doctor who looked like she'd barely graduated from high school? Maybe this nurse was one of those rotating nurses who filled in sometimes. That might explain the uniform.

She came closer to check her IV. Maybe Robin had hit her head harder than she realized. The nurse's hands felt ice-cold. Then again, the air-conditioning in the hospital was ridiculous.

"Can I get another blanket?" Robin shivered.

"Sure thing."

Robin felt slightly queasy. "I'm feeling a little nauseated."

"When was the last time you ate?"

"I don't remember."

"Let me get you some juice, but I'll let Doc McMurty know about that too." She rearranged the pillows behind Robin but didn't adjust the bed. "Maybe get you some pudding. Might be good for your tummy."

Robin barely registered the words the nurse was saying. Something was wrong. Something was very wrong. Her eyes were fixed on a spot of red that had appeared on Nurse

Hawkins's crisp blue uniform. It was right below her pointed white collar.

The red grew darker. It spread.

"There's something..." Robin couldn't breathe. She felt like she was drowning again. Everything in the room was cold. Her heart was racing.

"What's that, honey?" The nurse's voice was muffled, as if Robin was hearing her from underwater.

"Your shirt." Robin looked up.

All the color had leached from the woman's face. The single red spot had been joined by another, brighter, scarlet stain.

"I don't..." Robin's voice was a whisper. "I don't feel well."

Nurse Hawkins frowned and her pale white forehead crinkled in concern. "I can see that. Let me run and get the doctor. I think you may need something for the pain after all."

She turned to walk to the door, and Robin choked back a scream. On the back of her blue nurse's uniform were two bloody wounds, one in the shoulder and one in the chest. Gunshots. She'd been shot. The blood was bright red, dripping down the back of her uniform, over the clean white belt, and onto her skirt. She moved toward the door, reached out, and walked straight through it.

Robin tore off the oxygen mask and screamed.

DR. PATEL WAS STARING down at her, a tiny line marking the space between her perfectly groomed eyebrows. Robin let her gaze follow the doctor's finger as instructed. She tried not to blink when the light flashed in her eyes.

"Your eyebrows are really great," Robin muttered. "Do you do them yourself?"

"Oh no," Dr. Patel said. "I do the threading thing."

"Really? I tried that once, and it hurt like a mother. I decided to stick with wax."

Dr. Patel smiled. "I'm used to it." She shut off the light. "I definitely want to do an MRI. I'm a little worried that the oxygen deprivation was more severe than we originally thought."

"You think I have brain damage because I saw a nurse walking around with bullet holes in her back?" Nurses had rushed into her room as soon as she'd started screaming, but it had taken hours before anyone listened to her.

Her parents were waiting in the hall while she talked with the doctor. Grace Lewis had finally put her foot down and raised holy hell with the staff until someone came and talked to her daughter about the strange incident.

"I don't think you have brain damage." Dr. Patel stepped back. "You suffered a near-drowning incident, and though it was likely a very short time, your brain *was* deprived of oxygen. It's very common to have hallucinations after brain hypoxia. Add the trauma to that, and I'd be surprised if you *weren't* seeing and hearing strange things."

"She was here in the room. It was cold, and I had a conversation with her." Robin shook her head. "It was more than strange."

"It must have been terribly upsetting, and I wish I could tell you it won't happen again," Dr. Patel said. "But it's very likely that you might have strange dreams. You might see or hear things that aren't there. You might overreact to things that normally wouldn't bother you." She handed Robin a pamphlet that had WHAT IS POST-TRAUMATIC STRESS DISORDER? on the front. "PTSD doesn't only apply to soldiers coming home from war or survivors of violence. Your body and mind survived something very traumatic last night, and that can jolt brain chemistry in ways we can't predict. I encourage you to see a psychologist at some point."

Robin tapped the pamphlet. "Thanks. I'll... I'll check it out."

What she really wanted was to talk to Val and Monica. Mark had texted her mom that things were looking good for both, but she wanted to see them. Wanted to talk to them herself.

Dr. Patel started toward the door. "I want to keep you for a full twenty-four hours and complete those tests. So just sit tight and try to get some rest."

"Right." Robin nodded. "Get some rest."

So super easy to do with nurses—dead and alive apparently—waking her up every hour or so. The last time she'd been in the hospital was when she'd given birth to Emma, and she'd hated it then too. She wanted to be in a dark room with a comfortable bed and no one poking or prodding her.

"Dr. Patel!" Robin caught her before she closed the door. "Can you tell me anything about my friends? The ones who were in the accident with me? Val—Valerie Costa and Monica Velasquez?"

Dr. Patel gave her a rueful smile. "I can't. I'm sorry. I believe they have some family in the waiting room though. Maybe ask your parents to track them down."

"I'll do that. Thanks." Robin settled back into her bed

and had just closed her eyes when a nurse tapped on the door. Again. Philip Lewis, Robin's dad, followed after her.

"How are you, honey?" Her dad kissed her forehead. "Was it all a weird reaction to the medication or something?"

"Probably something like that." Robin felt instantly at ease around her dad, which was the opposite of how she felt with her mother. "They're going to run more tests. Where's Mom?"

"Talking with Val's parents in the waiting room. She'll be a while. Why don't you try to sleep more?"

The young nurse at Robin's bedside looked familiar and was wearing the colorful scrubs worn by most of the nurses on the floor. "Sorry to interrupt with all this. I'm Lucy." She walked over and started in on the routine. "I'll try to make this quick so you can sleep. You want me to close those shades?"

The sun had risen, and Robin was in an east-facing room. "Please."

Lucy walked over and pulled the chain to close the shades while her dad picked up a magazine and settled in the corner. Robin checked out the nurse's back. No bullet holes. Nothing weird. That was a relief.

"You know, you probably heard about it when you were a kid." Lucy kept her voice low and soothing. "My mom's a nurse." Lucy pointed to her scrubs. "Family business. She was working here when it happened."

"What?" Robin was so exhausted she could barely keep her eyes open. "When what happened?"

"Debbie Hawkins. The nurse you thought you saw?" The nurse slipped the blood pressure cuff over Robin's arm. "She died in... eighty-two, I think my mom said? Early eighties anyway. You probably heard about it when you were a kid."

Philip lifted his head. "You know, I do think I remember something like that."

"Huh." It didn't sound familiar to Robin. "Who was she?"

"She was a nurse," Lucy said. "Older than my mom. It was so sad. Her picture is still on a plaque in the lobby." She shook her head. "She was shot and killed by her ex-husband. She was working emergency one night, and he busted in and shot her in the back. It was awful. One of the waiting rooms is dedicated to her."

"She died right here in the hospital?"

Philip nodded. "I do remember that. It was in the newspaper. She was seeing one of the doctors here, correct?"

Lucy glanced at him. "Yes. Tragic, right? All those doctors and nurses around, but they couldn't save her. In fact, the doctor she had just gotten engaged to—that's why the ex-husband went crazy, I guess—was the one on call. Can you imagine?"

"Dr. McMurty," Robin murmured.

Lucy's eyes went wide. "Oh my gosh, how did you know that?"

"Must have read... remembered it." Robin felt all the blood drain from her face, and her body went cold again. "That's awful."

"I know." Lucy shook her head. "If it makes you feel better, you're not the first person who's seen her." She lowered her voice to nearly a whisper. "One of the nurses swears that Debbie Hawkins still does night rounds sometimes. She was always really sweet with the babies—I guess she couldn't have kids—and they find rocking chairs moving on their own in Maternity sometimes."

Robin blinked. "Seriously?"

"I guess. I don't really believe in any of that stuff, but I don't know." She shrugged. "I know a couple of nurses who swear she's the friendly ghost of Bridger City Memorial." Lucy finished up her notes and hung the clipboard back on the end of Robin's bed. "Well, I'm done here. Sweet dreams. Try to get some rest."

Her dad snorted a laugh.

"Right," Robin said. "Sleep."

Sure. Okay. No problem.

Robin had nearly drowned and was now seeing ghosts.

Apparently.

Who could possibly have trouble sleeping after that?

CHAPTER 4

*V*alerie Costa could hardly speak. "Mom, I cannot..."

No words. There were no words. Her mother had invited her ex to see her at the hospital, and the man'd had the nerve to say yes.

"Looking good, Val." Josh smiled. "Like the hair."

Val refused to talk to him. She refused to even look at him. She glared at her mother. "Why would you do this?"

"He was on the phone with Andy when you called, sweetie." Marie Costa smoothed Val's hair back and held her hand. "What was I supposed to do? Not tell him? The boys were upset."

Josh held out his hands. "Uh... I'm here. In the room."

Val finally turned her eyes on him. "Shut up, Josh. This has nothing to do with you." She pushed the call button. "But since you're here for once, why don't you make yourself a tiny bit useful and help your kids find some breakfast."

Everything about her was mixed up. Her head was cloudy, and she could hardly keep track of her thoughts. Her mom and dad were here. Josh had followed them. Her dad was sorting through paperwork and trying to talk to the police, who were in and out of the hospital. Andy and Jackson were roaming the halls of the hospital, looking for food, which was par for the course with an eleven- and fourteen-year-old. They were always, always eating.

"How are there so many people here?" The press of voices began to wear on her. She wanted the night to come back. She wanted darkness and quiet.

"Try to relax." Marie squeezed her hand. "As soon as Dad gets back, I'll tell him to take the boys back to our house."

"No, I want the boys here." She didn't want to let them out of her sight. "Has anyone been able to talk to Robin and Monica yet?"

"Dad said Grace and Philip are in with Robin, and all of Monica's kids are in the waiting room, taking turns going in and out."

"Okay." She closed her eyes and focused on Marie's hand in hers. It steadied her, which was weird because Val had never been the touchy-feely daughter. But in that moment, her mom's hand felt like a lifeline to normal.

Her mother was great. Val loved her mom. She was the most conventional woman on earth—probably the reason Val had as many tattoos as she did—but Marie was a maternal kick-ass. She was a killer wife, mom, and grandma. She did all the church fundraisers and volunteered for everything. She and Val's dad had been married for fifty years, and they still liked each other.

Her mom was also convinced that Val and Josh would eventually reconcile. Because her heart was too big to let go of anyone, including a son-in-law who was fidelity-challenged.

Ignoring her request to take care of the boys—*shocker*—Josh reached to the chair behind him. "Hey, I got you something."

Val and Marie exchanged a wordless conversation.

Can you get rid of him?

He's trying to be nice.

I don't want him here!

Honey, you almost died. Marie's eyes filled with tears she blinked away. She cleared her throat and patted Val's hand. "I'm going to track down Dad and the boys. I'll be right back."

"Don't leave me with him."

"I'll be right back!"

Josh cleared his throat. "Yeah, I'm still here."

Val swung her eyes toward him. "The question is why."

Josh looked uncomfortable. And hot. He was still so damn hot, which pissed Val off so damn much. He should have grown warts on his nose or developed middle-aged acne or something. Instead, the lines around his eyes were handsome and the silver stubble that flecked through his beard was attractive.

Asshole.

Her oldest, Jackson, was the spitting image of his father, which meant she couldn't even hate Josh's face, because it was her son's. It was all so weird and complicated.

Why was it so noisy? The minute her mom stepped into the hall, the volume in her hospital room had been turned up to eleven. Monitors and beeping and her skin was aching.

And Josh was sitting beside her with a glittery purple bag in his hands.

Val rolled her eyes and held out her hand. "What did you get me?"

Josh gave her his best crooked smile and reached into a bag. "You're gonna love this." He pulled out what looked like a rolled-up blanket and held it out to her.

She unrolled part of it. "Is this *Coraline?*"

"Yep."

She was... surprised. And pleased. "Seriously?"

It was a gorgeous blue, purple, and black throw blanket with images from one of her favorite movies and books. Val spread her hand over the soft picture. "Josh, this is perf—"

She blinked, and in the space between opening and closing her eyes, she saw an image of Josh handing the blanket to a blond girl with dark eyeliner and pouty lips.

"What's this?"

"A Coraline *blanket."*

"What's Coraline?*"*

Valerie blinked again and lifted her hands from the blanket. "You got this for Rachel."

Josh frowned. "What?"

Val shoved the blanket away. "You got this for Rachel, and she didn't like it, so you're giving it to me?"

She saw the truth flash like flip-cards in his eyes. Shock. Irritation. Denial. Shock. Denial.

"I didn't— She wouldn't even like— Why would you say that?" He grabbed the edge of the blanket and started rolling it up. "Rachel doesn't like shit like this."

"No, 'cause she's an infant." Josh's girlfriend wasn't an infant, but she was twenty-six, which was ridiculous when

Josh was forty-four. "Why would you give me a secondhand present? That's just gross. You didn't need to get me anything, so why—?"

"You know what?" He stood and shoved the blanket back in the bag. "I saw it and bought it because it was cool. You don't want it? Fine." He picked up the bag. "I shouldn't have come."

"No, you shouldn't have." She had the weird urge to scratch every inch of her skin, and she didn't know why she was so certain Josh had given the blanket to Rachel, but she was sure of it. It was as if she'd been in the room when Rachel turned her nose up at the beautiful blanket. "I'm fine."

His smile was grim. "Of course you are. You always are."

"I've had to be."

Jackson and Andy walked into the hospital room, both holding foil-wrapped burritos and looking between Josh and Val with wary eyes.

"You guys cool?" Jackson stepped in front of Andy by half a step.

Josh cleared his throat. "Yeah, we're cool."

Andy's eyes were wide and hopeful. Jackson's gaze was skeptical.

"Dad, are you gonna stay for a while?" Andy walked to Val's bed. "There are breakfast burritos in the lobby. I can get you one if you want. I have money."

Josh looked between all three of them and cleared his throat. "Uh, I think your mom wants to sleep. She had a rough night so..." He motioned toward the door with one hand in his pocket.

Val almost felt sorry for him. At the end of the day, Josh was a giant adolescent who needed to be the center of attention and had never really grown past his early twenties. He still thought he could skate through life with a crooked smile, good looks, and charm. He'd been a great boyfriend. He sucked as a father and husband.

She took Andy's hand and squeezed it. As soon as she took his hand, the itching sensation in her skin calmed down.

Andy was her baby with a heart as big as a mountain. Jackson was her capable and responsible partner in crime, but Andy was her big squishy heart. Probably the only heart Val really had.

"Right." Jackson was matter-of-fact. He walked over and grabbed the bag with the blanket from Josh's hand. "I'll take care of this."

Josh let it go. "Yeah, okay."

Jackson sat in the seat by the window and returned to his burrito. "Mom, are they bringing you breakfast soon? Do you need anything?"

"I think Grandma was going to check on breakfast." She kept her eyes on Andy, holding his hand tightly. "I'm fine, kiddo."

"Okay." Jackson got his phone out, his father forgotten.

Josh walked over and mussed Andy's hair. "See ya, kid."

Andy's expression fell a little, but he tried to hide it. "Yeah. I'll call you later, Dad."

"Okay cool." Josh walked out of the room without a backward glance, which was the way he'd left Val when she confronted him about cheating.

Gone.

Exit stage left.

See ya.

Val took a deep breath and tried to remember what was

going on in her life. "So this whole accident makes me kind of a badass, right?"

Jackson smothered a laugh. "Yeah, right."

Andy rolled his eyes. "Mom, seriously?"

"I mean, I kicked my way out of a sinking car and swam fifty feet to the surface of the lake in the middle of the night, dragging my friend with me. I think that's pretty badass." She scooted over so Andy could sit on the edge of her bed. "Did you bring me a burrito?"

"You're not supposed to eat burritos." Jackson flipped through a magazine. "That's why they bring you food."

"It's probably gonna suck," Val whispered to Andy. "Go steal Jack's burrito for me."

Andy giggled, and everything was right in her world again.

Except the minute her son slipped away to use the bathroom down the hall, Val's skin started itching again. Was her nervous system on edge? Was it some kind of weird reaction to the painkiller they'd given her?

She rubbed her face with both hands.

"Mom, you okay?"

"Yeah." She looked up and took a deep breath. "Just tired, I think. Just... really tired."

MONICA VELASQUEZ WAS NOT TIRED. Not even a little. But that didn't stop her from keeping her eyes closed and pretending she was. It was a tactic the mother of four had used often in the twenty-six years since her oldest son had been born.

If you couldn't find real sleep, fake it on the off chance they'd leave you alone.

If she kept her eyes closed, maybe she would dream again. In the watery, sporadic dreams she'd experienced since waking up, she'd seen beautiful things.

She'd been back with Gil, walking down the dirt road behind their house. He'd been teasing her that he was growing a beard since she wasn't there to demand he shave his stubble. He'd kissed her, and it had been the same warm thrill she remembered.

She'd been dreaming about her oldest, Jake. Only in her dream, he'd been telling her about a girl he'd fallen in love with and Monica was ecstatic. She loved this new girl, and she was so happy.

Sylvia was walking across a stage, graduating with honors.

Samuel and Caleb flashed in and out. Caleb had a beard. Samuel was talking about a new job. All her kids were in her dreams, but they were never with Gilbert. She didn't know what that was about.

"Mrs. Velasquez?" Monica felt a hand on her shoulder. "Mrs. Velasquez?"

She forced her eyes open, and there was a white halo around the edges of her vision. "Hmm?"

"Mrs. Velasquez, I need to take your blood pressure."

She opened her eyes fully and saw all the wires and monitors around her. "Oh right." She forced herself to sit up and remembered her arm was broken. "Ugh," she groaned. "I'm a mess."

"You're actually doing great. Don't stress." The nurse

slipped the cuff over her nonbroken arm. "How are you feeling?"

"Like I fell in a lake?" She glanced at the two chairs by the window. Jake and Sylvia were sleeping in them. Caleb and Samuel must have gone out to the waiting room. "What time is it?"

"Still pretty early," the nurse said. "I see your entourage hasn't left."

"They won't until I go home," Monica said. "Their dad would tell them off if they left me."

The nurse smiled. "Where's your husband? Is he out of town?"

"He's dead." Because twenty-five years of utter happiness was all she was allowed, apparently. "About six months ago."

"I'm so sorry to hear that." The shocked nurse scrambled to recover. "Your kids must have been really scared when you were brought in."

"Yeah." She hadn't even thought about that. No wonder all the boys had been so clingy. Now she felt bad for wishing a couple of them would go home.

Mom-fail, Monica.

The nurse was writing something on her chart. "You and your friends were so lucky."

"Yeah." She frowned. "Wait, how are they? Are they okay? I haven't heard anything—"

The door creaked open, and Monica spotted Val's mom. "Marie! How's Val?"

Marie held her hands out and walked over to Monica. "Asking the same about you, of course." She saw Monica's arm. "Does it hurt?"

Everything hurt. Her body hurt. Her head hurt. Her arm hurt. She wanted Gilbert and he was gone, and that hurt too.

She nodded and fought back tears. "Yeah, it hurts. I'll be okay though. The doctors told Jake that my MRI looked normal and my blood pressure and blood oxygen are good. I don't remember anything after I lost consciousness, but they said that's normal."

"Do you remember waking up in the hospital?"

I wanted to kill myself. I thought about taking sleeping pills after Gil died because I couldn't imagine my life without him. I thought about the future and there was just... nothing. There was nothing without him.

She remembered everything in the car and nothing after until the dreams came. Nothing lucid until she'd woken in the hospital with her arm in a cast and monitors hooked to what felt like every part of her, and she was still holding on to the dreams.

"It's strange," Monica said. "I feel strange. But I'll be okay. Tell me about Val. How's Robin?"

"She's fine. They're both fine. Robin had a weird scare earlier, but it was just a reaction to being unconscious I think. Something like that. She's resting now that I managed to see her and tell her about the rest of you girls. Mark took Emma home. I told him Eddie and I would keep an eye on you girls and call if he needed to come back."

"Do you know how long they're going to keep us?"

"Oh, sweetie." Marie put her arms around Monica. "You three drove into a lake and nearly drowned! Don't be in such a hurry to leave. Let them take care of you for a while."

ROBIN DRIFTED in and out of sleep. She could hear voices in the background, but they were mostly nurses. The television was off. She slept for hours, glad to finally have some quiet. The curtains were drawn, and the room was dark when her eyes flickered open.

She saw him sitting in the corner of the room, perched in one of the chairs next to her napping father. Was she dreaming? Was she imagining things? Was this another hallucination, like Dr. Patel had said she could expect?

It was the man from the lake, she was certain of it. His hair was dark, and Robin had the same feeling as the first time she'd seen him. He was familiar. She'd seen him before.

Nothing about the man frightened her. He didn't speak. He didn't fidget. He was reading a book. What book? She couldn't see. Why was he reading? Where did he even get a book?

The man looked up, caught her eye, and smiled.

The cold spilled over her, but it was familiar now, like a gust of fresh air in an overheated room. Robin closed her eyes and slept.

CHAPTER 5

 *wo weeks later*

"I SWEAR, no one ever closes a door or turns off a light switch in this house except me." Grace Lewis's voice cut through the shop and landed exactly as Robin knew her mom had intended—square on her daughter's shoulders.

Robin instinctively looked up to see what she'd forgotten. There was one light on in the storeroom, the one she was working under.

Robin's mother—the previous owner of Glimmer Lake Curios—walked into her daughter's office, a converted galley kitchen with a bathroom attached.

"Hi, Mom." Robin looked up, but she didn't stand.

"Why was the door standing open to God and everyone?" Grace asked.

"I don't know. I shut it. Do you want coffee?"

"You shut it? So it was the fairies?"

"Ha ha." She pointed to the counter. "There's coffee made if you want some."

It was a long-standing family joke that Robin had seen "fairies" when she was young. In reality, Robin had a normal childhood imagination that her mother had done her best to stamp out by the time Robin entered first grade.

"The door keeps blowing open." Robin paged through new auction catalogs. "I think there's something wrong with the latch."

"It doesn't feel loose." Grace unwound her delicate silk scarf and walked to the coffee maker.

"I know, but it keeps blowing open, so I think it must be something with the hardware." She shrugged. "It's an old house."

"It is." Grace poured herself a cup and sat across from Robin. "How was yesterday?"

"It was fine. I was exhausted by the end of the day, but I managed. And I slept really well last night."

"That's good. It was a Sunday."

"And it's the fall." Sunday had been the first weekend day that Robin had watched the shop by herself since the accident. She was surprised at how exhausted she'd been, but in the middle of the fall season the shop didn't get too crazy. By the time snow fell, she'd better be back to one hundred percent. "I'm sure I'll be myself in a couple of weeks."

"Good. You know I don't mind helping out, but I worry about missing sales," Grace said. It was Tuesday morning, and the new pieces her mother had picked up at a Sacramento auction house would be coming in.

"If you want to go back to buying only, I can find someone else to—"

"No, no!" Grace waved a hand. "I'm fine."

You hate working in the shop. Robin thought it. She didn't dare say it.

As Grace had gotten older, she'd grown worse and worse about customer service, especially when new people moved into town and didn't realize who Grace Russell Lewis was. Daughter of Gordon Russell, owner of the largest lumber mill in the mountains and founder of Glimmer Lake, Grace was nothing if not proud of her family and her town. She was short with customers from the city and could be incredibly judgmental.

"Did the woman on Saturday come back?" Grace sipped her coffee. "She had... interesting ideas."

"Nope. Never came back."

"That's a shame."

You definitely do not think that.

The customer had proposed staining the gold birch of a Depression-era desk with a darker color. The look on Grace's face had suggested the woman wanted to murder puppies.

"Don't worry." Robin sipped her tea. "You scared her off."

"I suspect..." Grace raised another eyebrow. "...that the prices scared her off more than I did."

"Mom, really?"

"Did she look like a serious customer to you?"

And that was why Robin was desperate to feel like herself again. She had to get her mom out of the shop. Grace had been driving customers away with her passive aggression, veiled insults, and dismissive attitude. Sure, Robin liked the original finish on the desk the woman had been looking at, but if it didn't match her house, it didn't match. She'd much rather a sell a piece—especially one that had been sitting in the store for six months—than keep it because she had philosophical differences with a buyer about furniture finishes.

Better for Grace to go back to buying, where she could charm auctioneers and find the best bargains for the store.

"I don't think you need to be here today," Robin said. "Nothing much going on except the shipment, and Brent said he could help me move stuff."

Brent Russell was her neighbor at Suffolk Realty next door. He was also her second or third cousin and was great about helping her move big pieces.

"Brent?" Grace frowned. "Is he strong enough for that?"

"Brent? Of course he is, Mom."

"Are you sure?" She leaned forward. "He's just not the same since Easton left him."

"What?"

Grace raised her carefully groomed eyebrows meaningfully.

"I honestly don't know what your eyebrows mean right now."

Grace whispered dramatically, as if Brent could hear through the walls and across the parking lot, "He's put on a lot of weight."

Robin closed her eyes, determined to get her mother out of the shop before Brent came over to help. "How's Grandma today? Did you go by already?"

Robin's grandmother, Helen Russell, was still living in Russell House, the home where she'd raised her children, but it was beginning to look more and more like a bad idea for her to live alone.

"I'm going to have to fire the maids," Grace said.

"What? Why?"

"They're lazy. And Mother can't see well enough to spot the dirt anymore."

"Shoot." Robin hadn't had a great feeling about the new cleaning service, but since Carla, her grandmother's longtime housekeeper, had retired, it had been one service after another, none of which understood how to clean an old home as large as Grandma Helen's.

"I think it's time for her to move," Robin said. "She's ninety-five, Mom."

"I know how old my mother is," Grace said. "Where do you think she's going to go? Is she going to move in with you and Mark?"

"I mean..." The thought hadn't occurred to her, but it wasn't out of the question. "If she wants to, we can manage. Emma will be gone in the fall, and Austin's room is empty."

"And on the second floor," Grace said. "Mother would hate living with you or me. She's too independent, and she'll never leave Russell House. It's her home."

"What about Partridge Valley?"

Grace looked offended. "Russell women do not move into old-folks' homes, Robin."

"It's a retirement community. Val's grandmother loved living there."

"Absolutely not." Grace rose. "We just need to find some live-in help."

Her grandmother was rolling in money, so it wasn't out of the question. "Should I ask Uncle Raymond what he thinks?"

"Don't be ridiculous." Grace's eyes were scorching in their disapproval.

"It was just a suggestion. She's his mother too."

Robin wished her mother had a better relationship with her Uncle Raymond, but that bridge had burned long ago, and Robin had never been sure why. Uncle Raymond had never gotten along with her grandfather, who'd been a hard, unforgiving, and judgmental man with exacting standards for everyone in the family.

Not unlike his daughter.

Robin sighed and stood, ready to face the shop and the day.

In the weeks since the accident, Robin had been trying to be more focused on her family, which meant more time with her mother and father. Mark and Emma were still in their own worlds. Austin had called a couple of times, but the conversations hadn't gone well. Robin felt out of sorts, discombobulated, and she wasn't sleeping well.

They were raising her car this week, and Robin was hoping that something about seeing it and settling the insurance mess would allow her to move on. Plus she really needed a new car. She was tired of borrowing Mark's truck or asking for rides, but she also couldn't decide what sort of car she wanted.

The world around her seemed like it was covered in gauze some days. Nothing was clear or urgent. It was difficult to concentrate, and she often lost track of time.

Both Val and Monica seemed fine. They still texted regularly, and they talked on the phone. They'd been busy, but everything seemed normal. Why was it so much harder for Robin to get back to her life?

She was still haunted by the face of their rescuer. Despite fleeting glimpses on the edge of sleep that she put down to posttraumatic hallucinations, she hadn't seen him. No one had seen him. Val and Monica had no idea what she was talking about. She'd stopped bringing it up because she was starting to feel crazy. None of the police had seen anyone matching her description at the scene. No one appeared at the hospital, ready to take credit for saving three women from drowning.

Nothing.

She had to move on. She didn't have a choice.

After an hour of prodding, Robin convinced Grace that she was fine and didn't need any help. No doubt the lack of customers helped her argument. It was a Tuesday morning in the middle of fall; Robin wasn't expecting much.

She filled out online orders and texted Brent when she heard the delivery truck arrive.

"Okay," Brent huffed as they moved the midcentury desk. "Where are we putting this beauty?"

Robin pointed at the corner. "Right there."

"Where there is already a dresser." Brent's face fell. "Are we stacking them now?"

Robin smiled. "No, we're moving that one out and waiting for Monica to come pick it up."

Brent cleared his throat and shuffled adorably. "Oh. Monica?"

Her cousin had had a crush on Monica when she'd still been Monica Morales and the prettiest girl water-skiing on the lake.

"How's she doing?" Brent asked. "I mean, with the accident and all."

"She's fine. I think her cast is coming off next week."

"That's good."

"Jake is driving her, but can you hang around to help us move the dresser into her truck? Or are you busy?"

"I'll be around."

"Thanks." She glanced at him from the corner of her eye. "I'm sure she'll appreciate it."

"No problem."

They finished rearranging the new pieces, moved the old dresser to the loading area in the back, then Robin redecorated the street-facing window with bold fall decorations and waited for Jake and Monica to arrive.

Mark called her halfway through the morning. "You busy?"

"I have a few minutes."

"How are you feeling?"

Mark had been unusually attentive in the past two weeks. He'd been paying extra attention to her, though he was still leaving the bed before she woke. But he'd call to check in on her and was making dinner more.

"I talked to Austin this morning while you were walking."

Robin just barely kept from rolling her eyes. "What's going on?"

She hadn't been able to walk up and down hills with her newly sore knee, so Mark had pulled his old treadmill out of the garage and cleaned it so she could walk. It was better than nothing, but Robin missed her morning air.

"He's taking an art class this fall to fulfill his fine arts requirement," Mark said. "And he's doing really well."

"That's good." She sketched on the edge of a notebook. "He never took art in high school."

"Not once. But he's doing it there, and I guess he's doing really well."

"Drawing?"

"Sculpture."

"Really?" She shrugged. "That's cool."

"He was talking this morning about…"

Robin's stomach dropped. She knew what was coming.

"…changing majors," Mark finished. "To fine arts."

Robin took a deep breath. "Are you kidding me, Mark?"

"Okay, I know it's another change, but this time—"

"This time he's moving from his third major in two years to another major. Only this one isn't kinesiology or business, both of which could theoretically result in a job if he actually followed through on them. This time he wants an *art degree?*"

"Hey, *you* have an art degree," Mark said.

"And I'm working in an antique shop!" Robin stood, nearly overcome with anger at her son. "And I took class after class in high school. And before that, I did summer programs. I drew relentlessly. I taught myself how to paint from library books. He takes one art class—"

"You know what?" Mark said. "Don't yell at me about it. Yell at your kid." He hung up the phone and Robin was still fuming.

She picked up her phone and nearly dialed Austin's number; then she thought twice. She needed to calm down. She needed to cool down.

She went back to her desk and flipped a page in her notebook before she closed her eyes and put her head in her hands.

Everything about her life felt like it was dangling on the edge of a cliff. Like her car was balancing precariously over Glimmer Lake, ready to fall in and sink to the bottom if she couldn't pull it back in time.

That's where she lived now, balanced on the edge, ready for the last little weight that would make her topple over and into the depths.

Her phone buzzed. It was Mark.

I'm sorry I yelled. I have my doubts too.

Robin didn't know what to text back, so she didn't text anything. A few minutes later, another text came through.

The sheriff called and they're pulling the car up today. They said the crane was free a day early.

She felt her sigh of relief on the inside, as if seeing her car would finally put a ghost to rest. Move her past this hideous chapter of life.

She texted back: *I'll let Monica and Val know.*

He gave her a thumbs-up emoji.

She went back to sketching, not even thinking about what she was drawing. She was thinking about Austin as a little boy. He'd loved drawing with her but had quickly become distracted by any shiny new thing. Had she missed natural artistic ability?

Had Austin played with clay? He'd loved his LEGOs, but what did that mean? Every kid loved LEGOs.

She sketched and sketched, not realizing what her hand was doing. By the time she looked up, she realized that once again, she'd sketched a portrait of the man who had rescued them from the lake.

Dark hair. Dark, deep-set eyes. Heavy eyebrows and high cheekbones.

He was handsome, she realized. Rough, but handsome.

Why was he rough? How did she know that?

His hands had looked work worn. He'd had blisters and a cut on his knuckle.

Robin was staring at the sketch on her desk when the bell over the door rang.

Monica walked in with a bright smile. "Hey!"

Robin put down her pencil and walked over, wrapping her arms around her friend. "You're here."

Monica hugged her back. "You okay?"

"Just... having a day." She released her friend. "Austin is changing majors."

"Again?"

"To art."

Monica let out a cackling laugh. "Oh, I bet you love that."

Robin raised her hands in surrender. "You know... I think I just give up with that kid. Tell me what to do, mother of three grown boys."

"Honestly?"

"Honestly."

"Ignore him." She raised a finger. "As long as he's making good grades in school, keep helping him with tuition, but he should be paying some of it."

"He is."

"Good." Monica shrugged. "Then ignore him. It's his life. You can't figure it out for him anymore. You and Austin have always been too close in personality. Let it go."

Robin took a deep breath. "I'll try."

"Good place to start."

"How are you feeling?"

Monica shrugged. "Eh. I'm okay. I haven't been sleeping well."

Footsteps came from the back, and Jake walked through the door with Brent. "You didn't mention the sleep thing, Mom."

Monica shot her a look. "Because you're my kid and not my doctor," she said. "Hi, Brent. How are you?"

Brent rubbed the back of his neck. "I'm good. Sorry to hear you're not sleeping well. I think we got that dresser loaded up. Do you want to come take a look?"

"Sure, I—" Monica glanced at Robin's desk and her face froze. "Robin, who's that?"

"Who's—?" She saw where Monica's eyes were. "Oh, remember the guy I thought I saw in the lake? Doctor said he was a figment of my imagination."

Jake leaned over the desk. "Wow, you're a really great artist, Robin."

Brent said, "She won a state competition in high school."

"That's so cool."

Robin kept her eyes on Monica. "What's going on?"

Monica shook her head. "I don't... I'm just... I'm sure it's nothing. Let me go take a look at the dresser, and then we should get going."

Robin got her phone as soon as Monica walked to the back and texted her friend. *You better tell me what you saw.*

A text came back almost immediately. *It's nothing. It's probably nothing.*

Stay here for lunch. Tell Jake to come pick you up later. We need to talk.

CHAPTER 6

*V*al dropped three sandwiches on the table in the shop kitchen. "Okay, this better be good. My cook is pissed at me for abandoning him right now. Today is crazy."

"Something weird is happening." Robin flipped the sign on the front of the shop and walked back to the kitchen. "We've barely talked since the accident, but something is going on."

Robin had made another pot of coffee. It was fall in the mountains, and once it got cold enough, she could drink coffee all day. Monica was sitting at the table, staring at the sketch in Robin's notebook.

"So what's going on?" Val looked at the sketch. "Who's that? Robin, are you drawing again? It's about time."

Robin said, "It's the mystery man. Remember him?"

Val rolled her eyes. "This again? The doctor said—"

"I saw him." Monica raised her eyes to Val. "I saw him too."

"Where?"

Monica looked down. "It was in a dream," she said quietly. "I don't know him. Why would I see him in a dream?"

Val opened her mouth. Shut it. "I don't know. Robin probably told you what she saw and you—"

"I didn't see a guy kinda like him, Val. I saw *him*." Monica raised the notebook and pointed at the detailed sketch. "I saw this guy. Exactly him." She punched her finger into the notebook. "In one of my crazy dreams."

Val frowned. "What crazy dreams?"

"The ones I am having like every single night since the accident," Monica said.

Robin said, "I've had nightmares about the car too."

"We almost died," Val said. "Of course we're having nightmares."

"They're not nightmares." Monica shook her head. "I do have nightmares about being stuck in the car, but it's more than that."

Robin sat next to her. "More like how?"

Monica was frustrated. "It's just... they're dreams, right? But they're super vivid, and it's like I'm there. I used to dream about Gil all the time, which my therapist says is totally normal."

"See?" Val rolled a sandwich toward both of them. "We're all stressed out and that's all this is. Eat. Robin, I got you turkey because we're almost out of chicken."

"I don't care about the food." Robin set the sandwich to the side. "Monica, you said the dreams were weird. Weird how?"

"They're weird in that they're not weird. Does that make sense?"

Val and Robin exchanged a look.

"No."

"Not really."

"Okay, okay." Monica drummed her fingers on the table. "Okay, so you know how dreams are kind of all over the place? Like you're in one place, and then all of a sudden you're in another place, and it makes perfect sense in the dream, right? You don't even notice it."

"Okay and...?" Val unwrapped her sandwich and began to eat. "I don't know about you two, but I haven't had anything but coffee today and I'm hangry."

"Eat." Robin unwrapped her sandwich too. "I get what you're saying about dreams, so how are these dreams different?"

"They're linear. Like a scene out of a movie, only I just caught a bit in the middle and it doesn't make sense. But everything happens in order. I can hear people. Like really clearly. I can hear other things too. Like I can hear background noise and I notice it. Who does that in a dream?"

Val swallowed a large bite. "Don't ask me. I don't dream."

"Everyone dreams," Robin said. "You just don't remember."

"Either way, I have no idea what a normal dream is."

Monica said, "Well, I've always dreamed a lot, and these are not normal dreams. And I see the same ones over and over."

"Recurring dreams?" Robin took another bite of her sandwich. "How is that weird?"

"I can't explain it, but they just feel more real than normal dreams."

Val raised an eyebrow. "What does that mean?"

"I mean maybe they're not dreams?" Monica looked unsure.

Robin felt unsure. Of everything.

"If they're not dreams," Val said, "what would they be?"

"I don't know!" Monica threw up her hands. "I'm Catholic. I don't believe in psychics and visions and stuff."

"But a virgin birth is no problem?" Val narrowed her eyes. "Or a guy coming back from the dead?"

"It's not the same, Val!"

"Stop." Robin held out her hands. "We're not having this argument right now. Let me..." She took a deep breath. "Okay, something happened at the hospital, and I didn't tell anyone about it. Not Mark, not you guys. No one."

Monica's eyes went wide. "What happened?"

"I saw..."

A nurse with gunshot wounds who's been dead for over thirty years.

A little girl on the edge of the forest with bare feet.

A man sitting in the corner of a room.

The bell over the door rang and Monica rose. "I could have sworn we locked that."

Robin sighed and took a bite of her turkey sandwich. "We did."

Monica walked out to the shop and walked back. Her eyes were locked on Robin. "The door was locked."

Val frowned. "Is there someone in back?" She reached into her purse. "I have my pepper spray."

"It's locked in back too," Robin said. "There's no one here but us. It's probably just the vents or something."

"What were you talking about?" Val said. "What happened at the hospital?"

Robin's heart began to race. "I saw someone who wasn't supposed to be there. Someone who had already died."

"You saw a dead body?" Val grimaced. "Sorry. That's not fun. But, I mean, it is the hospital."

"No. I mean... she was kinda dead?"

Val shook her head. "You're not making sense. You did or did not see a dead body?"

"I saw her... but she wasn't dead. But she was."

Monica's eyes bugged out. "What?"

"There was a nurse in my room." Robin took a steadying breath and put her sandwich down. "I talked to her. We had this whole conversation, and she checked my vitals, but I didn't realize..."

Val was staring at her. "You didn't realize what?"

Robin reached for the notebook and flipped forward a few pages. "I talked to this woman." She showed them a portrait she'd sketched. "But then she turned around, and I saw gunshot wounds in her back."

Val and Monica both stared at her with their mouths open wide.

"I screamed," Robin continued, "and the nurses came in and the woman was gone. I don't remember her leaving. I don't remember the door opening until the other nurses came through. They told me I was hallucinating because of PTSD."

"Which you were," Val said. "It's completely normal, Robin. I mean, having it after an accident is normal. You know what I mean."

Monica murmured, "That doesn't seem normal to me."

"Or me," Robin said. "Why would I see someone or dream someone I'd never seen before? Never heard of before?

Then later, one of the nurses who came in told me about this woman—this other nurse—who was murdered in the emergency room in 1982."

"So you must have heard the story somewhere," Val said.

"I never heard her name or saw her face until that day." Robin looked hard at Val. "Look up her name on your phone. Look for Debbie Hawkins murder. 1982. Bridger City. It's her. I looked it up after they told me her name. I'm not crazy."

"I'm not saying you are."

"Your eyes are saying it."

Monica said, "So you think you saw a *ghost*?"

"I don't know. But I saw Debbie Hawkins in the hospital. She took my blood pressure. I felt it. And I saw a man in the lake." She tapped the picture Monica had been staring at. "I saw this guy—the same guy you saw in a dream. He broke the window in the car and got us out. And then he wasn't there."

Both Val and Monica were silent.

"I know it sounds crazy! But so does having..." She gestured toward Monica. "Visions. Or premonitions. Whatever."

Val shrugged. "I mean, weird things happen, Robin. Are you saying you believe in ghosts? If that guy in the water was a ghost, how could he have broken the window like you say he did?"

"You think I broke the window myself? With what?"

Monica said, "Everyone calm down. Robin, we're not saying you made him up. We're just saying..."

"What?" Robin asked. "For real, what are you saying? Because if you have a better explanation for all this, I'd love to know." Robin pointed at the door. "I hear that damn bell all

67

the time. Sometimes the door is open. Sometimes it's not. But that bell goes off all the time and no one is there."

Val and Monica didn't say anything.

"What about you?" Robin shoved Monica's foot under the table.

"Ow!" Monica sat up straight. "I'm sure I'm just imagining things."

"Did you see this guy in a dream or not?" Robin asked.

"Yes." Monica was looking paler and paler. "But" —she spoke carefully— "maybe—"

"And it wasn't just his face," Robin said. "Tell Val what you saw us doing."

Monica's hand traced over the notebook. "He was with Robin, and they were walking in the woods by the old mill, not far from where the car went in the water."

"That is not a dream," Robin said.

Val's eyes shot between the two of them. Suspicious, pragmatic Val. She wasn't buying any of it. "So what do you think it is?"

Robin didn't speak. Neither did Monica.

"Okay, let me get this straight." Val pointed at Robin. "You are saying you can see ghosts." She turned to Monica. "And you're saying that you are having... visions? Premonitions?"

"I think premonitions would be the more accurate term," Robin said quietly.

Monica added, "I googled it."

Val rolled her eyes. "Forgive me. It's been a while since I watched *Charmed*." She turned to Robin and held up her phone. "I looked. Your sketch is dead-on. Good job. It's Debbie Hawkins."

"I told you I didn't make her up."

"Because you saw this story somewhere!" Val said. "You remembered it—maybe not consciously—but when you ended up in Bridger City Hospital, your brain pulled it out—"

"I didn't suddenly remember a murder from 1982." Robin fought to keep her voice even. "I was eight in 1982. I wasn't watching the news or reading the paper."

"Your brain was reacting to stress," Val said. "That's it. That's all this is."

"And what about Monica?"

"She's dreaming. She's dreaming about weird, intense stuff—"

"Last night I dreamed about a hunting knife, and it had dried blood on it," Monica said. "It was in a dark place with stained glass windows. Is that a normal dream? I don't know any place that has stained glass except the church. I have *never* dreamed violent things. Never. I have happy, silly dreams. Sometimes sad dreams. But now I'm dreaming about Robin walking with a mystery man and bloody knives?"

"Will you just stop and listen to what you're saying?" Val put her phone down. "You're saying that you're seeing ghosts, Robin. *Ghosts.* That you can even have conversations with them, and they do stuff." She turned to Monica. "And you're having *visions.*"

"Premonitions."

"Whatever you want to call them, you're saying you get previews of the future? Really?" She looked between them. "I mean... *really?*"

Robin didn't say anything. She could see the skepticism

on Val's face, but nothing else made sense. She'd been turning it over in her head for weeks.

"I know I'm not crazy," Robin said. "And I know this doesn't seem like something I'd believe—"

"You're like the last person who would believe bullshit like this!"

"I know. Because I'm practical, sensible Robin." She looked Val dead in the eye. "So doesn't that mean something?"

Val stood and walked around the kitchen. "I want to get this straight so I can be sure how much counseling you both need. You—my two normal, nonflaky friends—had near-death experiences, and now you think we've all developed psychic powers, and *that's* the most logical explanation? Not that we're all dealing with post-traumatic stress disorder. You think you're psychic?"

Robin leaned on the table. "What did you say?"

"It's PTSD, Robin. I'm saying—"

"No." Monica narrowed her eyes. "The thing before."

Val frowned. "What?"

Robin and Monica exchanged a look.

Did you hear that?

Uh, yeah. I heard that.

Robin turned back to Val. "We've *all* developed psychic powers?"

CHAPTER 7

"We've *all* developed psychic powers," Monica said. "That's what you just said, Val."

"I didn't say that."

"Yeah, you did," Robin said. "What's going on?"

Val blinked and stared straight at her. "Nothing."

Robin narrowed her eyes. "You are lying so hard right now. You are lying harder than when you told Julie Gulling her parents wanted to adopt you."

"That was so mean," Monica said. "You scared that girl."

"She deserved it," Val said.

Robin was not going to let Val and Monica go off on a tangent. "Don't distract us, Val. You just said, 'We've *all* developed psychic powers.' Tell us what is going on."

Robin was positive something was up with Val. She glanced at Monica. Monica knew it too.

"What are you feeling, Val?" Monica used her calm-yet-firm mother-of-four voice. "We've been honest with you even when it's been embarrassing."

"Nothing." Val let out a forced laugh. "I'm stressed out.

We all are. We almost died. Have you thought about that? *Really* thought about it? That's why we're having PTSD. We were terrified and nearly died and had to face the fact that our lives are a lot more precarious than we all thought."

Val lifted her chin as she sat back at the table and picked up her sandwich. "And to be honest, I'm still a little offended that Monica wouldn't marry me if we were lesbians because I don't fold laundry."

"Don't try to change the subject," Monica said.

"I'm just saying that seems like a really minor thing to focus on when we were almost going to die."

"But we didn't die, and I bet you still have laundry on your couch from before my birthday!"

"Are we in seventh grade again?" Robin rubbed her temple. "Both of you. Stop."

Was Val right? Was Robin imagining all this?

No. She wasn't an imaginative person. She hadn't been since she was a child.

"We probably all need to see therapists," Val said, "but my craptastic insurance doesn't do that, so I'm up shit creek. I'll be fine. I'll just drink more wine. Cheap wine."

"Yes, that's definitely a healthy strategy to nurture mental health," Robin said.

"Better than avoiding everything, which seems to be your go-to."

Bitch. Robin didn't say it, but her glare seemed to get the sentiment across, because Val was glaring too.

Monica reached for both their hands. "This is not accomplishing anything. Val, for the record, if I liked girls, I would consider you a great catch."

"Thanks, Monica."

"But I would insist on hiring someone to do laundry. Don't argue with me, you know I'm right."

Val shrugged. "Fine."

Robin said, "I'm so glad you got your completely fictional marriage sorted out."

Val flipped her off.

Monica shot Robin a look. "Before we start bickering again, tell us what's going on, Val. Even if you think we're full of shit, tell us what's going on."

"Nothing!" Val pulled her hand from Monica's and rose. "I'm telling you, this is PTSD. Do you remember how crazy I was after Josh left? This is worse, okay? I'm edgy all the time. I don't want to be in my shop. I'm losing patience with everyone, and don't even get me started on all the shit people leave behind."

"What?"

"Just... stuff! Have you ever noticed how much crap all of us have?" She walked over to the table. "Purses! Why do we carry purses everywhere?"

"Because women's pants don't have decent pockets because fashion designers are men who suck?" Robin said. "I don't know. Having a purse never bothered you before."

Val pointed to the kitchen. "All these... what do you call them? Little decorative things? Doodads? Fiddly shit? I don't know."

"Small decorative items?" Robin asked.

"Art?" Monica appeared confused.

"Stuff!" Val exploded. "We have so much random stuff! People leave phones and purses, and they're fucking careless with their stuff, okay? It's annoying as hell. And my boys are pigs lately. Just pigs. I feel like my house exploded."

"Your boys are always messy." Monica's voice was steady. "It's never bothered you before."

"Well, it's getting worse."

"What on earth is going on with you?" Robin was struggling to figure this out. Her friend had always had a short temper, but being annoyed at purses? That was just... weird.

"I'm telling you," Val said, "we're all feeling it. This is a normal reaction to nearly dying. I'm irritable. Robin's seeing things from the past and thinking they're something weird. Monica is dreaming disturbing things, but these are all symptoms of—"

"I really don't think it's PTSD," Monica said quietly. "But I do think something is going on with you. Why won't you tell us?"

Val paused and leaned back on the counter, only to pull her hands away as if she'd been burned.

"That." Robin pointed at her. "What was that?"

"Nothing."

Going with a sudden instinct, Robin reached for a pen and tossed it at Val. "Catch."

Val spread her hands, as if afraid the pen would bite. The pen clattered on the hardwood floor and Val's eyes went wide.

Robin stood. "Why aren't you touching anything?"

Monica pointed at her. "Something happens when you touch stuff, doesn't it?"

"I'm fine." Val paced back and forth in the small space, keeping her distance from Monica and Robin. "It's stress. I'll be fine."

"You keep saying that, and you're obviously not," Robin said. "Stop bullshitting us."

"What happens when you touch things?" Monica asked.

"I just..." Val bit her lip.

"Oh, for fuck's sake," Monica said. "It's us, Val!"

Both Robin and Val turned to Monica with wide eyes.

"She said fuck," Robin muttered. "You know how mad she has to be to say that word. You better tell us."

Val actually looked offended. "You never say fuck."

"I do when one of my best friends is lying to me. Spill."

All three of them were standing in the middle of the kitchen, staring at each other.

"Josh brought me a blanket in the hospital," Val blurted out.

Monica wrinkled her nose. "Ew. Why was Josh at the hospital?"

"Did your mom invite him?" Robin asked.

"Yes, of course she did, but that's not the point. He gave me this blanket. It was actually kind of perfect. It was a *Coraline* blanket—"

"Oh my gosh!" Monica grinned. "That's your favorite. I didn't think he was that smart. That's actually cool."

"I thought so too, until I grabbed the blanket and I just had this..." Her hands went to her temples and made exploding motions. "I just had this flash, and I saw him—I *saw* him—handing that blanket to his little girlfriend, and I could hear them. And she asked him what it was, and he said it was a *Coraline* blanket, and she said, 'What's that?' And I heard them, you guys. I *heard* them. It was like I was in the room."

"Like my dreams," Monica said.

"Or my imagination." Val put her hands on her hips. "So I tossed the blanket back at him and said I knew he'd gotten it for Rachel, and his face completely gave it away. He got it for her and gave it to me and I saw it. I saw it when I touched the blanket and..." Val seemed to deflate. "This is bad, you guys. If you're right and this isn't some weird thing my brain is doing because of stress, this is so, so bad."

The gravity of what Val was saying finally sank in. She was seeing things—visions—when she touched things. Pens. Blankets. Counters. Any. Thing.

"Oh shit," Robin said. That could be a nightmare.

Monica asked, "Does it happen when you touch other stuff?"

Val nodded, crossing her arms like she was trying to hide her hands.

"Like what?"

"Uhhh... keys this morning. I knew a guy at the café was cheating on his girlfriend when I picked up his keys. His side chick handed them to him when he left her house."

Monica made a face. "Ew."

"Yeah, tell me about it. I know his girlfriend, and I know the side chick too. They're both customers. But then, not all keys make me react. Uh... books. Most books do, but I usually just see someone reading them, so it's not that bad. Purses." She took a deep breath. "Purses are hit and miss."

"Phones?"

"Not anything electric," Val said. "Not so far. I kind of experimented at home a couple of nights ago. I touched Jackson's phone and I didn't get anything, and he's on that thing all the time."

"What about if you touch people?"

"Nothing." She let out a breath. "Thank God."

"But stuff?"

"Some stuff. And not electronics."

"Is it just people you know?" Monica asked. "Like maybe it's only people you know in your daily life?"

"I don't know, Monica." Val looked lost. "I haven't asked anyone about this. I kept hoping it was some weird reaction to stress, but what if it's not? What if it's permanent? I don't want this!"

Monica muttered, "I don't particularly like these dreams either."

"You think I like seeing ghosts?" Robin asked. "It's freaky. What if I start seeing more? What if I can't *stop* seeing them?"

"Why did this happen?" Val asked. "Why us? What are we supposed to do with... supernatural powers?" She shook her head. "I feel ridiculous even saying that."

"Why *not* us?" Monica leaned her chin on her hand. "I mean, if you think about it, we're at the perfect age. All those shows where teenagers get magic powers are dumb. Remember how stupid we were when we were sixteen? I'm much more capable of being a superhero at this point in my life."

"If my knee wasn't acting like crap lately, I'd totally be on board with being superheroes," Robin said. "But as it is, I can barely walk five miles on the treadmill right now."

"You better not be getting any ideas about spandex suits, Monica," Val said. "And I don't think seeing visions when I touch random crap is much of a useful skill. How am I supposed to live that way? Think about having two teenage boys. I'll basically never be able to enter their room ever again."

Monica cringed. "They're definitely going to have to start doing their own laundry."

"How does it work though?" Robin sat up straight. "Is it everything? You said some keys don't make you see anything."

"I don't know," Val said.

"I have an idea. Follow me."

Sandwiches forgotten, they headed toward the door and into the main floor of the antique shop. Robin pointed to the new desk in the corner. "Touch that piece. It's from an estate sale in Sacramento. See if you get anything."

Val was wary. "An estate sale? Like, from someone dead?"

"I don't think anyone died *on* the desk or anything. You're not gonna see anything gross." *Probably.* "We just moved it in today. Maybe we can figure out how this works."

"But I touched it too," Monica said. "And Jake and Brent. And the delivery guy."

"Exactly." Robin patted the edge of the desk. "Give it a feel. See if you get any of us, or just the elderly lady it belonged to."

Val walked over and put her hand flat on top of the desk. She closed her eyes and her shoulders visibly relaxed. "She wrote letters here. She loved writing letters. She looks happy. Nothing bad."

"You saw that?" Monica asked.

"Yeah." She shrugged. "Okay, I guess it's like what you were describing. Like watching a scene from the outside. Like a movie."

"Okay." Robin nodded. "Okay, so you can touch things

and know something about their owner." She pointed to another desk. "Now try that one."

Val put her hand on the next desk and frowned. "Kind of... a feeling? But nothing specific."

"It's from the old high school home ec classroom," Robin said. "So it didn't really belong to anyone. It would have belonged to lots of different people, but I doubt any of them were attached to it."

"Oh," Monica said. "I see what you're saying. So Val can feel if a thing *belonged* to someone, but not if it was kind of a general thing that lots of people used. Or something someone just touched for a minute."

"If that's true, then it's a huge relief," Val said. "I was worried about the tables in the café because so many people touch them all the time. I have to clear dishes. Handle cash. It's kind of a nightmare. I've been wearing gloves as much as possible."

"Which is good anyway, because money is disgusting," Monica said. "I saw a report about it once on the news."

Robin heard a buzzing from down the hall and realized she'd left her phone on the table. She walked back into the kitchen and saw her phone rioting on the table with two missed calls and a bunch of text messages.

She picked up the phone and answered. "Mark?"

"Is anyone at the shop with you right now?"

"Yeah. Val and Monica came by for—"

"Good. Perfect. Get the girls and go down to the lakeside where the car went in. The sheriff just called. They found something weird in the car."

CHAPTER 8

When Robin, Monica, and Val pulled up in Val's truck, Mark met them at the road. A group of police and a large crane were sitting on the edge of the lake while people milled around behind the equipment. At the lakeside, Robin saw her old Subaru looking remarkably intact. All four doors were open, and water dripped onto the narrow, sandy beach while people in uniform milled around.

Mark walked over to her, took her shoulders, and kissed her forehead. "You okay?"

She frowned. He was being... weird. "Yeah. I was just having lunch with Monica and Val. Did they find any of our stuff?" They'd left all their clothes and purses in the car.

"Your purse is in the back and they've found a few other things, but that's not really why the sheriff called." He kept his voice low. "Robin, was there anyone else in the car with you? Anyone?"

She frowned. "What?"

"Was there anyone—"

Val broke in. "Are you trying to accuse Robin of something? We were in the car alone. Just us. What the hell is this about?" She put her fists on her hips.

Mark kept his voice low. "Just... you do not have to say anything right now, okay? Remember that."

Robin spotted Sheriff Sullivan Wescott striding over to them. Sully was a few years older than she was, but she remembered him a little from school.

"Hey, Sully. What's up?"

Sully was an old-fashioned guy. He was a tall man with broad shoulders and a square jaw. He had a rifle rack in the back of his truck and a full row of lights on the top. If someone wanted to imagine "small-town mountain sheriff," they could just look at a picture of Sully.

"Robin." He tipped his hat. "Monica. Valerie."

"Just Val," she muttered. "For the hundredth time."

Sully ignored her. "Before I get into details, I need to know if there was anyone or anything in the car with you a few weeks ago when you went in."

Robin frowned. "I mean, we had our clothes and purses. I think there's some fishing stuff in the trunk. Maybe a camp knife? What are you—?"

"Not worried about a camping knife," he said gruffly. "Shit, ladies. I know all three of you. This doesn't make any damn sense, but I have to ask."

Monica cocked her head and stepped forward. She was small, but she was Gil Velasquez's widow, which meant every civil servant in town treated her with a degree of deference.

"Sully, what the heck are you talking about?"

He turned and waved at them to follow. "Just... see for yourselves. Don't touch anything."

Mark grabbed Robin's hand as they walked to the car. Val and Monica walked behind them.

"Do you know what he's talking about?" Robin murmured.

Before Mark could answer, Sully was shooing people from the car and pointing to something in the back.

Monica gasped audibly.

"Holy shit," Val muttered.

Robin's jaw dropped.

She didn't say a word. She couldn't. It didn't make sense. None of it did. The car was intact, save for the driver's window, which was shattered. Broken glass littered the floor and seat. But lying in the back of the car, stretched across the bench seat, was a rotting skeleton, mouth gaping, a loop of rusted metal chain wrapped around its legs.

Val said, "Who the hell is that?"

Sully turned to her. "Yeah, we're pretty curious about that too."

ROBIN WAS at the sheriff's station. She'd never been to the station before, except once when Austin was a baby and she couldn't figure out how to buckle his car seat into their old Ford Explorer properly. She didn't want to get a ticket and the highway patrol office was all the way down the hill, but the sheriff's deputy had shown her. She sipped her coffee and waited for Sully.

He'd been taking statements from Monica and Val before he got to Robin. But before they could talk, Sully and Mark had gotten into a low-key argument when Sully said he needed to question her about the accident.

Mark had drawn him away, and she couldn't hear anything clearly until Sully growled, "For fuck's sake, Brannon, I'm not gonna arrest your wife for murder. Calm down."

Robin's eyebrows went up. Murder?

Well, that was definitely not boring. Maybe she should have felt more worried, but she was too confused about what had happened.

How on earth did a skeleton get into the car? If it had been in the bottom of the lake, had it drifted through the window? That didn't make sense. It would have been in the front seat then. The back windows weren't open.

Sully finally sat across from her. She wasn't in an interrogation room or anything like you'd see on a TV show. Did Glimmer Lake even have an interrogation room? The sheriff's office didn't even look like it had a meeting room. She and Robin and Val were all just sitting at different desks.

Mark was pacing in the hallway. Should she be worried that her husband was worried about her being questioned?

Did Mark secretly think she was capable of murder?

He has seen you when you haven't eaten all day and after an estate sale day with your mom.

Fair. She couldn't dispute that.

Sully finally sat across from her at the too-small desk that likely belonged to a woman, judging from the flourishing houseplant and the line of framed pictures.

"Hey, Robin."

"Hey, Sully."

He took out a yellow pad of paper. "Okay, first off, I don't think any of you three are likely to murder anyone unless they were gonna hurt your kids."

Robin glanced over her shoulder. "I don't know. Mark's kind of driving me crazy with the pacing."

Sully cracked a smile. "Eh, he wanted you to get a lawyer before you talked to me."

"Should I?"

Sully rolled his eyes. "This is not a new crime. I don't know if you noticed that chain around the guy's... girl's...? I don't know. That's for the state medical examiner to say. But I know chains and I know locks. That setup was old as hell."

"How old?"

"Old old. Like, they were selling that before our parents were born."

"So the bones are old?"

He took a deep breath. "Probably. We're sending everything to the state medical examiner tomorrow. We don't have any missing people reports in town, so it's likely whoever it is has been dead for a long time."

"So weird."

"Agreed." He was jotting down notes. "But tell me, for the report, what were you and your friends doing the night your car went into the lake?"

"It was Monica's birthday. We were headed up to the lodge for drinks and karaoke." She kept her voice low. "You know, it was her first birthday since Gil—"

"Yeah, Valerie brought that up too." He glanced across the room. "How's she doing?"

"Monica?" Robin shrugged. "Good days and bad."

"That was a fucking tragedy. Excuse my language."

"Agreed. We wanted to take her out and do something

fun. Which didn't exactly turn out the way we'd planned. I just... it was bad. It was a really bad night, and now I've spoiled her birthday too."

"It wasn't bad," Sully muttered. "If you'd died, it would have been bad. But you lived, so now you just have a really cool story to tell."

Oh, Sully, you have no idea.

He continued, "Tell me about the guy you saw."

"What guy?"

"The guy in the lake." He looked at his notes. "The night of the accident, you told the EMTs a guy swam down to the car and smashed the window with a rock to get you guys out. I saw the shattered window. There're lots of rocks down there. The glass is in the car, not outside it." He looked up. "So your story checks out. Tell me about the guy."

Robin blinked. She'd been expecting Sully to say she was hallucinating. "You believe there was a guy?"

"Yeah. The glass was broken from outside, and now there's a body in the back of the car. Whoever swam down and rescued you might know how it got there. Was he in a suit?"

Robin shook her head. "A swim suit?"

"Diving suit. It's pretty deep where you went in. And it's cold."

"No, nothing like that."

"What did he look like?"

Robin held out her hand. "Let me see your pen."

Sully frowned and then shoved pen and paper toward her.

"I'll draw him. That's easier than describing him." Robin sketched out a picture that was closer to what she'd seen in mug shots or on television. Facing forward, neutral expression.

"Wow," Sully said. "You'd be a good sketch artist."

"I doubt it. Drawing portraits from people's descriptions is a completely different skill than drawing from my own memory." A few minutes and she had a decent sketch of her mystery man.

Sully took it and frowned. "He looks familiar, doesn't he?"

"I thought so too. Like maybe a weekender?"

"Maybe." Sully drummed his fingers on the table. "I'll put one of the guys on it. See if anyone else has seen him around. Thanks, Robin."

"No problem. Is there anything else?" She'd never finished her sandwich, and now she was ravenously hungry. Nothing good could come of that. "Can I collect my pacing husband and go home?"

Sully squinted at the picture. "Your family's been in town for a long time, right?"

"Since before it was a town, I guess. We owned the land up in the hills. The dam just turned it into lakefront property."

His eyebrows went up. "Lucky for you."

"Lucky for my grandparents maybe." Robin shrugged. "Most of it's still logging land. The real estate market in Glimmer Lake isn't exactly booming."

"I know," Sully muttered, paging through his notes. "That's why I like it."

He'd worked in Southern California for a while. Robin had forgotten that. After working in LA, Glimmer Lake must be a snooze. Of course, maybe that's why Sully liked it.

Val and Monica walked over. "You ready to go?"

She glanced at Sully, who nodded.

"Yeah." Robin rose. "I'll probably just go with Mark though. He's been waiting."

"Okay." Monica gave her a hug. "So weird and random."

"I know."

"See you, ladies," Sully said. "I'll call if I have any more questions."

"Please do," Monica said.

"Please don't." Val hooked her purse over a shoulder and put on her black aviators.

Sully glanced at her, and the corner of his mouth turned up. "You going to start offering a law-enforcement discount at the café, Valerie?"

"Do I look like Denny's?"

Monica pulled her away and headed for the door. "Bye, Sully. Call us when you find out about the bones."

"That could be months," he said. "Possibly years."

Robin walked toward Mark. "Ready to go?"

He ran his fingers through his hair and reached for her hand. "Yeah. You okay?"

"Sure." She threaded her fingers through his and glanced over her shoulder. "It's not the city. It's Sully. He knows I'm not a murderer."

Mark let out a sigh of relief. "It's just so strange. All this is..."

"I know." She squeezed his hand. "Come on. Let's head home. I still haven't eaten lunch."

Robin walked out of the sheriff's station feeling... kind of badass.

She'd survived a horrible car accident.

She'd seen a ghost. Probably. Or she was going crazy. Either way, not boring.

Now there was a dead body, and she'd just been questioned by the sheriff and given him evidence.

"This has been the strangest month I can remember in a long time," Mark said.

"I know." A smile lifted the corner of her mouth. "It's kind of exciting, right?"

He muffled a laugh and unlocked the car before he opened the door. "I mean... I guess. But I'd rather you not have life-threatening accidents to liven up our lives, okay?"

"Fine." She sighed dramatically. "If you're going to insist on being boring..."

Mark barked out a laugh and shut the door after she climbed in the car. He walked around and Robin closed her eyes in the sun-warmed cab of his pickup truck.

Warm. Lovely. She felt warm. She felt... alive.

Mark got into the truck and started it, letting the engine warm up. He looked at her with an odd expression.

"What?"

The corner of his mouth twitched. "I don't know. You seem different."

"Me?" She shrugged. "Still me."

"Thank goodness."

She wasn't sure what that meant, but she checked her phone while the truck warmed up. A few texts from her mother. Another from a customer wanting to know about the new desk she'd put on the shop's social media feed.

As the truck pulled out of the parking lot, Robin glanced up. She saw the face of her mystery man appear in the dappled shade of the woods behind the sheriff's station. Before she could open her mouth, he was gone.

Again.

She didn't say anything to Mark. What could she say?

Hey, honey, so I've started seeing ghosts.

No, no. It's fine. Pretty sure it's just an early menopause symptom. Like hot flashes or weight gain.

No, I don't think hormone replacement therapy is going to help with this one.

She felt her phone buzz and touched it to open the group text between her, Monica, and Val that had been going for roughly ten years, ever since Val finally gave in and got a mobile phone.

Monica had texted: *Okay, so I have a super-gross job for Val, and she's refusing to do it.* Another text a moment later. *She can't text because she's driving, but she says I'm being unreasonable.*

What is it?

She needs to touch those bones they found in the back of the car and find out if they're related to the weird stuff we're experiencing. But she won't because she says I'm being gross.

Robin winced. It was actually a really good idea. But also horrible. But also maybe helpful? She texted back: *V said she doesn't get anything from people though. Are bones people?*

Good point. I'll bring that up. A pause. *She's agreeing with you, bc of course she is.*

Robin texted, *Maybe she can touch the chains?*

I'll suggest it.

A few minutes later, another text came in. *Okay, she says she'll touch the chains and the lock, but we have to go with her because it could be super horrible, which is fair.*

When?

Tonight.

Tonight?

Tonight. Remember S said the bones were going to the crime lab in Sacramento tomorrow.

"Right." Robin bit her lip. "Mark, can you pick Emma up from the library tonight?"

"She really needs to get her license," he muttered. "We never had to chauffeur Austin when he was a senior."

"Austin also didn't get grades like Emma, so maybe we shouldn't compare—"

"You know what? Agreed. Let's not get into comparing Emma and Austin. Yes, I can get Emma. You need to go over to Monica's?"

To Monica's... and the morgue. "Yeah. To Monica's."

"No problem."

She texted back: *Tonight is a go. Let's break into the morgue and make Val touch some old gross bones.*

Monica texted back: *Val says chains only. She only touches old gross bones if they belong to millionaires who want to pay her mortgage.*

Robin bit her lip to keep from laughing.

CHAPTER 9

"*D*oes Glimmer Lake even have a morgue?" Val asked. "Where are we going?"

"The hospital." Monica was driving her minivan into Bridger City because how else would three middle-aged possible psychics go out investigating the bones that had mysteriously ended up in their car when they drove into a lake?

"Are we sure driving your minivan is the best idea?" Robin said. "Should we park around the block maybe?"

Val turned around, her eyes narrowed. "You think someone is going to be suspicious of a minivan in a hospital parking lot?"

"Well…"

"You know, a lot of private detectives use minivans in their work because they're both inconspicuous and also have a lot of cargo room." Monica read a lot of true crime and it showed. "Also, they're very comfortable when you have to wait a long time."

"The legroom is pretty great." Robin sighed. "I'm going to have to get a new car eventually."

"I hate that," Val said. "Can you buy one online?"

"Can you?"

Monica said, "Gil always bought our cars at the end of the year and the end of the month. He said you get the best deal during that time. Something about sales quotas."

"I inherited the Subaru from my mom. I loved that car."

Val pursed her lips. "You probably shouldn't have put it in the bottom of a lake then."

"Thanks. Great advice."

Monica's low chuckle broke the tension in the car. Val looked over her shoulder and winked at Robin. Monica didn't laugh much lately. Hearing it put a smile on Robin's face even if Val was being kind of bitchy.

The forty minutes into Bridger City flew by, and pretty soon they were pulling into the familiar hospital parking lot. Robin had been there countless times to visit friends who were having babies or whose parents were in the hospital. Both her kids had been born in Bridger City. Austin had broken his arm when he was eleven. Emma had her tonsils out at thirteen.

She knew they'd blend in with all the other visitors, but she still felt conspicuous as Monica led them into the lobby and down a hall, not once stopping or pausing for anyone to question them.

"Where are we going?" Val asked quietly.

"Just follow me," Monica said.

"Do you know—?"

"Val, shut it." Robin knew why Monica knew where the morgue was. She was only surprised Val didn't remember.

Monica hadn't been home when Gil had died. Jake had been the one to find him. Robin had been the one to drive Monica into Bridger City to join the boys because they'd taken Gil's body to the hospital morgue.

They walked through corridors and through doorways, following Monica silently.

What was she feeling? The last time she'd been here had been maybe the worst day of her life. Why had she suggested coming back?

They reached a door that simply said Morgue on the door.

"Do you think it's locked?" Val whispered.

"Probably."

Monica reached for the handle. "We're not going to know until we try." She gripped it, pulled down.

And the door swung open.

"That can't be legal," Val said. "You just leave a morgue unlocked?"

"I mean, it's Bridger City," Robin said. "Not LA."

"Weirdos are everywhere, Robin!"

Robin was watching Monica's face. She had the door handle in her hand, but she hadn't pushed it open. She hadn't gone inside. "We don't need to do this," Robin put her hand on Monica's shoulder. "We're probably just imagining—"

"Do you want to find out what's happening to us?" Monica's eyes cut her. "I do. I want to find out how that body got in the back of your car. I want to find out why this weird guy who's maybe a ghost is in my dreams."

Robin nodded. "Okay. I saw him again this afternoon by the sheriff's station. Just for a second. You realize—"

"The bones in there might belong to the mystery man?" Monica asked. "Yeah. I had the same thought."

"Yeah."

Val took a deep breath and put her hand on Monica's. "Okay. Let's get this over with."

Monica and Val pushed the door open, and all three of them stepped into a dark room that smelled like disinfectant.

"Lights, lights, lights."

Robin pulled out her phone and flipped on the flashlight. "Is this enough?"

"No," Val hissed. "There are dead people in here! Turn the overhead light on."

"People will be able to see from outside," Robin said. "There's a window in the door."

"No one is out there!"

"Do you want them to find us? They're going to think we're the weirdos!"

"Will you just—"

The lights went on. Monica walked over and shoved a piece of paper in the little window at the top of the door. "Stop arguing. Let's find them."

Monica walked to a wall of square doors.

"That looks exactly like it does on TV shows," Val said quietly.

"Well, yeah." Monica squinted. "Why wouldn't it? Darn it, I forgot my readers. Robin, do you have an extra pair?"

"I didn't bring them."

Val shoved both of them to the side. "Okay, old ladies, get out of the way and let the young eyes in."

"Right." Monica drew out the word. "I've seen you on your phone, Val. But keep lying to yourself. That's fine."

"This one has a name on the door," Robin said. "We'd be looking for like... John Doe or something, right?"

They all took different rows. Val was the tallest and read the top row. Robin the middle. Monica the bottom.

"Jerri West," Monica said. "Isn't that Dorrie's sister? From the salon?"

"Oh, maybe. That sounds familiar."

"That's a shame. I wonder what happened."

"Let's not find out."

"Focus," Robin said.

Val said, "Here's a John Doe." She opened the door and quickly slammed it shut.

"What is it?" Robin frowned. "What happened?"

"Just... definitely not bones."

"Okay." Robin decided she didn't want to know.

"Found it," Monica said. "It just says Glimmer Lake Bones. That's more obvious than I would have expected."

"But accurate."

Robin and Val walked over, and Monica opened the door.

She gripped the edge and pulled. A long metal shelf slid out from the wall with a black body bag lying on top. It was pretty flat, but then there was far less body in the bag than normal.

Robin bit the inside of her lip and stepped forward. "Okay. Let's do this."

She pulled the zipper and the bag opened. There another bag around the bones, but they were visible through the plastic, brownish grey, still looking like they'd been bathing in mud.

Val scrunched up her nose. "Still gross."

"But less gross," Monica said. "They're dry at least."

Robin tried to hold her breath, but it was impossible. "Slightly less... gooey."

"Oh my God, did you have to say *gooey*?" Val had a hand over her mouth. "I can't touch those."

"Just like... a finger," Monica whispered. "Just try a finger."

"His finger or hers?" Robin asked.

Val stomped her foot. "That question is gross too!"

"When Jackson had a compound fracture, you held his arm together all the way to the hospital, Val. This can't be grosser than that," Monica said.

"It was equally gross, but Jackson is my kid and I'm legally required to handle his gross bones." Val pointed at the skeleton. "I am not legally required to touch his!"

Robin reached out for Val's hand, took it, and held it over what remained of the body. "One finger," she said. "Just try. You need to know."

Val took a deep breath and nodded. She reached out with two fingers and touched the least gooey part of the skull she could find, closing her eyes.

Robin held her breath for what felt like a minute but probably was only a few seconds.

Val withdrew her hand and shook her head. "Nothing."

"Okay, so now you know—whatever this weird thing is—it doesn't work on bones."

Monica quickly zipped up the body bag and reached for what looked like a white garbage bag that lay at the foot of the body. "I'm hoping the chains are in here."

"Would they be?" Robin said. "Or would Sully have sent them from his office?"

"They're here." Monica reached in and pulled out a clear

plastic bag with a white sticker on the front. "It's just one of those giant Ziplocs."

"Is it sealed?"

"Nope." Monica pulled it open. "I am not very impressed with our local chain-of-custody procedures, I can tell you that much."

"This isn't exactly a hot case," Val said, peeking over Monica's shoulder. "Okay, let me touch those. Not nearly as gross."

"Really?" Robin said. "Because these were around Dead Guy's legs. They're probably the reason—"

"Shut. It." She held up a hand. "The less I think about it, the better." She nudged Monica out of the way and reached into the bag. "Here goes."

Robin didn't know what Val saw when she touched things, but she knew whatever happened in the next moment wasn't good. It was like her friend's whole body seized.

"Hold her!" Monica got behind Val and held her around the waist. "Hey, honey. I got you. I got you, Val."

Robin ran to catch Val's shoulders. The woman was stiff as a board. It was like she'd received an electric shock and her entire body had frozen.

"Val," Robin said firmly. "Let go of the chains."

"She's not letting go."

"See if you can get her fingers loose."

Monica reached around and pried Val's fingers from around the rusted chain while Robin eased Val back and away from the drawer.

"Okay, I got it." Monica carefully put the chains back in the bag and sealed it while Robin caught Val, whose knees had given out as soon as she let go of the rusted metal.

"You got her?"

"Yeah." Robin eased Val down to the linoleum floor. "Monica, can I have your sweater?"

"Yeah." She threw a cardigan at Robin, who laid it under Val's head.

"Bag," Val murmured.

"What?"

"Gonna puke." She was swallowing hard. "Get me a bag."

"Right." Robin shot to her feet and dove for the row of cabinets by the sink. She couldn't find anything plastic, but she found a paper bag like the ones they had on airplanes. "Do these actually work?"

"Robin!" Monica held out her hands, and Robin tossed the bag to her. Monica caught it and got it to Val's mouth just in time.

Robin grabbed a few more bags and placed them next to Monica while she took care of Val. Next, she stood and tried to put everything around the bones back as they'd found it; then she pushed the metal drawer back into the wall of bodies and shut the door.

She walked over and grabbed a paper towel from behind the sink, wet it, and brought it back to Val, who was on her second bag.

"We're gonna have some cleaning up," Robin said quietly.

"She's almost done."

Robin knelt next to Val and rubbed her back.

"Have you ever thought about how many bodily fluids we've dealt with over the years?" Monica asked. "Between poop, puke, and blood, moms have to have the sturdiest stomachs in the world."

Val spat and reached for the paper towel. "Speak for yourself."

"Was it bad?"

"Yeah." Val's eyes were haunted. "Let's get out of here."

"Agreed." Robin quickly grabbed more paper towels and managed to salvage a plastic bag from under the wastebasket. She and Monica quickly cleaned the floor, hid all the towels and puke bags in the bag, and hurried out of the morgue, dragging Val between them.

"Where should we throw this away?" Robin held Val around the waist, the plastic bag in the other hand.

They had made it through the twisting corridors and were starting to pass nurses and other hospital employees in the hallway.

"We'll find a dumpster," Monica said quietly. "Oh shit."

"Wha—? Oh *shit*. Val, look sicker and keep walking."

Sully Wescott was walking through the double glass doors and into the lobby just as the three of them were entering the lobby from the hallway. Robin could see the moment Sully caught sight of them. His eyes widened, then narrowed.

Robin kept her eyes forward. "Monica, wave. Don't talk. Keep walking."

"Got it."

Robin's hands were full of the plastic bag, and she had one hand around Val, who looked near to death. If they were lucky, Sully would assume Val had the flu and they'd had to rush her to the hospital or something.

"Is he coming over?"

"He's debating."

"Keep walking. Quick. But don't look like you're being quick."

They made it through the lobby and out into the chilled night air. Val took a deep breath as if she were coming up for air, then straightened. "Where's the car?"

"This way." Monica steered the three of them through the parking lot and toward the minivan.

Robin threw the plastic bag in the back while Monica helped Val into the passenger seat, and then she started the car.

Within minutes, Robin, Val, and Monica were driving through the deserted streets of downtown Bridger City. They stopped at a filling station near the highway and dumped the plastic bag in the trash behind the dark store; then they got back in the minivan and turned toward home.

As soon as the van was pointed east, Monica turned to Val. "Okay, what did you see?"

"Him," Val said, looking over her shoulder to Robin in the back seat. "Your ghost. The one in your visions, Monica. Mystery Man is the bones in that body bag."

CHAPTER 10

"Tell us." Monica kept her eyes on the road, but her voice was low and intense. "What did you see when you touched the chains?"

"He was someplace underground. Like... it looked like a cabin, but I knew it was underground. A cave maybe? Something like that? But there were lamps and there were books and I saw a bed—more like a cot, I guess. And I saw him. His feet were chained to a big post, and he was desperately trying to get out."

Robin got her sketchbook out and tried to draw what Val was describing. "The chains were around his feet? What was he wearing?"

"Yes. He was sitting down, and they were around his feet. He was wearing... ordinary clothes. Jeans. A flannel shirt. Normal stuff."

Jeans and a flannel shirt was the de facto uniform of eighty percent of the men they knew. Jeans and a flannel shirt would not narrow down when the man died.

"What about his hair?"

"It looked like what you drew in the picture. His forehead was bleeding. I could see that through his hair. Someone had hit him on the head."

Monica said, "Probably so they could chain him up."

Robin talked as she sketched. "Tell me more about the post."

"It was wood. Thick. Square. You know what?" Val's eyes went wide. "I think he was in a mine shaft. That's what it looked like. It was in the middle of the room. It looked like one of those supports in a mine shaft."

"Lots of old mine shafts around here," Monica said. "Remember when we lived in that house on Cypress Loop? We had to warn the boys to stay out of them all the time."

"Cypress Loop isn't all that far from where we went into the lake," Robin said. "Val, was he saying anything? Was he shouting for help?"

Val shook her head. "No. Not a word. He was alone." Her voice got smaller. "He was so scared."

"But he was trying to get free?"

"Yes. His hands were bleeding, but he didn't have anything. Didn't have any tools. He reached for something I think, but he couldn't reach it. It was just a flash, but I got the feeling..."

"What?" The highway ended, and Monica took the turnoff toward Glimmer Lake.

"I heard a noise. There was a smell maybe. I'm not sure, but I think it was water." Her eyes were haunted. "He was afraid of the water. The water was coming, and he knew he was going to drown."

Robin tried to remain impassive as she finished her sketch. She'd pictured what Val was telling her and tried to translate it onto the page.

She passed the notebook up to Val. "How close am I?"

Val ran her fingers over the page. "Pretty close."

"Could you see anything more of the room?" Robin asked. "Did I miss anything?"

"Do you think it matters?" Monica asked. "Isn't it obvious what happened to Mystery Man?"

Robin knew in her gut, but she felt sick saying it. "Someone chained him up in an old mine shaft, and he drowned when they flooded the canyon. That's why he was at the bottom of the lake."

For years she'd had dreams about the old town of Grimmer lying under the serene waters of Glimmer Lake, rotting away as decades passed, a ghost town in the deep.

A ghost town with a real ghost.

"Maybe where he died isn't far from where our car went in," Val said. "Maybe that's why all this is happening."

"So if we find out what happened, do you think it'll all go away?" Monica asked. "Do you think our lives will get back to normal?"

"Maybe?" Robin said it, but she didn't believe it. "Either way, whoever that man was saved our lives. We owe it to him to find out who killed him."

"How the heck are we supposed to do that?" Monica said. "We're not detectives, Robin. We don't know how any of that stuff works. Reading crime novels does not mean I'm a cop."

Val looked over her shoulder and handed the sketchbook

back. "Seriously, Robin, what do we know? We're a home-maker, a coffee shop owner, and an antiques dealer. We don't know how to solve a decades-old murder."

"You can't think of it that way." Robin knew in her gut that they needed to do this. She felt more alive than she had in years. More confident. She had purpose. She had a goal. "We're a medium, a touch telepath, and a seer. Or something like that. Also, we have Monica's kick-ass minivan, and she already told us that's what private detectives use a lot, so we'll be fine."

Monica snorted and Val cracked a smile. "You've already kicked into super-organized-mom mode, haven't you?"

"Yes."

Monica turned in to her driveway. "Super-organized Robin is a fearsome thing."

"Think about it," Robin said. "Between the three of us, we've handled three marriages, one divorce, one ex-husband, eight mostly great kids, and two successful businesses. Not to mention all the laundry and the Parent Club meetings."

"And being a room mom."

"And planning funerals," Monica said quietly.

Robin continued, "We have stayed up to all hours nursing babies and finishing science projects on things we knew nothing about twelve hours before they were due. We know how to find information when we need it. Plus we have all the psychic stuff now."

"Okay," Val said. "But where do we even start with this? This isn't a middle school science project."

"No, but I think we can start the same place." Robin got out her calendar. She knew most people kept everything on their phones now, but she liked the visual and tactile experience of keeping a paper calendar. "Monica, you're really good at online research. Why don't you start with finding out everything you can about why they decided to flood Grimmer Canyon? There's got to be stuff online. When the café closes tomorrow, maybe you and Val can go to the library and see what they have there."

Monica nodded. "I can do that."

"Café closes at two," Val said. "I'll have a couple of hours before I have to pick up the boys. They both have practice after school right now."

"And I'll go talk to the only person I know who was alive when our mystery man was drowned." Robin closed her calendar. "I'm about due for a visit to Grandma Helen anyway."

IT WAS NEARLY midnight when Robin walked through her door. Mark was sitting at the kitchen counter, drinking something steamy.

He looked up. "Hey."

Robin glanced at the clock. "Hi. You're not in bed?"

Mark frowned. "You were gone a long time. Everything okay with Monica?"

Robin scrambled. She had expected Mark to be in bed. He was usually an early riser, so he went to sleep by nine or ten at the latest. "Uh... she's okay. Just haven't had time to really catch up with her since the accident."

"Val there too?"

"Yeah." She swallowed. "It was just the three of us. Hanging out."

"Huh." He flipped his phone over and over. "I texted you and you never got back to me. I was kind of worried because you were out so late."

Shit. She'd forgotten about his text. "I'm sorry. We were in the middle of something, and I forgot to text you back."

To be fair, it was right after they'd tossed the bag of Val's post-psychic-vision puke in the dumpster in Bridger City. Robin hadn't been thinking about anything but how to get that smell out of the car.

Mark held up his phone. "When I got worried, I looked on the family locator app we got when Austin got his phone and... you weren't at Monica's. Why were you in Bridger City?"

Robin's jaw dropped. "You were *spying* on me?"

"Spying?" Mark's eyes went wide. "It was past ten thirty and you weren't responding to texts. Your car went into a lake three weeks ago, Robin. I was *worried*. And now you're lying to me about it."

"I'm not lying to you! I was with Monica and Val. We were hanging out."

"In Bridger City?"

"Yes." *Looking at gross old bones and touching rusted chains from murder victims.*

Mark tossed his phone on the counter. "I don't believe you."

Robin didn't blame him. It wasn't exactly in character for her and her friends to randomly drive into Bridger City for no reason. If they wanted to go out for a drink, there were bars in Glimmer Lake. The only thing Bridger City had was more people, bigger grocery stores, and a hospital.

"Okay." She thought quickly. How to lie without lying? She didn't want to lie to Mark, but then she really didn't want to have to explain being suddenly psychic with her two best friends. "It's Val," she blurted.

He frowned. "Val?"

"Val needed to go to the hospital in Bridger City. I can't tell you why. It's not my place to tell you." None of those things were a lie. "Monica and I went with her."

Mark's face transformed from pissed off to worried. "Is she okay?"

"I think she'll be fine. She was doing okay when Monica dropped me off."

"Does she need help? Are the boys okay? Does she need help with anything around the house?"

Gil and Mark had stepped up for Val when Josh walked out. If there was anything she needed that her parents couldn't help with, Gil and Mark were always happy to lend her a hand. More than one fall, they'd spent a day or a couple of days at Val's, helping her and the boys get the house ready before snow came.

And with Gil gone, it was just Mark now.

"No." She tried to soften her tone when she heard the worry. "It's nothing with the boys. It's personal. And... she'll be fine."

"Are you sure?"

Robin was suddenly reminded that—even though he might ignore her sometimes—Mark was a good guy. A solid guy who stepped up for his friends. He liked being the hero, and that wasn't a bad thing. "She'll be okay, but thanks."

"Okay." He wiped a hand over his face, looking exhausted. "I'm sorry if it seemed like I was spying. I wasn't. I was just—"

"Worried." Her tone softened more. "I get it."

"We're all on that app, by the way. You can always see where I am too."

Oh technology, you double-edged sword. Robin would have to think up reasonable excuses for anywhere she went now. She hadn't even thought about that.

"I'm not..." Mark looked up. Sighed. "We've been kind of distant lately. I feel like we're both really busy, and I can't even remember the last time we went for a night out."

They hadn't gone out for a date in... Robin couldn't remember. Not since Gil had died, that was for sure. Before, the four of them would go out, but Robin and Mark rarely went out just on their own.

Robin shrugged. "It's fine."

"I don't think it is. I think it's... not fine." His eyes stayed on her, and Robin felt like Mark was seeing more than she was comfortable with. Of all the times for her husband to start paying attention to her, right when she was trying to figure out weird psychic powers was not ideal.

She gave him a tired smile. "You ready for bed? I am."

He looked surprised, but she could see he was tired too. "Yeah, I guess... Yeah, we should probably go to bed."

Robin patted his shoulder as she walked by and wondered what Mark would say if she told him the truth. He'd probably think she was a lunatic. He'd probably roll his eyes. He'd probably tell her to call her mom and get her head straightened out.

He would definitely not support the idea of Robin baking

cookies the next morning and running up to Russell House to interrogate her ninety-five-year-old grandmother. Maybe *interrogate* was the wrong word. Question? Coerce?

Whatever word she used, Grandma Helen was no pushover. Double-fudge brownies were definitely in order.

CHAPTER 11

ouble-fudge in hand, Robin made her way up to Russell House after she'd dropped Emma off at school and whipped up a batch of brownies. As usual, Mark was in his office before she woke, so she hadn't seen him that morning. She'd also swung by the shop and put a note on the door. It was the middle of the week. Glimmer Lake could wait to buy antiques until after lunch.

Gordon Russell had built his house on a wide sweep of lakefront property that overlooked what had been Grimmer Canyon. He'd built it three years after the dam had been completed and the lake was mostly full. He'd already moved his lumber mill up the hills and near the new road that led into the mountains and serviced the quickly growing town of Glimmer Lake.

Over the years, the Russells had built a library, a social hall at the Lutheran Church, purchased several stores, and built rental properties. By the time Gordon had passed away when Robin was a girl, the family was past comfortable and well into rich.

And yet, for her entire life, Helen Russell, Robin's grandmother, had worn a serene sadness on her face. She'd taken joy from her children and tolerated her bombastic and domineering husband. She'd encouraged her daughter Grace toward independence and played referee between her son Raymond and his father, who had never come to terms.

More than anything, she had enjoyed painting and her grandchildren. Helen came to life behind an easel and doted on both Robin and her older brother Jack, who lived near Lake Tahoe. She enjoyed being a great-grandmother even more.

Robin drove through the granite-decorated gates of Russell House and into a carefully managed forest that was Helen's other passion. Thick pines dense with an undergrowth of delicate ferns gave way to sweeping meadows of wildflowers.

It was all natural but carefully managed, just like the land where Russell Lumber still logged. Jack ran the logging company statewide, and Robin was proud of her brother's work. He'd taken Russell Lumber into the twenty-first century with sustainable practices. Conservation hadn't been high on the list of Gordon Russell's priorities, but Jack had made the company his own.

Because of Jack's good business management, Grandma Helen was living—and would continue to live—very well. Robin parked in front of a house that could only be described as a luxury mountain estate.

Russell House was a combination of granite rock and cedar, three stories looking over Glimmer Lake with a sloping lawn leading down to the water's edge where a boathouse and dock dominated the shore. If Robin hadn't grown up visiting, she would have thought it was a small hotel.

Robin rang the doorbell before she walked in. "Grandma Helen?"

She looked right, but her grandma wasn't in the front parlor where the light warmed the room, so Robin turned left from the grand entryway and walked through the dining room and into the kitchen.

Helen looked up from her cup of coffee. "Robin!" She held out a wrinkled hand. "I wasn't expecting a visit today."

"I know." Robin set the brownies on the kitchen table. "But I baked these, so I thought I'd bring you some."

Helen's eyes lit up. "They smell like they have walnuts."

"They do, but I cut them up really, really small, so you should be able to eat them and not bother your teeth."

Helen motioned Robin down. She bent over and her grandmother kissed her cheek. "You're such a good girl."

Robin turned her face and kissed Helen's wrinkled cheek. "I learned it from the best girl."

"Get some coffee," Helen said. "Your mother just brought up more of the little pod things."

Grandma Helen loved her coffee, but Grace and Robin didn't love her making it on her old percolator. They'd bought her a single-serve coffee maker, and Helen had grown to love it.

"How many cups have you had today?"

"Enough to keep my heart going," Helen said with a tiny bite in her voice. "Don't you worry about me."

"Have you been painting anything?"

"Just a few watercolors." Helen's complaints about aging

weren't wasted on her wrinkles or her glorious sweep of grey hair. They were reserved completely for arthritis and fading eyesight. She'd had to stop painting with oils in her seventies. The fumes gave her an awful headache. She'd switched to acrylics for a time but had eventually settled on watercolors, painting more and more landscapes through her eighties. Though she no longer finished many pieces, she still enjoyed it, and she liked taking her easel outside. She just sat instead of standing.

"And what have you been drawing?" Helen asked. "Anything new?"

Robin smiled. "This and that."

"Oh?" Helen looked surprised. "That's good." Helen had never approved of Robin moving back to Glimmer Lake. She'd told Robin to stay in the Bay Area and keep working on her art. But when Austin had been born, all Robin had wanted was the familiar. She wanted her friends and her family. Wanted cold clear air and wide-open skies.

There was no excuse for stopping her art. She'd just gotten busy.

"Have you been sleeping well?" Robin brought her coffee to the table.

"Yes. It's finally getting cold."

"I know you like that."

Helen was a mountain girl through and through. Her family had lived in Grimmer before the dam was built. Her father had been a rancher who worked in timber during the off-season. She loved the cold weather and the snow.

"Is your little heater working?"

"Perfectly." When Helen hit ninety and Carla retired, she'd moved into Carla's old room, which was on the first floor, just off the kitchen. It made for a comfortable living area, but it also meant that most of the house was unused.

"Mom says we need to hire you some full-time help."

"Oh, I don't know if I want anyone puttering about the place," Helen said. "Where would they stay?"

Robin laughed. "Grandma, there's like seven empty bedrooms upstairs. This place could be a hotel."

Helen's eyes sparkled. "That's a good idea. Do you and Mark want to move in?"

"You want to come live at our house?"

"And leave my view?" Helen gestured to the lake in front of the large bay windows that surrounded the kitchen table.

"I didn't think so." Robin smiled. It was an old argument. "But you know Mom is right. You need someone to keep you company."

"Someone who likes to garden might be useful," Helen said. "I can't do as much of the gardening as I used to. And the lawn service only maintains. They don't know how to prune the hedges properly. And there's a drip in the bathroom upstairs. I heard it last night."

"I'll ask around. Maybe someone Austin's age would be good." If they could be responsible. And would actually help out. And not throw parties at the giant, fancy house.

Okay, maybe not someone Austin's age.

Helen didn't need nursing. Yet. Once she did, she'd need a woman's help. But for now she just needed someone to keep an eye on things and make sure she was okay.

"Hey, Grandma." Robin reached for a brownie. "How old were you when the dam was built?"

Helen glanced away from the window. "What has you thinking about that?"

"Um... Val and Monica and I are doing kind of a history project. I thought I might put something up at the store to draw more customers in. Maybe put something on the website too."

"Oh, that was so long ago." Helen waved her hand. "No one wants to hear about that."

Robin set her coffee cup down. "I do."

Helen tasted a brownie. "I was twenty when they finished. It took years to build, of course, but it started during the Depression and went through the war. They were government jobs, so they had lots of men working on it over the years." Her eyes took on a dreamy quality. "For the longest time, we thought it wouldn't happen. Then all of a sudden it did."

"Were people in favor of it?"

"Of course not!" Helen looked affronted. "All my daddy's grazing land was flooded. All the farms and ranches down in the valley. The only people who liked it were people like your grandfather who got permits to log all the lumber from the valley and then had access to more land farther up in the hills. They knew when the new road went in, it would only be a benefit. So the timber people liked the dam. The rest of the town didn't."

"Where did people from Grimmer go?"

Helen's eyes took on a hollow quality, like she was looking at something in a dark room. "People went everywhere. Most down to Bridger City, I suppose. Some up to Sacramento. Lots and lots of boys were going into the army, of course. My brothers all moved away, and three of them were drafted. A few people stayed and built up the new town, but most people left."

"And you and Grandfather stayed."

Helen's face was carefully blank. "I married your grandfather right around the time the town was breaking up. Of course I stayed."

And were pretty miserable until he died. Robin didn't say it. She didn't have to. Her grandmother had been a stunning woman, and Gordon Russell had treated her like a trophy. Robin didn't try to understand their relationship. It was probably not uncommon for that day and age. Helen was a poor, pretty girl from a decent family that lost most everything during the Depression. Gordon was a rich man's son who gave her a good life. Robin couldn't judge.

"Did people have a lot of warning?"

Helen frowned. "What do you mean?"

"I mean, when they finished the dam and started flooding the valley. They gave people lots of warning, right?"

Helen's smile was sad. "How fast do you think a lake fills up? It takes months. Years even. Don't you worry. Everyone had time to move."

Unless they were chained up in an old mine shaft.

Robin took a chance and flipped open her sketchbook. "Do you recognize this man? Was he someone you knew?"

Helen reached for her reading glasses, put them on, and froze when her eyes reached the page where Robin had drawn their mystery man.

Froze. As in Robin actually checked if she was breathing.

"Grandma? Do you know him?"

"Where did you see this man?" Helen was barely audible.

"I think... it was in an old picture." Robin watched her

grandmother. Helen definitely knew who it was. Whether she'd say more was another question.

"He was a boy from Grimmer." Helen closed the sketchbook and took her glasses off. "I think. Don't remember his name. Nobody important."

"You didn't know him?"

"Oh, everyone knew everyone." Helen waved her hand again. "Grimmer was that kind of place."

"But you don't know this man's name?"

"No." She took a deep breath. "I'm old, you know. I've known too many people over the years. Can't remember everyone."

"But this man—"

"Can you be a lovely girl and get me another spot of coffee?" Helen held out her cup. "Then tell me everything that girl of yours has planned for next year. Has she settled on a college yet? Last time your mother came by, she said Emma had early admission to three different ones already."

And that, Robin knew, was all she'd get out of her grandmother that day.

"Okay, so Grandma Helen definitely knows who it is." Robin set her knapsack on the library table where Monica and Val were huddled over some old books and what looked like card boxes. "She didn't tell me a name though."

"She doesn't have to." Monica slid a picture over to Robin. "His name is Billy. We're not sure of a last name."

"Wow, already?"

Val walked around the table. "There was a government

photographer up here when the dam was built. Something about documenting it for Congress? We think it's him."

Robin grabbed the magnifying glass Monica held out. She held it over the photograph, which was in a plastic sleeve.

A large group of men were standing in front of the half-finished dam. They were wearing jeans and button-down shirts, but all their hats had been removed. All the men wore a grim expression.

"Huh," Robin said. "They weren't a happy crew."

"It might have just been the time period." Val spread a bunch of yellowing photos over the table, all of them in clear plastic sleeves. "It seems like 'serious and grim' was the going expression for most people in pictures."

"Or they weren't too thrilled about building a dam that was going to flood their hometown," Robin said. "Helen was pretty clear on that. Other than timber men like my grandfather, no one wanted the dam."

"Why did they build it?" Monica asked. "Was it for the electricity?"

"Mostly," Val said. "And water for farming."

Robin found the face she was looking for. It was hidden in the back row. He'd been a tall man, younger in the picture than when Robin had seen him.

"He's younger." She looked at Val. "You think?"

Val nodded. "He looks a few years younger in the pic than when I saw him, yes."

Robin looked at the date of the picture. 1942, three years before the dam had officially finished. "And his name?"

"Look at the bottom."

"Oh right." There were dozens of names on the bottom of

the picture, but counting across the page led her to one name to go with the familiar face.

"Billy G." Robin looked up. "Do we have any idea what the G stands for?"

Monica shook her head. "Not so far. But we have a name at least."

"I'm just frustrated that Grandma Helen wouldn't tell me who he is. It's obvious she knows him."

He was handsome. His dark hair was unruly and his jaw was square.

And familiar.

Why did he look so familiar? There was something about him that kept tickling Robin's memory. Did she know Billy G's relatives? Did they still live in town, or had they all moved away like Grandma Helen had said?

"I know you guys need to get going," Robin said. "But I think I'm going back to the lake. I want to see if Billy shows up again."

CHAPTER 12

"You're purposely going to look for a ghost?" Val asked. "Are you insane?"

"Maybe he can talk to me," Robin said. "He saved our life. I don't think he's a mean ghost."

"Because we all know so much about how ghosts work." Monica cocked her head. "Seriously, Robin?"

"Why not? What's the worst that could happen?"

"He could decide he's sorry he saved you and throw you back in the lake?" Val said. "He could... get stuck to you. And then you'd have an old ghost with you all the time instead of just sometimes."

"How do you know he'll still be hanging around the lake?" Monica asked. "Maybe his ghost stays with his bones."

"It's worth a try." Robin handed the picture back. "Oh, also, I have to figure out excuses for everywhere I go now."

Val frowned. "Why?"

"Because Mark can see me on the Find Your Family app or something. He asked about Bridger City last night. I had to make an excuse about Val needing the hospital." She looked at Val. "Sorry. But I figured you were the one who looked sick if Mark or Sully happen to mention it to each other."

"Wait," Val said. "He's following you on this app?"

"It's not really following," Monica said. "We have it activated on our family plan too. For security. You don't have that app for your boys' phones, Val?"

Val threw up her hands. "I never know what's going on with my phone. Jackson usually does all that. Do you think he's been hiding stuff?"

"He's a fourteen-year-old boy," Robin said. "Of course he's hiding stuff."

"Probably stupid, mostly innocent things," Monica said. "Don't panic. But I'm not exactly surprised that he hasn't told you about it." She held out her hand. "Unlock your phone and I'll show you how to turn it on."

"And while you're doing that," Robin said. "I'm going to the lake."

"Wait!" Monica said. "Give me a minute with Val and I'll come with you. She's got stuff to do, but I don't want you going alone."

While Monica showed Val the necessities of twenty-first-century parenting, Robin pulled out her phone and called Mark.

"Hey." He sounded surprised. "You aren't at the shop today. I came by with lunch, but you were gone."

He came by with lunch? That was... weird. "Sorry I wasn't there. I went to visit Grandma Helen this morning. Didn't know how long I'd be."

"Is that why there's a mess in the kitchen?"

"I'll clean it up later."

"Nah, I got it." She could hear him doing dishes. "Did she like the brownies?"

"Yeah. She did."

"Did you save any for me and Emma?"

"They're in the breadbox."

"Yes!" She smiled when she heard the victory in his voice. "I'm eating all of them before the kid gets home."

"Speaking of that, I wanted to go up to the lake with Monica." She thought quickly. "She lost a bracelet, and she's thinking the EMTs might have taken it off when they got her out."

Monica looked at her and Robin mouthed, *I'm sorry.*

"A bracelet?" Mark sounded skeptical. "Kind of a needle in a haystack, don't you think? How are you going to find a bracelet on that beach?"

"It's not that big. And she at least wants to try. I offered to help. Can you pick up Emma from the library?"

"Yeah, sure. What am I cooking tonight?"

Mark would cook, but Robin had to plan everything out and make sure all the ingredients were on hand. She'd tried to get him involved in meal planning years ago, but he'd complained that he liked to be spontaneous when he cooked. That led to various interpretations of pasta and jarred sauce three times a week, so Robin had taken it over and held his hand.

At least he cooked. Most of the married men she knew did nothing to help around the house.

"There's ground beef in the fridge," Robin said. "I thought you could make meat loaf."

"You got it."

"Okay, bye. I'll see you later."

"See you."

She ended the call and walked back to Monica and Val. "Okay. Who wants to go ghost hunting?"

ROBIN SAT on a large granite rock on the edge of Glimmer Lake and stuffed her hands under her arms. "It's cold."

"Yeah, pretty cold." Monica's teeth had chattered a couple of times.

"Do you think we should move back into the woods?" Robin asked. "M-maybe he won't come out in the open."

"I know nothing about ghosts. Maybe he can't come out when it's daytime."

"I saw him during the day by the sheriff's station."

"Okay" —Monica turned to Robin— "speaking of the sheriff, were you getting vibes from him and Val?"

"Vibes? Like... what do you mean?"

Monica raised an eyebrow. "Seriously?"

"What? I didn't notice anything. Like they're mad at each other? Why would they be mad at each other?"

"Not mad!" Monica huffed out a breath. "Like *vibes*, Robin. Like his boy parts would like to hang out with her girl parts, and maybe they already have?"

Robin's eyes went wide. "What?"

"You don't get that at all from them?"

"No! I mean, I haven't looked."

Monica rolled her eyes. "That's 'cause your own girl parts are probably desperately in need of attention."

Robin's mouth dropped open, and Monica reached over

and tapped her chin. "Do that the next time Mark is naked. You'll both have fun."

"Monica!"

"What? I can tell it's been way too long. You're super uptight lately. What is going on with you guys?"

"Why are we talking about this?"

Monica threw her head up and groaned. "Because we're sitting on the edge of the lake waiting for a ghost to magically appear, and I'm cold and I'm bored, and also you've been kind of bitchy lately and I think you're not getting laid enough."

"When am I supposed to get laid? He's in bed at nine thirty and awake at five in the morning. We're never awake in bed at the same time." She could feel her cheeks burning.

"Aha." Monica's expression was triumphant. "So you *are* orgasm deprived. I knew it."

"I've been orgasm deprived for like five years."

Monica's eyes went wide as saucers. "Five years?"

"I mean... we've had sex. It's just been kind of... blah."

"Oh." Monica put her hand on her chest. "Blah is not okay."

"I don't know." Robin could still feel her cheeks burning. "Isn't that just kind of how it is? We've been married for twenty-three years. Everyone has dry spells."

"Not five-year dry spells. That's just wrong." She patted Robin's hand. "You need to make time for sex."

"Says who?"

"Says your body. It's not healthy to go that long without an orgasm. And I promise Mark's not happy either. He's probably just trying to ignore it."

"He ignores me, that's for sure."

"Since when?"

"Since..." Robin shrugged. "I don't know. Since a long time. I can't remember. I've honestly wondered whether he's just going to leave me when Emma's out of the house. He has no friends here anymore. He ignores me. He pays more attention to his work friends online than he does to me."

Monica was staring at Robin with wide eyes. "You think Mark's gonna leave you?"

"I mean... maybe."

"Robin, how do you say a thing like that like it's no big deal?" Monica glared at her. "'So I've been thinking we might get a fake Christmas tree this year. Also, I think I might paint the living room, and oh, Mark might leave me when Emma goes away to college.'"

"It's not... Don't overreact, okay? I'm not saying he will."

"Do you *want* him to leave?"

"No." Robin shrugged. "I don't know. He's messy."

"He's messy?"

"Yes. He leaves socks everywhere. It's annoying."

"You're willing to let go of a twenty-three-year marriage because he leaves socks lying around the house?"

Robin took a deep breath. "Maybe the question is, is it inevitable? Why am I holding on to it if it's not working? Can anyone stay together for that long and still like each other?"

"It happens! Look at your parents. Or Val's mom and dad. And what about me and Gil?"

She glanced at Monica. "I'm not talking about you and Gil. You guys were special."

"No, we weren't."

"Yeah, you were."

Monica turned on her rock to face Robin. "No. We were

not. We got sick of each other too. You think having four kids that fast and that young is easy? We just went through our shitty stuff when the kids were young."

"So what's the secret?"

"The secret?" Monica huffed out a breath. "I don't know that there's a secret or anything."

"Not helpful." Robin took a deep breath. "Maybe—"

"Are you still interested in him?"

"Who, Mark?" Robin frowned. "He's my husband. Of course I'm—"

"No, I mean... Imagine if you weren't married to him. Would you still consider him an interesting person? If you were introduced at a party, would you be curious about him? About what he does and who he is?"

Robin opened her mouth. Shut it. "I think so. He does interesting work. He helps companies expand their platforms internationally, so he works with people all over the world and he travels quite a bit. And he really likes outdoor stuff. Camping. Hiking." She shrugged. "Yeah, I think he's an interesting person."

"Good to know. Now, do you think *you're* an interesting person?"

No.

The answer came to her so quickly she felt her heart sink. "I don't.... I mean, how do you judge that for yourself? It's impossible."

"No, it's not."

"I don't know, Monica."

"Liar."

"Fine." Robin swallowed hard. "No. I'm not interesting. I'm practical. I'm always on time. I'm boring. I'm a boring, middle-aged mother of two with an antique shop and two kids who barely acknowledge me and a husband who can't be bothered to look at my face when he walks through the kitchen in the morning." She coughed to clear the lump from her throat and fought back tears. "Happy?"

"No. Because you don't see yourself at all." Monica slid her arm around Robin's waist. "You're a passionate, talented artist who runs a thriving business and doesn't make enough time for herself. You're generous to a fault, will do anything for your friends, and have raised two amazing children."

Robin stared at the water. The sun was starting to sink, and the bugs were coming out, but the water was like a mirror, reflecting the forest and mountains that surrounded her.

"But I don't think I'm interesting," Robin said. "And you're right. Why would Mark like me if even *I* don't think I'm interesting?"

"You are not understanding me at all. I think he sees the same things I do. But you need to make it clear to him that you're not fine." She raised a hand quickly. "And don't tell me you have because I know you haven't. You are terrible at telling people when you need help. I have many theories about this, mostly revolving around your mother, but the fact is, Mark loves you."

Robin raised a skeptical eyebrow.

"Don't give me that look. He does. I've seen him watch you when you're not paying attention—which you do a lot, by the way. You get wrapped up in details, and you don't pay attention. So pay attention to this: you need to make time for yourself, and you need to recognize how great you are."

"But Mark and I—"

"Just shut up, because you're alive." She blinked back tears. "Both of you. You love each other and you're alive. So fix things while you can, so you don't lose something precious."

Robin put her arm around Monica's shoulders. "I'm sorry. You're right. I shouldn't waste time because I think my life is blah."

"Your life is not blah! If you don't recognize that, you're going to end up pushing everyone away."

Robin took a deep breath. "My life is not blah."

"It's not. On top of all the cool things I mentioned before, you see ghosts now. And that's like the opposite of blah."

"Do I though?" Robin looked around. "I'm not having much luck calling Billy."

"Are you really calling him though?" Monica looked around.

"No. I mean, I don't know how I'd call a ghost. Do you? The other times he just kind of showed up."

"How to call a ghost...?" Monica pulled out her phone and tapped. "Okay, no, that's about a weird malware thing in mobile phones."

"Malware thing?"

Monica waved her hand. "Wait, this is better. Twenty ways to summon spirits." She frowned. "We don't have a Ouija board."

"I'm not going to use a— Monica, seriously?"

"It's at the top of the list!" She pointed to her phone. "Okay, summon a witch, don't need that. Summon a demon, definitely don't need that. Summon the grim—you know, there's not actually much about summoning ghosts. Google, you've failed me."

Robin stood and brushed her hands off on her pants. "Okay, clearly I don't know much about being a medium." She turned around. "So why don't we just…"

A man stepped out from between the trees.

Robin froze. "Monica?"

"I think a Ouija board might be the—" Monica yelped when Robin tugged on her hair. "Ouch! What are you looking at?"

"Ghost." Robin's voice was tiny. "Seeing the ghost."

"Oh wait." Monica scrambled to her feet. "Like right now? I don't see anything."

"Nothing?"

"She can't," the ghost said. "But you can. I wasn't sure. I thought I'd imagined it when you saw me in the water." He stared at Robin, who was still frozen. "Sorry you were waiting so long, but it seemed like an important conversation, and I didn't want to interrupt."

"Considerate for a ghost," Robin murmured.

"I try to be."

"Robin?" Monica asked. "What are you seeing?"

"Billy," she murmured.

The ghost smiled. "You know my name."

"Yeah." Robin stepped closer. "Why did you save our lives?"

The ghost shrugged. "Seemed like the thing to do. No use letting you drown in the lake. Drowning isn't a fun way to die."

CHAPTER 13

"You drowned," Robin said. "Val—our friend, the one with the short hair? She saw you. She touched..." She winced. Did the ghost remember the chains? Was it rude to bring up how he'd died to his face? Did ghosts get offended? "She touched something and saw that you were trapped and water was coming."

Billy's ghost looked remarkably human. There was a faint glow around the edges of his body, but she wouldn't have even noticed unless she was looking for it. He looked solid. Tangible. If she reached out, could she touch him?

Robin could see a swollen lump on the side of his head, but his dark hair hid the blood from the wound. He was wearing the same jeans and flannel shirt as the first time she saw him in the lake.

"Thank you." Monica was looking the same direction as Robin even though she couldn't see Billy. "Thank you for saving us. Me and my whole family are very grateful."

"You're welcome, ma'am."

"He says you're welcome." Robin kept her eyes on Billy.

"We found your picture in the paper. You helped build the dam."

His expression darkened. "God help me, I did."

"You regret it?"

"The dam killed everything. The animals. The forest. The farms." Billy shook his head. "And me."

"What's your last name? It starts with a *G*."

"Grimmer." Billy smiled. "They named the town after my grandpa. We had a big ranch back in the day." He glanced at the lake. "Of course, that's all gone now."

"His name is Billy Grimmer," Robin said to Monica.

"Oh! Like the founder of the town?"

"He says it was his grandfather." She turned back to the ghost. "If you hated the dam so much, why did you work on it?"

"Trying to make my mama happy. The government needed the electricity the dam would produce if it was gonna keep powering those factories for the war. So everyone had a choice."

"What kind of choice?"

"If you worked on the dam, you wouldn't get drafted into the army. I didn't mind signing up, mind you, but I was the youngest. My mama already had four boys in the war, and she couldn't bear to let me go. When I turned eighteen, she told me, 'Billy, you better stay here. You work on the dam so that war don't take all my boys from me. They're gonna build it with or without you.'" He offered Robin a small smile. "I might have had better luck in the army."

"He worked on the dam to keep from getting drafted during the war," Robin said, conscious that Monica could only hear one side of the conversation. "He was the last of his brothers left, and his mom insisted."

"That sounds like something my mom would do too," Monica said. "Is he Catholic?"

"Are you Catholic?" Robin asked. "Wait, I don't think that's important." She looked at Monica. "Is it?"

"You think I know?"

"I don't need a priest," Billy said. "I don't think."

"Why are you still here?" Robin asked. "Do you know?"

"Your guess is as good as mine."

"Do you remember what happened when you died?"

He shook his head. "It's all a little fuzzy. I remember waking up in the mine and I was chained up and had a big, bloody knot on my head. Don't remember what happened before that. There was something..." He frowned. "I was supposed to be somewhere that night. I don't know where or why, but I needed... I needed to be someplace."

"Like an appointment?" Robin asked. She glanced at Monica. "He says he doesn't remember what happened. Just remembers waking up in the mine. Someone must have knocked him out before."

"Do you know why you can see me?" Billy asked. "That hasn't happened for a good long while. Most people can't. Every now and then a little kid will see me, but their parents usually ignore them. And dogs. Dogs can usually sniff me out."

"That's so weird." Robin breathed out. "I'm not sure why I can see you. We just..." Robin looked helplessly at Monica. "We went in the water normal and came out—"

"Different." Monica smiled a little. "Just... kind of different."

"And you've never seen ghosts before now?" Billy asked.

"No."

"Are you sure?"

Robin thought back to the strange ringing bell in her shop. That wasn't recent. That had been happening for months. "I saw a little girl by the lake. Have you seen her?"

He shook his head with a soft smile. "We can't see each other. I can feel other spirits sometimes, but I don't see them. They don't see me. You're the only person I've talked to in... I don't know. Time is different here."

"Where is here?"

"I guess... I don't know how to explain that either." He shoved his hands in his pockets. "What's your name, ma'am? You from Grimmer?"

"They call it Glimmer Lake now."

Billy turned to the water and the corner of his mouth turned up. "I suppose that's a prettier name than Grimmer."

"Robin. My name is Robin Brannon. And yeah, I'm from here. I have the shop at the corner of Foreman Creek Road and Lake Drive. The big old log house. Does that sound familiar?"

Billy shook his head. "I'm not much for town; I like the woods. Always have."

Robin stared at him while the light grew dim. "Why do I know you?"

The corner of Billy's mouth turned up. "You've seen me a few times now."

"No, it's not that. As soon as I saw you—as soon as I remembered you—I could picture your face. It was familiar, like someone I've seen before."

"You got any Grimmer people in your background?

Maybe we're related. Probably not. All my people were on the way to Sacramento when..."

"When what?"

"I don't know." He shook his head again. "It's like there's this fog that comes down when I try to think of it. I was going with them. I'm sure of it. But there was some place I needed to be first. And then..." He pointed to his temple. "Quite a thing, isn't it?"

"Yeah." Robin saw his outline beginning to fade. "You can touch things. How does that work? You broke the car window. Can you feel my hand?" She held it out and Billy reached for it, but their hands passed through each other with nothing more than a gust of cold air.

"Guess not. I think I have to want something real hard to do that," Billy said. "And I wanted to save you. I saw your face, and it reminded me..." His voice drifted out and his tenuous outline seemed to shimmer in the setting sun.

"Billy? I reminded you of what?"

His mouth was moving, but the sound of his voice was gone. Billy Grimmer reached out his hand and Robin tried to close her fingers around his, but they were gone.

"He's gone." Robin stared at the place where he'd been. "And we still know nothing."

"We know his name." Monica put her arm around Robin's shoulders. "That's something."

"Do you think I did it right?" Robin said. "Maybe there are ways to help him remember stuff better. Do you think that's what I need to do? Does his soul have to... I don't know. Find peace?"

Monica looked over the deep blue water of the lake. "It's pretty peaceful here."

"Not for him." Robin walked to the edge and watched the evening breeze whip up small whitecaps. "For him, this is his grave."

THEY WERE PULLING onto Robin's street when Monica suggested it. Robin thought she was hearing things.

"Wait, what?"

"I think we should talk to Sylvia," Monica said. "Don't you think that would be good?"

Robin's eyes went wide. "Sylvia? Your Sylvia? The daughter who is getting her masters in psychology? Um, no. I don't think it's a good idea. I think that sounds like a recipe for us being committed."

"Oh, come on," Monica said. "Maybe she'll know how we can get rid of this."

"I'm sorry." Robin reached out. "Are you still having dreams?"

"Every night."

"Every night? Why didn't you tell us?" Robin couldn't imagine seeing ghosts every day. It was bad enough that she saw them sometimes. "What are they? Are you seeing Billy? Something about his death? Are you—?"

"I had a dream that my car battery went dead this morning." Monica turned right on Robin's road. "And it was true. I got up and my battery was dead. Jake had to give me a jump start."

Robin waited. "And…?"

"And nothing. That's the kind of stuff I'm seeing. And you think you're boring. I get a premonition that the casserole is going to burn. Or the car battery is dead." She stopped the car abruptly. "A deer is gonna cross the street right in front of the Millers' house."

Seconds later, a deer bounded across the road and into the brush along the road.

"See?"

Robin stared at the dark space where the deer had disappeared. "Okay, but the deer thing is really useful."

"I'm not denying that. But the rest of it is just kind of annoying. Also, I live in terror of seeing something really bad. I don't know what I'd do, Robin. Would I call the police? Would they believe me? Of course they wouldn't."

"Probably not." Robin stared at her house, which was lit with glowing gold lights. "You want to get rid of it?"

"The visions? Yes! Don't you?" Monica parked in the driveway. "I don't want to know what the future holds. Not little boring things or big scary things. Do you want to keep seeing ghosts everywhere? That sounds scary as hell."

"It's not bad so far," Robin said. "Though, admittedly, I've only met nice ghosts."

"And you know they can't all be nice. Assholes are everywhere. Even on the... spiritual plane or whatever you call it."

"So your solution to this is to call Sylvia?"

"She does brain research! If she doesn't know about psychic stuff, maybe she can find out. Maybe there are studies. I heard the military uses psychics. Maybe there are research papers."

"Maybe?" Robin still felt skeptical. "Our kids don't take us seriously, Monica. Sylvia's going to think we're nuts."

"My daughter loves me."

"Yes, and she's also a twenty-two-year-old grad student. She thinks she knows everything."

Monica's lip curled up. "I want to say you're wrong, but you're probably not. I still think we should ask. She'll probably suggest we get our heads examined, but we can ask."

Robin opened her car door. "Fine. But if we get kidnapped, put in an isolated government bubble house, and our brains get experimented on, I'm blaming you."

"Go have sex with your husband!" Monica shouted. "I'll call you tomorrow."

"Say that a little louder maybe?"

"Go—!"

Robin slammed the car door and spun toward the porch. *Go have sex with your husband...* Monica was so full of it. She and Mark had sex. Sometimes.

Okay, it had been a while.

She opened the front door and toed off her shoes. It wasn't snowy or muddy yet, but her shoes were covered in dirt from the lake.

"Emma!" She unwound her scarf. "Mark?"

"In the kitchen, Mom!"

She walked back and found Mark and Emma cooking dinner together. Mark was pressing meat loaf into a pan while Emma dumped some frozen green beans in a glass bowl.

Her daughter looked up. "Hey, Mamacita."

Robin walked over and pressed a kiss to Emma's cheek. "How's my favorite girl?"

"Good." Emma flashed her dimples. "I got an A on my history project."

"Oh, sweetie! That's so awesome!"

School didn't come easy to her daughter like it did for her son. Emma worked twice as hard to get half the GPA Austin got without trying.

Mark looked up with a smile. "She called me from school, so I swung by the store and got her a chocolate pie."

"Yessss." Emma danced across the kitchen to put the glass bowl in the microwave. "And I get half."

"Half?" Robin laughed. "No one needs that much sugar."

"I do."

Robin hadn't even said hello to Mark. He was humming along to a song under his breath. Something upbeat. He was cooking dinner. He'd bought their sweet daughter her favorite pie.

She walked over and stood on her toes, pressing a kiss to his cheek. "How's my favorite guy?"

He turned his head, surprised. A smile flirted at the corner of his mouth. "I'm good."

"Cool." Robin felt suddenly shy. Why? She kissed Mark all the time, didn't she? Maybe she didn't.

"Did you find the bracelet?"

"The what?"

He frowned. "Monica's bracelet? The one you were going to the lake to—"

"Oh! Right." She shrugged. "We could hardly see. But we ended up having a good talk about some stuff she's been dealing with, so it's all good."

"I'm glad." He turned to the sink to wash his hands. "Bummer about the bracelet though."

"Yeah." Robin opened the oven door and slid the meat loaf inside.

"She needs to call a psychic," Emma said. "You know, like those people on the TV."

"Right," Mark said. "'Cause those are so real. I think a metal detector might be more useful."

"But far less cool," Emma said. "What do you say, Mom? Psychic or metal detector for finding lost things?"

Well, this was awkward. "Metal detector," Robin said. "Definitely. You can rent those down at Glimmer Lake Sports. I don't have any idea where you'd rent a psychic."

CHAPTER 14

Shopping for cars had to be Robin's least favorite thing to do ever. But since the Subaru was totaled from the crash, she needed a vehicle. Something sturdy. Something good in snow. She'd been depending on friends and borrowing Mark's truck for way too long.

"What about this?" Mark pointed to the largest SUV on the lot.

Robin glanced up at him. "Are we moving someplace that doesn't have any roads?"

"It's nice, right?" He opened the door as the hopeful salesman hovered in the distance. "Leather interior. This has all the modern guidance systems—"

"Most of which won't work up here because there's no cell signal," Robin said. "I don't need anything fancy."

The salesman's face fell.

Mark slammed the car door shut. "We're not getting you a piece of junk."

Emma was leaning against a neighboring pickup truck, playing on her phone. She'd be no help.

Robin said, "I think there's something between a giant luxury tank and a piece of junk, Mark. What about another Subaru?"

Mark made a face. He'd never liked the Subaru.

"Subarus are very safe," Robin said. "Maybe they're not sexy-looking but—"

"I don't care about sexy." Mark walked to the next giant SUV. "I just want you driving something... substantial."

"Substantial?"

"Big, okay? When it comes to being in accidents, size does matter."

Emma snorted.

"Hey," Mark barked. "You're not supposed to think that's funny."

"Sure, Dad." She never looked up from her phone. "Mom doesn't like giant cars. She thinks they're hard to park."

Mark frowned at her. "You have no problem parking the truck."

"But I don't drive that every day. Plus it just seems wasteful. Emma's going off to school next year. Austin's gone already, along with all his football gear. I don't need a giant car. Buying all this seems silly."

"I don't think keeping you safe is silly." Mark left her and walked over to the salesman. "Which of your cars has the best safety rating? I mean, the absolute best. Do you have brochures about that?"

The two men walked back toward the office and Robin joined Emma, leaning on the truck opposite Emma's as she surveyed the car lot in Bridger City.

"He's just worried about you," Emma said. "You should probably let him get you a giant car."

"No, I shouldn't. I have to drive it every day. The only reason for me to have a big car is to take them to estate sales. And what happens when I go to an estate sale?"

"You take Dad's truck because you always end up getting tall stuff."

"Exactly."

Robin watched as a man in a retro-looking suit walked toward them. It took Robin a moment to realize the man was a ghost. He had the same faint aura Billy did, and his hair and clothes were straight out of the 1970s. He didn't look at Robin. He hadn't noticed either of them. He was strolling through the car lot like it was his regular routine. It looked like he might be whistling.

Had he died at the car lot? He carried no visible injuries. Had he suffered a heart attack? Stroke?

Why did some ghosts get attached to a place? Could they move? Travel? Or were they stuck in one place for eternity? Why had she only seen Billy's ghost near the lake or the sheriff's office? Could he move other places? Why had he become a ghost in the first place?

Obviously, not every person turned into a ghost after they died, otherwise she'd see way, way more of them. Counting Car Lot Man over there, she'd only ever seen four. Billy Grimmer, the little girl by the lake, Nurse Hawkins, and Car Lot Man. Why did ghosts stay in one place instead of moving on? Why did some seem to know what had happened to them, like Billy, and others not have a clue, like the nurse in the hospital?

Car Lot Man looked happy. He looked content even. He wandered up and down the rows of freshly washed vehicles, nodding at the living people he passed, not noticing or maybe not caring that they didn't wave or nod back.

He was happy. Maybe he didn't want to move on. Maybe the old car lot was his favorite place in the world.

"Where's the one place you feel most at home?" Robin asked Emma.

"Other than home?"

"Including home."

"Isn't that obvious?" Emma looked up from her phone. "I feel most at home when I'm at home."

"Good." Robin's heart was doing the warm-fuzzy dance. "Sadly, it's not obvious. I never felt all that at home in Grandma and Grandpa's house."

"That's because Grandma sees her house as a showroom."

How did her daughter get to be so wise? "I guess that's true," Robin said. "Half the stuff in my house growing up was for sale. I think she even sold my dresser once."

"And your dollhouse."

Robin stared at Emma. "You remember that story?"

"Dude." Emma looked at her phone again. "Mom, that was so wrong."

"Well, Grandma figured that Grandpa could make me another one, and she did give me part of the money."

"It was your dollhouse. You should have gotten all the money."

"This is your grandma we're talking about. I knew even at age seven that arguing was worthless."

"What about Grandma Helen's house? You had your own room at Russell House, right?"

Robin shuddered. "No. Russell House was never home."

That was probably why her mother had always been so mercenary about possessions. Her own father hadn't exactly created a warm and comfortable home.

Emma was staring at her phone. "You know, Mom, you need to tell Dad what you want. He can't read your mind or anything. He's not psychic."

"Ha ha." *The irony.* "I don't expect your dad to read my mind. I don't know what I want." She wanted her old Subaru station wagon back. It had moved beyond dated and into classic territory. Probably. "I want my old car back."

"Your old car was a relic," Emma said. "Get something cool."

"And safe," Robin said. "The most safe, apparently. Maybe your dad wants to get me a tank."

"Nope. That would have sunk a lot faster."

Robin winced. "Too soon."

Emma wrinkled her nose. "Yeah, I kind of regretted it as soon as I said it. Sorry."

Robin sighed, watching Car Lot Man walk around the lot. Up and down. Back and forth. Happy to be ignored. Happy to keep doing the same thing over and over for all time.

"So what kind of car should I get?" Robin asked.

"I don't know. What do you like?" Emma looked up. "*Other* than your old car?"

"Not a truck. Or one of these big things."

"Well, whatever it is, you need to pick something and tell Dad. He's waiting to get you something you want. He just wants you to be happy."

"I am happy."

Emma rolled her eyes. "Sure, Mom."

"I THINK you should just get a new version of the car you lost," Grace said. "Weren't you happy with your old car?"

"It was *your* old car," Robin muttered. "And yeah. I liked it."

Grace shrugged. "So get a new one." She held up a swatch of fabric. "This is too dark."

They were talking over the seasonal decoration for the antique shop. Robin usually let her mom take the lead getting Glimmer Lake Curios ready for the season. Grace had a wonderful eye for design, and she wanted to make new swags for all the windows, which took time.

Robin glanced at the fabric swatch. "So find something lighter. I just picked that one because I liked the red against the walls." The interior of the old house reflected the exterior. Log walls were bare through most of the living room that had been turned into the main showroom. Deep colors looked great. Pale colors disappeared.

Grace flipped through a giant ring of fabric samples. "It's your shop now. You should decide."

"Mom, don't do that."

"Do what?"

Don't try to make me guess what you want. The bell over the door rang and Robin walked into the showroom, only to find no one there.

"Robin? Who is it, honey?"

"Just the wind." She walked up and down the entry hallway. There were no cold spots. No gusts. Was it the wind, a ghost, or her imagination?

"We need something in a deep color," Grace said, "but

something that's light enough to pop against the permanent curtains."

Which were green. Robin knew exactly what Grace was doing. "Mom, you found one an hour ago."

"Honey, this is your decision."

You just want me to pick the one you already found! It was a cranberry red with a subtle snowflake pattern. It was nice. It was lovely, in fact. But Grace refused to make a decision; she wanted Robin to magically agree with her.

Just tell me you want the snowflakes!

Robin walked through the entry one last time and turned in to the showroom. She heard something, but she couldn't put her finger on it. It was faint, like a person talking at the end of a long hallway.

She walked to the window seat where she and Emma had created a kids' corner for children to play while their parents shopped. There was a dollhouse and a shelf of books. A small table with buckets of crayons and scrap paper.

She was crouching down to pick up a few crayons that had fallen on the ground when she heard the noise behind her.

Creak.

Creak.

Robin slowly turned to see the antique rocker she'd placed near the children's corner moving back and forth. There was a faint outline that grew more substantial the more she trained her eyes on it.

A woman appeared in the rocking chair. She was wearing a simple housedress, and her hair was frozen in crisp waves around her head. An apron covered her flowered day dress, the gingham trim popping against the bright blue pattern.

She was in her early thirties if Robin had to guess, and she watched the children's corner with sad eyes.

"Hey, Mom?" Robin kept her eyes on the woman in the rocking chair, wondering if she'd just found the source of her mystery bell.

"Yes?" Grace's footsteps came from the kitchen. "You know, when I look at this room in the middle of the day, I think you could get away with the darker red, but most of your shoppers aren't in the middle of the day until right before the season—"

"Mom, who built this house?"

Grace looked up from her fabric swatches. "What?"

"This house," Robin said. "You know most of the town history. Who built this place? It was back in the forties, right?"

"Oh yes, this place was one of the first permanent homes in town. Quite a tragic story actually. I haven't thought about it in years. The family was called the McGillises. What was his name? Hank? Henry? Something like that?"

Robin stared at the woman. "Was he married?"

The ghost hadn't moved, and she hadn't looked away from the children's play area. She was rocking back and forth, though Grace seemed oblivious to the movement of the chair.

"Yes, he was a bit older, but he married a young woman. She'd been a teacher at the school. She wasn't from here, but everyone liked her. I can't think of her name just now. That's so odd. I remember my mother talking about her. She was very well liked. A wonderful quilter, if I remember correctly."

"Did they have children?"

Grace smiled. "What made you think of all this?"

Robin scrambled for an answer. "You know, I had a customer ask me the other day about the history of the house, and I realized I had no idea. I just remembered and I thought it'd be good to know. So, did they have children? The McGillis family?"

"Yes." Grace's smile was sad. "They didn't have children for years and years. Who knows why? But then she finally did get pregnant, and she died giving birth to the baby."

Robin's heart broke as she studied the ghost watching the corner. "Did the baby live?"

"He did. And the family stayed for a while, but I think the husband and the boy moved away right around the time the little boy started school. The father didn't have any other family in town. They'd already moved away before the dam was finished. So it was just him, and after his wife died... I wish I could remember her name! You know, I think one of the quilts at the museum was made by her. If you're curious, you could go and look there."

"I think I will. I wonder if I could get a picture of them." She finally looked at her mother. "It would be good to put that up by the door, you know? The McGillis family home, then the Lewis family home. People love that kind of thing."

"You're right." Grace held up the fabric swatches. "Which one do you want? I've got to get started on these curtain swags."

"The cranberry red with snowflakes, Mom. You've had your finger stuck next to it for the past hour."

"Have I?"

Robin cocked her head, looking at her mother, who never asked directly for anything. When she wanted something, she nudged and hinted and pouted until she got her way. She always had, as long as Robin could remember. It worked with her dad. It worked with sellers.

"Why don't you ever just ask?" Robin sat in the window seat.

Grace frowned. "What?"

"You spotted that fabric an hour ago. You wanted to use it for the swags as soon as you saw it, but you didn't tell me that. You wanted me to pick it."

"Well" —Grace looked at the fabric swatches— "it's your shop and—"

"It's your shop too. I bought you out, but it's still your shop. You work here. You started it. I don't mind you having an opinion, Mom. You have a great eye for design."

"It's not my place to tell you what to do."

"Grandma does the same thing," Robin said. "Was it your dad?"

Grace's expression tightened. "My father was very opinionated. He had a certain way of doing things."

It wasn't hard to read between the lines. "So if you wanted something, you had to make him think it was his idea, didn't you?"

Grace waved a hand. "I've never thought about it. Why are we talking about this? If you like the cranberry and snowflake, then I'll order that."

"We're talking about this because…"

Because I've been walking through my life like one of these ghosts.

I've spent forty-five years making myself more invisible.

I've been expecting people to read my mind.

Just like you.

Robin stood up and walked to her mom. "I want you to

make the curtains with whatever fabric you want, Mom." She felt her chest get tight. "And I think you should tell Dad you want to go to Hawaii for Christmas."

"Don't be ridiculous." Grace looked flustered. "I don't want—"

"You do. You've wanted to do that for years. You never did when you ran the shop because it's impossible in retail, but you start looking at flights in October every year. And Dad doesn't notice because he loves the snow and he loves the mountains, but he wouldn't mind, Mom. He wouldn't. He loves making you happy."

Wait.

"...*you need to pick something and tell Dad. He's waiting to get you something you want. He just wants you to be happy.*"

It was rare for Robin to do an actual facepalm, but she did. Her palm was on her face. On her forehead, to be exact. Palm. Forehead. Sudden realization.

"I'm doing it too," she said. "I've been doing it for years, and I don't even remember the man. Grandma Helen married an asshole, and we've been walking on eggshells ever since."

Grace pursed her lips, but she didn't correct Robin for calling her father an asshole. "I do not walk on eggshells."

"But you kinda do," Robin said. "And so do I. We don't ever ask directly for what we want. You married Dad, who is like the opposite of Grandpa Russell, from what I can remember. He's a pushover for you, but you still make him play the guessing game."

And I've been doing it to Mark too.

"I'll order the cranberry with snowflakes," Grace said.

"But don't be so silly about Hawaii, Robin. It's Emma's last Christmas at home."

Robin stared at her mother's back as Grace returned to the kitchen. Maybe it was too much for her mother to recognize. Maybe she'd been living in unspoken wishes for too long. Or maybe she just didn't want to see how the actions of her father still haunted the woman she'd made herself.

But Robin could see it. Robin could see it as clearly as she saw the woman sitting in the rocking chair. Robin watched her rocking back and forth, staring at the memory of a little boy she never got to hold.

What was her name? Could she speak like Billy?

And maybe the most important question Robin had been pondering since she'd spotted the ghost of the man at the car lot.

If spirits could leave, what made them stay?

CHAPTER 15

*R*obin sat down at Monica's kitchen table in a huff. "I need to figure out what I want."

Monica paused pouring herself a glass of white wine. "I'm making green chicken enchiladas, so if you don't want that for dinner, you're on your own."

"Not dinner. Enchiladas sound amazing." She squeezed her hand tight, then reached for Monica's glass and took a long drink. "Thanks."

"That wasn't actually for you." She narrowed her eyes. "What's gotten into you?"

"I'm practicing taking what I want," Robin said.

"Okay, rah-rah Wonder Woman, but that was my wine."

Robin stood. "And I will immediately pour you a glass to thank you for it."

Monica shook her head. "Okay, weirdo."

Robin grabbed a long-stemmed glass from the cabinet. "I don't ask for what I want." She reached for the bottle of chilled wine. "Emma told me the other day while we were car shopping, and she's right. I'm starting to do the same thing my mom does."

"Which is?"

"Never directly asking for what I want and then getting annoyed when people don't guess correctly."

"Ah." Monica reached for the glass Robin held out. "Yeah, you've been doing that for a while."

"Why didn't you tell me?" Robin grabbed her wine again. "You know how annoying I think it is when my mom does that!"

"Oh yes, because we all love it when we're reminded that we're turning into our mothers." Monica rolled her eyes. "Yep, I can see that conversation going super well. Great idea."

Robin bit her lip for a full minute before she blurted out, "You're babying Jake like your mom babied your brothers, and you don't do it with Sylvia, just with your boys."

Monica's mouth dropped open. "What?"

"You always hated that your mom expected so much from you but she let the boys run wild."

"My boys are not running wild." Monica glared at her.

"No, but all three of them are kind of aimless and ask you for money all the time while Sylvia is getting her graduate degree and working and hasn't asked you for anything since she turned eighteen."

"Robin, you should know boys don't mature as fast as girls and—" Monica had her own facepalm moment. "Oh dammit, you're totally right. I'm exactly like my mother."

"No." Robin lifted a finger. "No, you are not. You always had the exact same rules for all four of them. But as they've gotten older, the boys definitely use you for a crutch more."

Monica sat next to Robin and took a deep breath. "Okay, since it's truth-telling time, you need to go easier on Austin."

Robin almost spit out her wine. "Why?"

"You're hard on him because he reminds you too much of yourself. And you think you made bad choices in life—which you have not—and you don't want the same for him. When he finds the thing he loves, he's going to be just as passionate and directed as you are."

Robin tried to hold in the snort and couldn't. "What am I passionate about?" She set down her wine. "Seriously, Monica. What do I have to be passionate about? My life is not exciting. My life just kind of happened and I ended up here."

"Do you seriously not see it?" Monica put her arm around Robin. "Your mother sold furniture like it was a competition, but you? People buy stuff from you because you have a great eye. But you also care about creating a home."

Robin felt her throat tighten up. "When I was Austin's age, I thought I was going to be an artist. I'm not an artist, Monica. Not even close."

"Wrong. I think you need to be doing more of your own drawing and painting because it's past time for you to take time for yourself again, but you make *home* an art. For yourself and for every one of your customers. That's a beautiful thing, Robin."

"Knock knock, bitches!" Val walked through the door and caught Robin's glassy eyes. "Oh fuck, did I miss a big emotional moment?" She held up a carton of chocolate ice cream. "I may be late, but I came prepared. Why do you always have the big emotional moments before I come?"

"It's not our fault you're always late." Robin wiped her eyes.

"Yeah, I told you dinner was at six thirty," Monica said. "The first half hour is for wine and emotional revelations, like the fact that we're all turning into our mothers."

Val scoffed. "That's not a revelation, Monica. That's the circle of womanhood. Maiden, mother, crone-that-sounds-exactly-like-your-mother."

"Robin has realized that she never asks for what she wants—"

"'Cause I don't even know what I want at age forty-five," Robin muttered.

"And also she's been letting life happen instead of taking charge of her own destiny," Monica continued. "And I realized that I've been doing the same thing—coddling my boys—that my mother did, and I hated it so much. What have you been up to?"

"Uh-uh." Val put the ice cream away and got a wineglass. "It's not my turn. I'm still choosing to live in denial. Robin, you don't know what you want?"

Robin took a breath and then let it out, her hands waving in hapless circles. "To be happy and content?"

"That's a bullshit goal," Val said. "Being happy is a side product of achieving goals."

"Fine," Robin said. "I want to start drawing again."

"Good." Val slapped her hand on the counter. "Done. That's an easy one. You just have to do it."

"And I don't want Mark to feel like a roommate. I want to be... wildly desirable again."

Val wiggled her eyebrows. "Ooh la la."

Monica nodded thoughtfully. "We can work on that.

You're going to have to retire some of your supermom purses, but your ass has only gotten better with time."

Robin blinked. "What?"

"I'm just saying it was always kind of skinny, so the lack-of-running thing isn't all bad."

Val nodded. "Agreed."

Robin felt for her ass. "It was too skinny?"

Monica said, "I mean, you worked it with the athletic supermom thing, but a little extra junk in the trunk isn't hurting."

Robin hadn't thought about her ass in years. Of course, maybe that was part of the problem.

Val said, "You need skinny jeans. Emma and I will take you shopping."

"Oh." Robin ignored the shopping idea. "And I want to find out why I'm seeing ghosts. I don't know if that has anything to do with this mini-midlife-crisis or anything, but I'd definitely like to figure out why we're all suddenly psychic in our midforties."

Val narrowed her eyes. "Has anyone else wondered whether this is an early symptom of menopause?"

Monica raised one eyebrow. "Do you mean have I wondered whether you being telepathic, Robin being a medium, and me suddenly developing foresight has anything to do with the natural aging process?"

Val rolled her eyes. "Okay, when you put it like that, it sounds slightly less likely."

"Just a bit."

ALL THREE OF them managed to find time the next morning for some research in the Glimmer Lake Library. Robin was looking through boxes of photographs as the librarian, Gail Carpenter, brought another box over.

"My predecessor was in the process of putting all these on microfilm when I took over. Luckily, I've been able to drag the library into the twenty-first century, but we still have a long way to go scanning all these old pictures."

"We're wondering about the Grimmer family," Val said. "Specifically, a man named Billy Grimmer."

Gail cocked her head. "It doesn't sound familiar."

"The Grimmers mostly moved away after the dam was built," Robin said. "According to some things we heard, their land was flooded by Glimmer Lake. I'm doing some research kind of related to a piece of furniture I found."

"Oh." Gail frowned. "So it's not a family connection?"

"No," Robin said. "Just general town history." She glanced at the sketch and the photograph of Billy Grimmer they'd found. "I know it was a long time ago, but—"

"See, I saw that picture" —Gail pointed at the sketch— "and all I could think about was your Uncle Raymond. I assumed you were doing something family related. Not that it matters to me, mind you, but I should get you some earlier boxes then. These are clippings and photos from the early sixties, when we were in high school."

Robin asked, "You knew my Uncle Raymond?"

"Oh yes," Gail said. "He was a grade ahead of me, but the school wasn't big. We all knew each other." She opened one of the boxes and rifled through. "Here's one I was remembering. See?" She handed the photo to Robin. "There he is in the back row. There was a youth fishing derby on the lake that summer."

Monica and Val walked around the table and hovered over Robin's shoulder as she looked at the black-and-white photograph of the young people gathered on the lakeside. A long line of trout was laid in front of them, and smiling teenagers jostled in a clump.

"There I was in the front," Gail said. "I was always short. But your Uncle Raymond was tall, even when he was young." She pointed to a blurry face in the background. "There he is. Not the greatest picture, but he's the first one I thought of when I saw the sketch you did."

Robin felt her heart start to pound as she reached for the magnifying glass. The young man in the picture wasn't in clear focus, but a cursory glance did seem to resemble the picture of Billy Grimmer.

What was going on here?

Val's hand squeezed her shoulder. "Are there more pictures of him in here?"

"I'm sure there are," Gail said. "Ray was very popular. Always had a bit of the rebel about him. The girls loved him."

"Right." Robin set down the picture and turned toward the box. "Thanks, Gail."

"Sure thing. And I'll look for whatever I have on the town before the dam," the friendly librarian added. "I know it won't be as much. Most of the families that were in Grimmer left when the valley flooded."

"Right. Thanks." Robin wasn't hearing her. All she could think about was finding more pictures of her mother's brother.

She'd never seen pictures of her Uncle Raymond when

he was young. She'd never seen many pictures of him period. Whatever had caused the rift between her mother and her uncle wasn't spoken of, not by her mother or her grandmother.

Val and Monica sat on either side of her.

"Robin?" Val's hand never left Robin's shoulder. "Your family has been in the town for ages. It's totally possible that your grandma's family and the Grimmers are related somehow."

"Uh-huh." She sorted through pictures, looking for any faces that looked familiar. Her mother wouldn't be in this set. She was four years younger than her brother and wouldn't have been in high school with him.

"Want me to look for a yearbook?" Monica asked. "I know where they are. And none of these pictures are labeled."

"Great idea," Val said.

Monica left, but Robin kept looking through the pictures. What had her grandmother said when she showed Helen the sketch of the ghost?

He was a boy from Grimmer. I think. Don't remember his name. Nobody important.

If Billy Grimmer had been a relative or a cousin, would Grandma Helen have been so secretive? Would she have looked away from his picture or pretended she couldn't remember him?

"Here." Monica returned. "I found 1962. That would be the year, right?"

"I think so." Robin opened it and flipped through the pages, looking for names she recognized.

Cartwright.

Kenrick.

Montes.

Russell.

"There." She ran her finger along the black-and-white pictures of the girls in black dresses and pearls. The boys wore suits and ties. Her finger stopped on the picture of a teenager with a hint of acne, unruly brown hair that had been imperfectly slicked back, and an unmistakable resemblance to Billy Grimmer.

Raymond Russell, class of 1963.

Monica let out a breath. "Okay, so there's definitely a family resemblance. Is Billy Grimmer related to you? Is that why you can see him?"

Val said softly, "I don't know if Robin is related to Billy Grimmer, but I'm betting her uncle is."

"Huh?" Monica's eyes went wide. "Ohhhh. Right."

"We don't know it's that." Robin slammed the yearbook shut. "But we're going to Grandma Helen's. Right now."

Val said, "I'll go grab some cookies."

"Chocolate," Monica said. "We're going to need chocolate for this."

CHAPTER 16

*R*obin parked Mark's truck in front of Russell House right at ten, just as the cleaning crew was exiting the building. The laughing group of three women stopped in their tracks when they saw Robin.

Mom was right again.

Dammit.

"Hi." Robin glanced at her watch and realized her mood could actually be put to pretty good use that day. "Don't you guys get here at nine?"

One of the women in uniform nudged another, who was standing at the front and had her hand on a cell phone. "Uh... yeah. We're just taking a break."

"An hour after you got here?" Robin glanced at the buckets and mops the women were carrying out. "With all your cleaning supplies?"

Two of the woman had red cheeks. They knew they'd been caught. The one who spoke doubled down. "We're good at our jobs. We finish fast."

"Which is it?" Robin was furious. "I've cleaned houses

before. I know how long it takes if you do it right. Were you taking a break or taking off because you're so good at your job?"

One of the women with red cheeks turned back to the house. "We can go back and—"

"No." Robin held out her hand. "Just because Grandma Helen is old doesn't mean you're allowed to take advantage of her. Give me the kitchen key and leave. I'll call your boss this afternoon and tell her we won't be needing your cleaning service anymore."

The one with the attitude lifted her chin and held out the key. "Bitch, you don't know what it's like to work for a living."

Monica gasped and Val put a hand on Robin's shoulder before she swiped the key from the cleaner.

"Bite me." Robin wasn't going to fight with these lazy girls. She had too much respect for how hard housecleaning work was to pay people who slacked off. "Leave and don't come back."

"Fine," the girl said. "We're done with your creepy-ass house anyway. And your crazy grandma." The trio of women walked off without another word.

Robin grabbed the key from Val and shoved it in her pocket. "I guess my mom isn't going to have to fire the cleaners after all."

"I have a customer who cleans houses," Val said. "She's awesome. I'm pretty sure she's fully booked, but do you want me to ask her for a recommendation?"

"Yeah, that would be great." Robin rubbed her temple. It was another thing she'd have to take care of, but she was relieved Grandma Helen wouldn't have to put up with those rude cleaners anymore. Her grandmother paid generously, and she didn't deserve being treated that way.

Monica said, "I wonder why they thought the house was creepy? This place is so beautiful."

"It is, but parts of the house can feel a little empty," Robin said. "That's probably all it is."

"What are we looking for here?" Val walked toward the kitchen door on the side of the house. "Are we confronting your ninety-five-year-old grandmother about her secret past?"

"No," Robin hissed. "We're just going to ask about Billy Grimmer. Maybe they were related. Maybe she just forgot his name because her memory is spotty. Plus we should look for more pictures of Uncle Raymond if they're here."

"I can go upstairs," Monica said. "Look on the walls for stuff. I love old houses."

"Perfect." Robin unlocked the kitchen door and walked inside. "Grandma Helen?"

Helen poked her head out of the bedroom. "I thought the cleaning girls were back."

"No. I fired them, Grandma."

"Oh." Her face fell. "One of them was very nice. She always made me coffee when she was here."

Probably because she felt guilty for not doing her job.

"I know, Grandma, but they weren't doing a good job."

Val was poking in the corners and shaking her head. "Surface only," she muttered.

"Hi, Grandma Helen." Monica walked over and gave Helen a hug. "Your house is so beautiful. I love your view from here."

"Thank you." Helen squinted. "You changed your hair and it looks very pretty."

"Thanks. I like yours. Did you just get it done?"

"My Gracie took me into town yesterday." Helen patted Monica's cheek. "How are you, sweet girl? I was thinking about Gilbert last Sunday. I remember him singing in the Christmas choir."

Monica swallowed hard. "Didn't he have a beautiful voice?"

"He surely did." Helen sat at the table. "And is that Valerie?"

"Yes, ma'am." Val put the cookies on the table. "I brought some chocolate-fudge cookies from my café."

"Oh, I do like chocolate." Helen turned slightly. "But I need some coffee."

"I'll make that." Val hopped up.

"And I'm going to call Jake about something." Monica walked toward the dining room door. "I'll be right back."

Helen sat at the table and looked out over the lake. "I'm missing the sun today."

"It's supposed to be clear tomorrow."

"That's good." She reached for Robin's hand. "You have a question for me."

"Do I?" Robin tried and failed to ask about Billy Grimmer. "I was thinking about Uncle Raymond the other day," she started. "Mom and he don't talk much."

A shadow of sorrow passed over Helen's face. "They were never close, which made me sad. No one ever understands you like your brothers and sisters. Even if you don't get along, they know you better than anyone."

"Is it because of Grandfather? Raymond and his dad didn't get along well, did they?"

Helen's chin tilted up. "Raymond was headstrong.

Gordon and he often disagreed when he got older. But Gordon was very kind to him when he was a boy."

Robin frowned. What an odd thing to say. "Kind?"

"Yes, Gordon was very kind," Helen said. "When Ray was older, they had a harder relationship. I think Grace tried to play peacemaker sometimes, but she wasn't very successful."

Val sat down with two cups of coffee. "Where's Raymond now?" she asked. "I can't remember Robin ever mentioning him visiting."

"He hasn't been back in a few years, but he writes very regularly." Helen pointed to a drawer. "Every week. Your mother never asks about him. He calls too, but not as often. He knows I don't like talking on the telephone."

"Is he married?" Robin asked.

"He is," Helen said. "His first wife wasn't a nice person, but his second wife is lovely. She has three grown children, and they're very much a part of Ray's life."

"That's great." This was all news to Robin. "So why did Grandfather and he fight so much, do you think?"

Helen turned to Robin with concern. "Are you and Austin fighting again?"

"No, Grandma, that's not why I'm asking."

"You shouldn't fight with your son. He's just taking his time. Sometimes the most interesting personalities like yours don't always know what they're meant to do right away."

Was that Robin's problem? Was she just a late bloomer? Forty-five was pretty damn late to be figuring out what she wanted in life.

Val asked, "What about Raymond? Did he know what he wanted?"

Helen laughed. "To be out of this house."

"And he never came back," Robin said. "Even after Grandfather—"

"Gordon was very kind to Raymond," Helen said again. "And he didn't need to be, you know. But he was. And Raymond didn't understand that, so their fights could be very bad."

There it was again. Robin and Val exchanged a look.

Weird?

Yeah, totally weird.

Why did Helen keep telling Robin how "kind" Grandfather Russell had been when everything Robin had heard told her the exact opposite? According to Robin's mother, Grandfather Russell doted on his daughter and fought like mad with his son. And who described a father as being "kind" to his son and said "he didn't need to be"?

Was there a reason for that?

Did it have to do with Billy Grimmer?

Grandma Helen reached for the drawer. "You should call your Uncle Raymond. His number is in there. He asks after you and Mark often. I know he'd be happy to hear from you."

"I think I'll do that." Robin took her grandmother's address book and snapped a picture of the page with her uncle's information. "Hey, Grandma, remember that town history project I was working on?"

"About the dam?"

"Yes, and the town of Grimmer." Robin watched Helen's face. "We keep coming across Billy Grimmer's name. Does that sound familiar to you?"

Helen took a sip of her coffee. "He was just a boy in town. Why is his name coming up?"

"He worked on the dam."

"Lots of boys did," Helen said. "Before the lake came."

"What happened to the Grimmer family?" Val asked. "Did they all move away?"

Helen stared out the window. "I suppose he went with them to Sacramento. I suppose he did. They went to Sacramento and... he was going to join them. I imagine he went there."

"So you did know him?" Robin asked. "Were you friends?"

Helen's smile was strained. "No. Why are you asking about Billy Grimmer? Such an old name and an old family. All the Grimmers are gone now."

Because he didn't follow his family to Sacramento, Helen. He drowned in Glimmer Lake and I'm seeing his ghost and he has something to do with our family.

Monica poked her head into the kitchen. "Hey ladies, do you have a minute?"

Robin leaned over and kissed Helen's cheek. "I'll be right back, Grandma. Monica needs our help with something."

"Okay." Helen reached for a cookie. "I think I'll have some chocolate."

VAL AND ROBIN followed Monica into the large, wood-paneled entryway.

"What's up?" Robin asked.

"Okay, I found this picture with Raymond's name on the back." Monica flipped over a picture frame. "Now, Robin, I

167

can't see Billy's ghost, but from what I remember in my dream—"

Robin reached for the picture, which appeared to have been taken post high school. "Wow, he was the spitting image of Billy Grimmer."

In the black-and-white photograph, Raymond was leaning against an old car and Grace was leaning next to him in a skirt, smiling. They didn't look like they were fighting. They looked like a brother and sister posing for a family picture. Grace was the mirror image of Helen, and Ray looked like a carbon copy of Billy Grimmer.

"Where did you find this?" Robin stared at it. "I've never seen it before."

"It was in a room upstairs in a dresser. Also, yeah, this house needs a lot of deep cleaning, and I'm going to have Jake come around tomorrow to deal with some leaks in the upstairs bathrooms. He's great at that stuff."

"Oh cool. Just tell me how much I owe him and—"

"Please. I cook for the kid every night. He can help out your grandma and bring her lunch."

"Grandma will love that," Robin said. "Thanks, Monica."

Val said, "I know talking with Helen is complicated—I could tell you were kind of struggling with how to bring all this up—but I definitely think you need to call your uncle. I have a feeling he probably knows more than anyone else in the family about how you might be connected to the Grimmers."

"Not related, but there's something else." Monica started up the stairs. "I can't really explain it, just... follow me."

Monica led them up the stairs and across the long landing where bedrooms branched off from the open entryway that overlooked the lake. The landing had a second staircase at either end, both leading to the third floor.

Robin, Val, and Monica walked up the flight of stairs, and Robin immediately felt the chill in the old house.

"Sheesh. I'd forgotten how cold the third floor is."

"Doesn't hot air rise?" Val was looking around the long hallway that ran between the two staircases. "What's up here?"

"Uh, the kids' rooms. Some storage. A maid's quarters from when they used to have full-time help. A sewing room. Stuff like that."

"So your mom and uncle were up here on the third floor with the domestic staff and the storage?"

"Children were to be seen and not heard," Robin said. "I never claimed it was a healthy home."

Monica stepped forward and pointed at a narrow hallway between rooms. "And what's that?"

The chill became more pronounced.

"That's the staircase to the attic," Robin said. "More storage." Just looking at the narrow hallway gave her goose bumps.

"Have you ever been up there?"

"No way."

Monica narrowed her eyes. "Never?"

"No."

Val said, "Really? I mean, not even when you were a kid to explore or snoop for Christmas presents or anything?"

"No one goes up there," Robin said. "I don't know. Not since Grandpa Russell died. We just don't. I remember my dad saying something about putting a bunch of Grandpa's things up there, but that's all I can really remember."

"So there's a room in your grandparents' huge old mansion that's super cold and creepy, and you never once had the urge to explore it?" Monica said. "Does that strike you as weird?"

"I don't know. I never thought about it."

"Can we go?" Val rubbed her arms. "I'd rather not hang out here. And I definitely don't want to touch anything."

"Okay," Monica said. "But I think you need to ask your dad about what all is up there. Because something about that hallway and that staircase seems off."

"If my grandfather's ghost was haunting his house, don't you think I'd have seen him by now?" Robin asked. "Monica, this time I think you're letting *your* imagination get away from you."

"Okay," Monica said. "But think about it. And definitely ask your dad."

ROBIN WAS LYING AWAKE, trying to get into the same mood as her husband, while her brain kept drifting to the old house and the cold room at the top of the stairs.

Mark kissed her neck while his hands traveled down her torso. "Hey."

It was Friday night and they'd gone out for dinner, just the two of them. It had been fun, and they'd talked about Robin turning Austin's room into a studio or possibly converting a room at the shop into a studio if the light was right. Mark had been great and enthusiastic, and it was the most fun Robin could remember having with him in months.

When they'd gotten home, he'd been eager to get into

bed. So had Robin. For the first time in months, she'd actually been feeling smart and sexy and desirable instead of old and tired. Mark hadn't been able to keep his hands off her in the car.

But as soon as they'd gotten in bed and he'd started his usual seduction, her brain had started to wander. Mark's hands were moving to all the places they usually did, and he was doing all the things that... usually did not lead to Robin having a good time.

If he could...

Nope. *Maybe if he did* that *longer she'd...*

Uh-uh.

If only...

"Stop," Robin blurted.

Mark raised his head. "What's wrong?"

Oh, why was it so hard to talk about this? She wanted to sink into the mattress and disappear. Or maybe just pretend it was working and get it over with.

No. Stop pretending.

You have to ask for what you want.

She spoke quietly. "I don't actually... like that."

Mark frowned. "What?"

"When you do the thing—"

"You mean...?" He moved his hand.

"Yes. That. I don't like it."

He blinked rapidly. "But I always do that."

"And I don't like it." She bit her lip. "Sorry. It just... it feels good at first, but then you don't do it long enough and you switch to something else and—"

"Wait so..." He pulled away and frowned. "That's not working for you?"

She shook her head slightly.

"Robin, I've been doing... *that* for like twenty years now. Probably longer."

She spoke as quickly as she could manage. "And everything used to work faster, but I don't know, it's just not happening like it used to and I think I need—"

"Wait." He propped himself up on one elbow. "Is this why you haven't wanted to have sex?"

"Maybe," she muttered under her breath.

She couldn't read his eyes, but she could tell his earlier enthusiasm was gone. "So you've been unhappy with... *that* for years now?"

She didn't say anything.

"And you didn't say anything?"

She let out a frustrated sigh. "Could you really not tell I wasn't having a good time?"

"Uh, no. I couldn't. I'm not a fucking mind reader, Robin."

He was pissed. More than pissed. He was actually angry. He got out of bed and crossed his arms. His boxers were still tented, but she could tell he was no longer in the mood.

"I can't believe this," he muttered. "You're unbelievable."

"I'm..." She sat up and held the sheet up to cover herself. "I am trying to communicate better, okay? It's not easy."

"It's not easy to say don't do that, do this?" He glared. "Really? What's so hard about that? Is it harder than shutting me down in bed for years?"

The burning in her chest was anger. It was also embarrassment. And frustration.

"You didn't exactly ask." Her voice was tight. "You just assumed—"

"What else was I supposed to do when you don't tell me anything?" Mark walked to the closet and emerged wearing a pair of flannel pants. He grabbed his pillow and walked to the door. "I'm sleeping in the guest room tonight. I have an early meeting tomorrow anyway."

"On Saturday?"

"Some of us don't get to only work when we feel like it."

And with that, the door slammed shut.

CHAPTER 17

*R*obin sat at the diner in Modesto, waiting to meet the uncle she hadn't seen in years. It had been a week since her disastrous date night with Mark, and he was still sleeping in the guest room. Emma had noticed, but she didn't say anything. Mark muttered something about not wanting to bother her when he had early meetings, and all Robin could do was nod.

This is it. This is your life.

This is the rest of your life.

She hadn't seen Billy's ghost again, not even when she'd gone out to the lakeside at dusk. She hadn't returned to Grandma Helen's house. She didn't know how to bring up her suspicions about Billy Grimmer with her ninety-five-year-old grandma, and she didn't even know why she was meeting her uncle.

This is ridiculous, a voice in her mind whispered. *You're not special, Robin. You don't have any special supernatural powers. What you have is an active imagination and a midlife crisis.*

Midlife. What did that even mean? Halfway through, that's what it meant. If she lived to be ninety, she was halfway done with her allotted time.

And what did she have to show for it?

A dead-in-the-water marriage.

Two kids who thought she was irrelevant.

A semisuccessful business that did nothing important.

She didn't make anything. She didn't create anything. She sold other people's old things. How pathetic was that? No wonder Mark didn't have any interest in talking to her. He probably had far more interesting people to interact with. Austin would probably change majors, study art, and become something amazing, no thanks to her. Emma would probably go on to do something glittering and fabulous, far away from Glimmer Lake, while Robin stayed forever, slowly becoming more irrelevant as she shrank into nothing.

You were stupid. There's nothing special about you.

This is it. This is your life.

This is the rest of your life.

"Robin?"

She schooled her face and turned to see a handsome, silver-haired man walking through the diner door with a broad smile.

Robin had to return his smile. "Hi, Uncle Raymond." She rose and walked into his hug.

"It is *so* great to see you." His arms were strong and reassuring. Her own father was a kind man, but he was a bit aloof.

Raymond said, "I can't believe how long it's been."

She put on her happy mask. "Same. It's crazy, isn't it? Sacramento, right?"

"North a bit. Roseville."

"Right. Thanks for driving down to meet me. You know, Austin isn't too far from you. He's going to school in Chico."

"Oh, that's great." Raymond smiled and sat in the booth across from her. "You know, Debby's oldest has a daughter at Chico. She's majoring in accounting. What's Austin studying?"

Robin blew out a breath. "What *isn't* he studying? He originally went in for business, whatever that means. And then he switched to forest management after the summer he worked with Jack—"

"Saw Jack last August," Raymond said. "Debby and I were up in Tahoe for our anniversary. He's doing great things with that company."

"You think so?" Raymond had been left out of his father's will, which had always struck Robin as horribly unfair. Her mother and grandmother had gotten everything, including Russell Lumber. "So there're no hard feelings?"

"Between me and Jack?" Raymond frowned. "Definitely not. I have no interest in timber. I'm surprised he didn't mention seeing me."

Robin waved a hand. "He's busy. We don't talk much these days."

"That's too bad." A shadow fell over Raymond's face. "You know, you shouldn't lose touch with your family. I've always regretted that your mother and I didn't get to reconnect after Gordon passed. But I know it's complicated."

She didn't miss the use of her grandfather's first name. "Gordon?"

Raymond raised one eyebrow, and he'd never looked more like the image of Billy Grimmer than he did in that moment. "Tell the truth, Robin. Why did you want to meet me after all these years?"

She took a deep breath. "Because I've been doing some research into family history."

"Uh-huh." Raymond didn't look surprised.

"It started out... It's a long story. But I came across some things that didn't make sense, and I'm hoping you can tell me what I'm missing."

"Like why Gordon Russell hated his only son so much? Or why I don't look anything like the rest of the family?"

He knew.

"Yeah," Robin said. "It's definitely along those lines."

"MY REAL FATHER's name was Billy Grimmer." Raymond was looking at the picture that Robin had copied, the one from the dam. "Of course, I had no idea until a few years ago. I never questioned that Gordon Russell was my father when I was growing up. After all, he was an ass to everyone, not just me. I don't know how much you remember about him."

"Not much."

Raymond waved a hand. "Our mother, his employees, even his friends. Gordon was not a nice man. But he cast a big shadow. After I left home, I had to go far away. No one in the mountains would hire me to wash their windows, much less anything approaching a real job."

Robin's eyes went wide. "He told people not to give you a job?"

"Yep. He said Glimmer Lake was his town. He made it and he controlled it. If I wouldn't work for him, I wouldn't work for anyone." Raymond shrugged. "And I was never going to work for Gordon Russell. So I made my way up to Sacramento, found odd jobs, and managed to finish school eventually."

"What did you do? Something with metal, right?"

"I've done a few things. I ended up studying material sciences and made it out of school just in time to get drafted. Ended up back in California after the war and found my way into the Cal State system, working as a metallurgist."

"That's interesting."

"It had its moments. By the time I got back from Vietnam, your mother was out of school and already dating your dad. I kept in touch with Mom, but Gordon made it clear I wasn't welcome back. I don't know if your mother knew how much he controlled that whole town. He told me not to come back for your mother's wedding, and honestly, I don't think she ever forgave me."

"Did you tell her?"

Raymond smiled sadly. "I was young and proud. I should have, but I didn't. I decided in my own head that Grace was on Gordon's side, and I didn't want to make life harder for Mom."

"Grandma Helen says you write every week."

"I started that when I was deployed," he said. "Guess I never really stopped."

"Does she write back?"

"Mostly. Not as much anymore, of course. Sometimes she'll just send me little sketches she's made." He pulled a paper from his jacket pocket. "This is one she did of you when you were little."

Robin took the paper and saw a picture of a smiling,

chubby-cheeked girl in a bright yellow swimsuit, playing along the edge of the lake. "I remember that bathing suit."

"She said you're quite the artist yourself."

Robin's smile fell. "I don't know. I took over Mom's shop."

"The antique store, right?"

"Yeah." She stared at the sketch. "I always think of Grandma Helen as a painter, but her sketching is a lot like mine."

"Or yours is like hers." Raymond smiled. "I'd love to see some of your work."

Robin hesitated; then she pulled out her sketchbook from her purse and flipped to the picture of Billy Grimmer.

Raymond blinked. "How about that? That's a very good likeness."

"How did you find out?"

"Because my wife thought it would be funny to do one of those DNA testing kits for a surprise on my birthday." Raymond looked up from the sketch. "Surprise!"

"Wow. But if you and Mom didn't both do the testing—"

"The Grimmer family contacted me," he said. "One of my cousins on that side is really into family history and research. She has the whole family up there. I guess they ended up in the Sacramento area after the dam was built in the mountains."

"But not Billy?"

Raymond shrugged. "According to the Grimmer family, I was part of the reason they went looking for their family tree. They knew that Billy was staying behind for a girl—that he had plans to marry her and follow them when he got the money together—but they moved, and year after year passed with no word. They figured something hadn't worked out and

Billy took off. They were looking for a lost branch, and they found me."

"But they had no idea that you existed before the DNA thing? They had no idea that Grandma Helen...?"

"According to them, Billy was the quiet type. And he was young. He and Mom probably had plans to run away together, but I have no idea what happened and neither do the Grimmers. They all moved out and started new lives. They were curious what had happened to Billy, but they didn't have many resources until DNA testing became more common."

"And they found you."

Raymond nodded. "You can imagine the shock, but when I saw the pictures they had..."

"The resemblance is pretty obvious."

"It is. And the minute I met some of Billy's brothers, I knew. I was definitely part of the Grimmer clan. I can't even tell you why, but I knew."

"Do you think Gordon knew?"

"I'm sure he knew eventually." He tapped his finger on the coffee cup. "I was born early, according to Mom. But I've seen my birth certificate. I was pretty big for a premature baby, if you ask me."

"So you think she was pregnant when she married Gordon?"

"Why else would she marry him? Mom and Gordon were never in love. I'm pretty sure she married Gordon because she was pregnant. Options for young single mothers were not the best in 1946."

"True." It would certainly explain why Grandma Helen stayed in such an unhappy marriage.

"Now," Raymond continued, "I don't know if Mom *told* him she was pregnant when they got married, but Gordon would have known Billy Grimmer. They lived in the same town. Once I got old enough, he could have easily put things together. Gordon and Mom were both blond, and I had dark brown hair before I went grey."

Robin leaned forward and said, "I was trying to talk with Grandma Helen about this last week before I called. She said something strange. She mentioned a couple of times that Grandpa Russell was *kind* to you. Her word. *Kind.* Which I thought was strange, because why would she mention that the man was kind to his own son? Plus, from what I've heard, he wasn't all that kind."

"That's interesting." He tapped his fingers on the table. "Kind?"

"Yeah. I thought it was strange."

"I suppose Gordon wasn't horrible to me until I got to be a teenager," Raymond said. "That's probably when it became more obvious that I wasn't his. Before then, he was mostly indifferent. But if Mom thought Gordon was being kind, then I think we have to assume that Gordon knew from the beginning I wasn't his son."

"He might have known she was pregnant when he married her," Robin said. "Do you think Billy knew she was pregnant?"

"There's no way of knowing," Raymond said. "We don't even know what happened to Billy. He didn't stay with Mom, that's for sure. He must have run off, but according to the Grimmers, he never got in touch."

Robin knew. She knew exactly what had happened to Billy Grimmer. She just didn't know how to tell Raymond

181

without arousing suspicion. Of course, some information was public.

"You know," she said, "I had a bad car accident a couple of months ago. My car went into the lake."

"Robin." Raymond reached for her hand. "Your car went in the lake? Thank God you're okay. What happened?"

"It's a long story, but when they were raising my car, they unearthed a body that had been at the bottom of Glimmer Lake for a long time. They think... maybe even seventy or eighty years."

Raymond's eyes went wide. "You don't think—"

"Maybe?" Robin took a sip of cold coffee. "I don't know. Nobody knows what happened to Billy. Maybe he ran off, or maybe he never left Grimmer."

"There's no way of knowing." Raymond was frowning. "What happened to the man in the lake? Do they know how he died? It could have been a boating accident or something to do with the dam. Is it even a man?"

"I'm pretty sure it was a man. The sheriff was sending the remains to the state crime lab in Sacramento," Robin said. "But Uncle Raymond, it wasn't an accident."

"How do you know?"

"There were chains around his ankles," Robin said quietly. "That's how they determined the age of the remains. Whether he drowned in the lake or was dead when he went in, someone didn't want his body to be found."

CHAPTER 18

*A*n hour after she'd left Raymond, Robin called Val. "Hey," she said. "I think I'm out of my funk."

"You were in a funk?" Val asked. "By the way, you're on speaker. Monica's here."

"Hey, Robin." Monica lowered her voice. "How are you so dense, Val? Yes, she was in a funk. The date with Mark did not go well."

Robin kept her eyes on the road. "The funk was not because of Mark."

"Uh-huh."

"Sure."

"Okay, maybe it's kind of because of Mark, but it was also because I felt like we were accomplishing nothing important, and this was all in my head, and we were being stupid about our supposed supernatural powers."

"Supposed powers?" Val asked. "I nearly lost my head earlier today because that cheating cheater who likes my danishes told his side chick he loved her the same day he told his girlfriend, and I saw it when I accidentally touched his keys. Again! I want to kick him out of the café, but seriously, I have no valid basis for calling him an asshole. God, people are the worst."

Robin cringed. "I'm so sorry."

"Yeah," Monica said. "I think you definitely got the worst power."

"Thanks?" Val said. "Maybe I just need to wear gloves all the time. And I mean *all* the time."

"Robin, have you thought about telling Mark what we're doing?"

Val yelped, "Wait, what?"

Robin shook her head. "You know, Monica, you say these things in your cute little voice, and they sound so reasonable, but then I think about *what you actually said* and realize that you are, in fact, nuts."

"Mark might not think we're crazy!" Monica said. "I decided not to tell Sylvia, but she's my daughter. Mark is Robin's husband. It's different."

"How?" Val asked.

Robin had the same thought. "Monica—"

"Plus he and Robin are going through things, and he's going to eventually realize that something is different. Let him help. He might want to help."

"Robin doesn't even trust the man to pick out a car for her," Val said. "She's not going to tell him about seeing ghosts."

"I do not..." Robin glared at her phone. "You act like I'm a control freak."

"You kind of are," Val said.

"I can't disagree," Monica said. "But I want to add that

you're partly a control freak because you're very good at managing things. I mean, it's not all negative."

"Thank you?" Robin sighed. "This was not why I called."

"Oh?" Val sounded like she was eating something. "Why did you call?"

"I got confirmation from my Uncle Raymond that he definitely is not Gordon Russell's son. Guess who he's related to."

Monica said, "Billy Grimmer?"

"Yep." Robin took the exit at Bridger City and turned east. "My grandma Helen and Billy Grimmer must have had an affair. Or a relationship of some kind. Raymond is pretty sure Grandma was pregnant with him when she married my grandfather."

"Wow! Grandma Helen, woman of mystery."

"That's so sad," Monica said. "Billy left her pregnant?"

"Did he?" Robin asked. "Remember when I saw him at the lake the second time? He kept saying he was supposed to be somewhere, but he didn't remember where. And according to Raymond, Billy's family thought he was staying in Grimmer for a girl. Maybe he was trying to get to Helen when he was killed."

Val said, "Oh, that's awful."

"If that's true," Monica said, "then your grandmother never knew what happened to him. She probably thought he abandoned her."

"That could definitely explain why Grandma barely acknowledges she knew him."

"...I suppose he went with them to Sacramento. I suppose he did. They went to Sacramento, and he was going to join them. I imagine he went there."

"Were you friends?"

"No."

Helen and Billy weren't friends. But they were lovers. And Helen thought he'd left her. Had he? Or had something or someone stood in the way?

"We need to find out why Billy is still here," Robin said. "What does he need? What does he want? Why hasn't he moved on?"

"Can we ask him?"

"If I can find him, I can ask him. But so far I'm super crappy at actually summoning ghosts. I don't seem to control it at all."

"Okay," Monica said. "So maybe that's job one. We need to figure out how you can summon ghosts. Then you can ask Billy questions."

"Do you think it has to do with solving his murder?" Val asked. "Do you think he needs to remember who killed him?"

"He may not know," Monica said. "Didn't Robin say he doesn't remember what happened before he ended up in the mine?"

"If he doesn't know, how do we find out?" Val asked. "It's not like we're police. We can't exactly question people, especially when this murder happened seventy years ago."

"First things first," Robin said. "We have to figure out how I'm supposed to summon ghosts."

THE NEXT MORNING they were back at the shop, and Robin was sitting in the children's area, thinking about the memory of the ghost she'd seen the week before. Robin sat on the ground, her eyes closed, facing the rocking chair and trying to meditate.

Val and Monica watched her silently. Neither of them had been surprised to hear a ghost lived in the antique shop. Val said she was pretty sure one was living at the café too. Monica suspected two at the library. Apparently Glimmer Lake was chock-full of ghosts if you kept an open mind.

Robin opened her eyes and sighed. "This is no use. Have you ever tried to empty your mind? It's impossible."

Monica tapped a finger on her chin. "Maybe if you think about her really hard. Picture her in your mind. Maybe you can focus just on her?"

"That's impossible."

"Why not? Just try to focus—"

"My brain is never that focused!" Robin nearly yelled. "I have to juggle too many things. Emma's schedule. She still hasn't decided where she wants to go next year, which means we haven't even started on financial aid stuff. Work, running the house, dealing with my mom, visiting Grandma. I still need to find someone to live with her and also a new cleaning crew. I have to get inventory up and the store decorated for the holiday season. We need to update the insulation around our outside plumbing before the snow comes, and Mark keeps forgetting. There's a leak upstairs at Russell House. Added to that, Austin has been trying to call me, and I've been putting it off because I know he wants to talk about switching majors and I just do not feel like I'm going to be able to have that conversation with him without yelling. And my knee is acting up again, and I'm sexually frustrated."

Val blinked. "Wow."

Monica's shoulders drooped. "I'm exhausted just listening to that."

Val grimaced. "Is there anywhere—*anything* you do or place you go—where you actually feel like your mind is empty? That you feel like you focus on one thing?"

Robin took a deep breath. "My morning walk when I can be outside. And drawing."

Val snapped her fingers. "Drawing." She ran to the kitchen and came back in seconds. She tossed Robin's sketchbook at her. "Draw her. Draw the ghost you saw."

Monica nodded. "That's a good idea."

Robin was skeptical, but she started sketching out the face she saw in her memory. She drew the curve of her cheek first. The line of her back sitting in the rocking chair. The draped skirt.

She heard the rocking chair begin to creak.

Robin kept drawing. She drew the crisply curled hair and the zigzag edging on her dress. By the time she looked up, the woman in the rocking chair was staring straight at her.

"You never bring the children anymore." Her eyes were sad.

Robin couldn't tear her eyes away from the woman who was speaking to her. There could be no mistaking it. The ghost saw Robin just like Robin saw the ghost.

"I'm sorry," she said. "The children grew up."

Monica and Val both jumped a little where they were standing, but Robin held up a hand.

"My little boy played there." The ghost nodded to the window seat. "I wanted to hold him so much, so I stayed. But they moved away and there were no children for a long, long time." The smile on her ghostly face was wistful. "But then you came, and you had your little boy. Then your little girl."

"Is that why you stayed?" Robin asked. "To see your son?"

"A son needs his mother." The rocking chair went back and forth. "I couldn't just abandon him."

Monica said, "Val, do you see the chair?"

"Yeah, I see it."

Robin kept her focus on the ghost. "Can you leave? Where would you go?"

"Oh, there's a place." The ghost's eyes took on a faraway gaze. "But what if he comes back and I'm not here?"

Your son is an old man now. Robin didn't want to say it; she felt the ache of longing from the ghostly woman.

"What's your name?"

"Clara." Her smile was soft. "My boy was named Paul, after my father. Henry did that for me. He named my boy Paul."

"That's good." Paul McGillis. Robin wondered if she could find out where he'd gone. "My name is Robin."

"I know," Clara said. "We all know."

"Are there many of you?"

"Oh, a few." Clara looked at her from the corner of her eye. "You haven't seen all of us yet."

"But I've seen you." And she'd gotten a few answers. Clara had stayed because she wanted to. Because she felt needed. Had Billy done the same? Was he stuck here because he felt an obligation? Was he waiting for his son too?

Robin put her pencil down and looked at the sketch she'd drawn. It was one of the best she'd ever done. Clara McGillis was rendered in clear swipes of the pencil; everything from her dress to her curls to her lips was perfect. Exactly as Robin had seen her.

When she looked up from her sketchpad, Clara was gone.

"She left," Robin said.

"That was so weird," Val said. "Monica?"

"Super weird." Monica sat next to Robin. "What did you see?"

Robin passed her the sketch. "What did *you* see?"

"You were staring at the rocking chair so hard, and then it started creaking. Not much, but it was definitely moving back and forth."

"Did you hear me?"

"You said one thing about the children growing up," Monica said. "But then nothing. You were just staring at the chair."

"But I had a whole conversation with her," Robin said. "With Clara. You didn't even hear me?"

"Nope." Val reached for the sketchbook. "Weird. It sounds like it was all in your head."

She turned to Monica. "But by the lake when I talked to Billy, you could hear me then?"

"Yes, but maybe it's a different connection there. Or a different method of calling him? Maybe if they reach out to you, you stay more in yourself. If you call them up, then it's internal."

"That makes as much sense as any of this." Val was staring at the sketch. "So what happens if you sketch Billy?"

"I don't know, but I'm thinking that might be the way to go."

"What happens if you sketch Billy when you're with Grandma Helen?"

Monica's eyebrows went up. "Playing with fire, Val?"

"Hey." She shrugged. "If we want to get answers, that might be the only way to go."

Robin felt her phone buzzing in her pocket, so she stood and brought it out. "It's Sully."

Val sat up straight. "Sully?"

Monica made an "answer it" motion with her hands.

Robin tapped on Accept Call. "Hey, Sully."

"Hey, Robin." He sounded tired. "So, we haven't gotten anything formal from state medical examiner's office. They as much told us that even though it's suspicious, it's a cold case, so we go to the bottom of the priority pile."

"But there must be something," Robin said. "Or you wouldn't have called.

"You could say that." He sighed deeply. "I don't know why, but I figured you might want to know that he—it's a male—was definitely murdered."

"The chains kind of gave that away, don't you think?"

"Well, whoever killed him definitely didn't want his body found, but that's not what killed him."

"Really?" Robin motioned Val and Monica closer. "He didn't drown?"

"If he did, he did it after surviving a pretty vicious slice to the neck."

Robin cringed. "He was stabbed?"

"More like his throat was cut. The initial visual exam just came back, and there's a cut right across his throat that went so deep it cut the bone."

Robin closed her eyes. It was so much worse than she'd imagined. "Horrible way to die."

"But they did determine the age of the bones is well over fifty years, so you and your friends are officially in the clear on that. This guy died long before you or I were born."

"I'll let them know. Thanks."

"See ya, Robin. Say hi to Mark."

"Will do." She tapped on the phone to end the call. "Did you guys hear that?"

"Not all of it," Monica said.

"Billy Grimmer's throat was cut. Whoever put him in that mine shaft must have come back to make sure he hadn't escaped and he—"

"Or she." Val shrugged. "What? It's possible."

"He or she didn't want to wait to let the water do its job. Billy's throat was cut so deep with a knife it left marks on the bones." Robin flipped to her sketchbook and stared at Billy Grimmer's face. "I think it's time that Grandma Helen and I had another talk. And this time I'm going to get some answers."

"Good luck with that," Val muttered. "She may be ninety-five, but she's cagey."

"I know." Robin looked at Monica. "We're going to need enchiladas."

CHAPTER 19

Grandma Helen was sitting outside in a wooden lawn chair, staring at the sun setting over the lake, when Robin, Monica, and Val arrived. Bright red autumn leaves were scattered across the lush green lawn, and the roses were eking out their last blooms before the frost came and forced them to settle down for winter.

Robin was reminded as she stared at the old woman sitting on the giant lawn, bundled in a fluffy coat, that her grandmother was ninety-five.

Ninety-five years had seen a lot. Ninety-five years had seen a Depression, a World War, atomic bombs, and nuclear scares. It had seen the transition from agriculture to manufacturing to technology. Grandma Helen had been born into radio and was ending with the internet.

Without a word, she and her friends went into the kitchen and dragged chairs outside to join Helen. They sat in the late-afternoon sun in silence. No one spoke, though Helen reached across the table and took Robin's hand.

Robin looked at her grandmother's profile. "Are you happy here?"

"I love this spot. I love the view." Helen glanced over her shoulder. "The house is too big. I told Gordon that, but he never listened. If we were going to have a house so big, we needed more children in it. But he didn't want more children."

Robin leaned closer to Helen. "One was enough for him?"

Helen didn't look shocked. She just smiled. "I always wondered if Grace suspected. Does Raymond know?"

"Yes."

"I never wanted him to."

"Debby gave him a DNA test for his birthday."

Helen frowned. "What is that?"

Val moved closer. "You can spit in a cup and send it in, and they'll tell you what your DNA profile is."

"Heavens," Helen said. "Why would anyone want to do that?"

"One of the Grimmer cousins did it to find out what happened to Billy and his family."

Helen finally looked at Robin. "Don't they know?"

"No." She shook her head. "They don't know what happened to him either."

The long, sad look returned to Helen's eyes. "I suppose no one did."

"Grandma—"

"I don't want to talk about sad things, Robin. What is the point of talking about sad things like this? I was poor and I had a baby on the way. No one was going to help me." She glanced over her shoulder. "And then Gordon came along.

He found me when I was sick. I was waiting in our cabin, crying over Billy, and he found me."

Robin made a mental note to look for a cabin—maybe the one Monica had seen in her dream—but she didn't interrupt her grandmother.

"I don't know how," Helen continued, "but he did. I hardly knew him, except to know he had a hard reputation. He was a businessman. Other men didn't like him much, but he was kind to me. And he said he'd marry me. Just like that. That very day. He said, 'I know your condition, Helen, but I don't much care. Marry me and no one will say a word against you. I'll build you a big house and you'll be a lady.'"

Monica said, "And he did. And you are."

"Yes." Helen smiled at Monica. "He did and I was. I didn't care much about the big house or the money, but I didn't want to shame my parents. They were good, honest people. They'd been well-off before the Depression, and I cared about their reputation. And Gordon took care of me and my family. My daddy didn't have to work again after that, except a little in Gordon's offices for appearance's sake. And my momma had new dresses and didn't have to take in clothes anymore. To his credit, Gordon never once mentioned it after the day I agreed to marry him. Not when Raymond was born. Not ever."

But you never loved him. Not even a bit.

And what was love when you were a desperate young woman? Robin reached for her grandmother's hand. "You really do have the best view in town."

"But I know why no one wants to live here," Helen said. "It wasn't a happy home." She squeezed Robin's hand. "You made a happy home for your children. Be proud of that,

Robin. That is a tremendous thing." She looked at Val and Monica. "And both you ladies did too. I know it. What girls are doing now is just amazing to me. I'm so pleased I've lived long enough to see everything you're doing in the world." Helen raised Robin's hand and shook it. "Girl power! That's what they say, right?"

Val and Monica smiled.

"Yep," Monica said. "That's what they say."

Robin watched her grandmother with new eyes. She'd always wondered what had led Helen to marry Gordon Russell. He wasn't a nice man, but maybe he'd been an honorable one. He'd married a woman pregnant with another man's child, and he'd never thrown that back in her face. That wasn't nothing.

"Grandma, do you want to know what happened to Billy?"

Helen's eyes didn't leave the sunset. "What difference would that make now?" She closed her eyes as the sunset reached the edge of the horizon.

"He might have had a reason—"

"What happened, happened. It was a lifetime ago." The sun slipped below the mountains, and the temperature dropped immediately. "Robin, can you help me back in the house?"

"We brought enchiladas, Grandma Helen."

"Oh, that sounds nice."

Monica got on Helen's other side while Val gathered the extra chairs on the lawn. They helped Helen back into the house through the side door and turned on the lights in the kitchen.

"It's cold in here," Robin said. "Is your space heater not working?"

"I might have forgotten to turn it on." Helen waved a hand. "It's not that cold."

"I'm going to check it, and I'll turn on the heat on the first floor, okay?"

"Don't fuss." Helen used her cane to walk to her favorite chair in the breakfast nook. "I'll be fine."

While Val and Monica were heating the enchiladas, Robin walked out to the entryway and turned on the heat for the first floor. She'd felt a gust of cold sitting at the bottom of the stairs, as if winter were creeping down from the top of the house to the bottom.

She finally had answers, but just as many questions remained.

Who killed Billy Grimmer?

What was the cabin Helen was talking about?

If the past was in the past, why was Billy still hanging around?

Robin got her phone out and tapped Mark's number, walking out to the front porch to watch the sky turn from deep blue to black.

"Robin?"

"Hey. I'm at Grandma Helen's. Monica, Val, and I brought her some enchiladas. I made a chicken casserole and put it in the oven before I left. Just turn it to 350 for like an hour or so," she said quickly.

"Is she feeling okay?"

"Yeah. I think something is wrong with her space heater though."

"I'll go by in the morning and take a look at it," he said. "It might need the filter cleaned."

"Thanks." She felt a wave of gratitude for her husband. He might not be perfect, but neither was she. When anyone needed help, Mark was always the first to volunteer. How many people could you say that about? He didn't always say the right things, but he *did* the right things. Most of the time.

She'd married him because she loved him. And he loved her. Did he still?

"Robin, you okay?"

She sniffed. "Just thinking about Grandma and Grandpa Russell."

"Is it wrong that I'm relieved I never met him? Your dad's stories would scare anyone."

"I know. It's kind of amazing he had the guts to marry Mom."

"Well, men do stupid things for love."

"Oh yeah?" Robin smiled. "What stupid thing did you do for love?"

"Moved to this little bitty town in the middle of nowhere."

"Oof," Robin said. "That's rough. No airport?"

"Nope."

"Movie theater? Major league baseball?"

"Nada," he said. "But it does have its attractions."

"Oh yeah?"

"The scenery is pretty great. Schools are good. And there's this woman."

Robin felt her heart clutch. "A woman?"

Mark spoke slowly. "Even after twenty years, she still

drives me crazy. Still keeps me guessing. I try to make her happy, but… after all this time, I'm still not sure I get it right."

Robin blinked hard. "Sounds like she doesn't make it easy on you."

"Well, she's got a lot going on. And she's always thinking about other people before herself."

Robin bit her lip. "Mark—"

"I can be an asshole when I don't know what the right thing to do is," he said quietly. "I need you to tell me things. Maybe that's dumb and male of me, but—"

"You're not dumb. Not even close to it." She swallowed a lump in her throat. "I need… to be better about communicating. That's on me."

"I think we could both improve in that."

"Yeah." Robin didn't know what else to say. "I should get back to Grandma Helen, but I won't be home too late."

"Good." Something chimed, and the weird mood he was in seemed to clear. "That's Emma. She said she'd text when she was done at the library."

Robin let out a long breath. "That girl really needs to get her license."

"I'm about ready to drop her off at the DMV in Bridger City and not pick her up until she has it."

"Right?" She squeezed her eyes shut. "Mark?"

"Yeah?"

Ughhhhhh. She bit the bullet. "Can you just buy me a car that you think I'll like and be done with it? I'm sick of asking for rides from everyone, and I hate car shopping so much."

"You don't care what kind of car you get?"

"I mean, I care. But you know what I like. I trust you to

get something good." *Kinda. She kinda trusted him. Leap of faith, Robin.*

"Good and *safe*."

"And safe, yes. As far as the details, I don't really care that much." She cared so much, but she genuinely did hate car shopping.

"Okay!" He sounded like someone had put sugar in his coffee. "Yeah, I can take care of that. I'll do it this weekend."

"Thanks." She saw something flickering at the edge of the forest.

What the...? "Hey honey, I have to go."

"Right. I have to get Emma. I'll see you when you get home."

"'Kay." She turned off her phone, slipped it in her pocket, and nearly ran across the lawn. By the time she reached the edge of the forest, Billy's ghost was walking away.

"Stop!" Robin was panting. Man, she really needed to start running again. Screw her knee, she hated feeling weak. "Billy, we know about you and Helen."

He turned and frowned. "What?"

"Helen" —Robin panted— "is my grandmother. I am Helen's granddaughter."

"Helen's granddaughter?" His eye went wide. "That's why you looked familiar. Are you—?"

"Not yours." She stood up straight. "I'm sorry. My mother was Helen and Gordon's daughter. But her older brother, my uncle... Well, he's—"

"The baby." Billy's face was the picture of grief. "We found out, and God forgive me, I was so happy. It was every dream come true."

For you, maybe. Robin had to imagine that being unmarried and pregnant wasn't Helen's idea of a dream come true. "Were you planning on getting married?"

"Oh yes. There was nothing more I wanted in life than to marry Helen Moore. She was sunshine. Smart as a whip and funny. She was scared at first—about the baby—but I told her we could just leave. Her and me. We'd get married and walk away from that old town. We could go up to Sacramento with my people."

"What happened?"

He shook his head. "I don't remember. I just can't remember anything."

Robin looked over her shoulder to the grand house on the edge of the lake. "Do you ever go see her?"

His smile was sad. "I can't. I can't even get close. But I can feel her, especially when she's happy. Something about her..."

Robin's heart felt like it was breaking. "Is that why you stayed?"

"I couldn't leave because there was something I had to do. I had to be someplace and I missed it."

"Did it have to do with Helen?"

He furrowed his brow. "I don't know. Maybe."

"The sheriff, he said you were murdered."

"We knew that already, didn't we?"

"No." Robin stepped toward him. "I mean, it wasn't just the drowning. You didn't drown in that mine shaft. They examined the bones on your neck. Someone took a knife and—"

"Whoa." Billy held up his hands. "I get the idea." He rubbed his neck. "That's unpleasant, for sure."

"Who would want to kill you? Did you have any enemies?"

"Not that I know of. A few fellows didn't like me much, but that's no cause for killing, you know what I mean?"

"Yeah." Robin did know what he meant. She wasn't a trained detective, but something in her gut said that whoever had chained Billy and then cut his throat had hated him with passion. Chaining someone up was killing from a distance. A knife to the throat was personal, direct, and very, very permanent. Someone wanted to make very sure Billy Grimmer was dead.

Robin stared at the ghost in the moonlight, the outline of his form getting murkier as the night grew deeper. He stared at the house, his eyes longing to see something just out of reach. "I just wanted her to know I tried."

"Tried what?"

He frowned. "I'm not sure. But I tried. I know that. I would have walked through fire for her. I would have done anything to make her smile." Billy turned to Robin. "You do look like her, you know. Not everything, but something in your eyes..."

He faded into the darkness. Robin was tempted to grab her sketchbook and try to make him come back, but she was tired and she was cold.

And Billy Grimmer wasn't getting any more dead.

CHAPTER 20

*V*al threw her pencil on the library table. "I don't know what we're doing."

Robin looked up. "What do you mean? We're trying to figure out who killed Billy Grimmer."

"Why?"

Monica and Robin exchanged a look, and Robin wasn't encouraged by what she saw in Monica's expression. Both her friends were having doubts.

Val said, "Whoever did it is probably dead. We've uncovered the secrets in your family. Your grandmother doesn't want to talk about it. We can't make her. Your uncle knows about it. I don't think anyone feels the need to tell your mom because why would we? And Billy—"

"Shhhh." Robin glanced at the librarian. "Do you need to shout?"

Val dropped her voice. "Billy is a ghost. He doesn't care. He doesn't seem to want to move on, so why are we doing all this?"

"All this" was box after box of old photographs and news

clippings that Val, Robin, and Monica were sorting through. They were also scanning a few of them as they went to help Gail out, but that was kind of a side job.

"I don't know what we're doing anymore," Val said. "It's been weeks since Sully found the bones, and I have a business to run. I have two boys, one of whom is failing geometry, and I don't know why because he's always liked math. And I don't think any of this is going to cure" —she dropped her voice again— "our conditions. I think we're stuck with them, because as far as I can tell, none of this is doing anything." Val pulled on the gloves she wore everywhere. "So I'm going home."

Monica tried to speak up. "Val—"

"No." She cut her eyes at them. "I know that both of you have free time. Monica is trying to find her new place in the world and all that. Robin is trying to come to terms with... whatever, I don't even know. But I have a business to run. I have two children. I have no backup plan. And I have an ex I still have to deal with and his pissy little girlfriend who's screwing with my life because she's an infant and has no idea what being a mother is." She threw her notebooks and pencils in a black backpack. "I do not have time for this."

Val stomped out of the library and into the darkening afternoon.

Robin looked at Monica. "What the hell?"

Monica took a deep breath. "Josh filed paperwork to increase his visitation."

Robin frowned. "Why? He doesn't make half his visits now."

"Val thinks it's because his girlfriend is telling him that if he has more custody, he won't have to pay as much child support."

"Again, he hardly pays child support as it is."

Monica threw up her hands. "I know. He's an ass, but he told the boys they were going to see him more, and now Jackson and Andy are both excited and Val feels like chopped liver for being the steady one all these years and getting no credit when Josh was being a dumb ass."

Robin closed her eyes. "Why are men the worst?"

"They're not all the worst. Let's keep this limited to Josh."

"Why is Josh the worst?"

"Because he thinks with his dick and not his brain," Monica said. "Just don't take any of that stuff personally. She's stressed. And when you top all that shit off with picking up random visions from personal objects, it's just been a bad couple of months."

"What about you?" Robin asked. "I mean... I guess I don't know why I'm doing all this, but it feels important personally. Why are you doing it?"

"Val's kind of right." Monica gave her half a smile. "I feel like the accident woke me up. I've been treading water since Gil died. I need to find something new. I don't have a career. I'm not an artist like you."

"I'm not an artist."

"But you are. You always have been. You've always had that *thing* that you're really good at. I've been... what? Gilbert's wife. Jake, Michael, Philip, and Sylvia's mom. I was on all the PTA boards and volunteering in classrooms, but what does that leave me with now?"

"Monica, you are so smart and funny and have so much to give—"

"To who?" She threw up her hands. "Seriously, Robin? To who? That's what I'm dealing with right now. My husband is gone. No one cares if I'm home or not. I mean, I know you think Jake is freeloading off me, but honestly, I think he's still there because he knows I don't want to be alone. I know how to make dentist appointments and juggle homework with studying, music lessons, and sports practice. None of that translates into a career once your kids are gone." She lifted her chin. "And I have *two* persistent chin hairs now instead of one. What is that about? They're grey too! I don't have a single grey hair on my head, but I get one on my chin? It pisses me off."

"Don't get me started on random chin hairs, because I'll never stop," Robin said. "And I don't know if my opinion counts for anything, but I think you're really good at being a psychic detective."

"Thanks. You're as much of an expert on that as I am. But thanks."

Robin closed her notebook and started putting pictures back in boxes. "Have the dreams gotten any better?"

"Nope. I'm not getting any new ones either. Just you and Billy by a house in the woods, and a bloody knife in a dark room with stained glass."

"Did you go to the church?"

"Yes." Monica rolled her eyes. "Every single church in town. None of them have stained glass like what I saw. It doesn't look like a church either. It looks more like... You know those Tiffany stained glass lamps they have at the lodge?"

"Yeah."

"Like that."

"Is it the lodge?"

"Nope. It's definitely a window. And yes, in case you were wondering, I drove up to the lodge too. They do not have any stained glass windows. They only have the lamps."

"This is maddening."

"Tell me about it. I think maybe the next step should be trying to find that cabin I keep seeing."

"Where do we even start with that?"

"With you learning how to call ghosts better." Monica threw her purse over her shoulder. "You ready to go?"

"Yep." They walked out of the library, waving at Gail behind the desk, and to the dark parking lot shared by the library, city hall, and the post office.

Monica grinned when they got to Robin's new car. "I love your car."

"Thanks." Robin couldn't stop her smile. "I'm starting to like it a lot. I'm not in love yet, but it's heading there."

"It's sexy."

Mark had jumped at the task Robin had given him and bought her a deep red, low-slung crossover SUV that was halfway between a station wagon and a Jeep with all-wheel steering, a state-of-the-art navigation system, and tan leather interior.

"It's very... red."

Monica elbowed her. "And you said your husband thought you were boring. That is not the car of a boring woman. That is a sexy car. It's sexy red."

"Monica—"

"And it has all the things you love, but it's not a boxy

Subaru. Just take the sexy car as it was intended and do bad things to your husband with your newfound sexiness."

"Could you say sexiness one more time?"

"Sexiness." Monica made a purring sound. "Sexy. Sex-ay. Sexy."

"This is bordering on disturbing now."

"Shut up, sexy."

TAKING MONICA'S ADVICE, the next night just before dusk, Robin went out to the edge of the lake where she'd seen Billy's ghost twice. She sat on the rocks with her sketchbook and started picturing Billy in her mind. She sketched him walking in the forest near the edge of the lake in his plaid flannel and worn jeans. The image was so clear in her mind her pencil flew over the paper.

As she drew, Robin felt like her mind opened. She could sense everything around her. The scent of lake water and pine. The cold clear air laden with the coming winter. The birds grew louder, then fell silent, and when she looked up, Billy Grimmer was there, looking more than a little disoriented.

"It worked." Robin couldn't stop her smile.

"That was strange."

"I did it. I called you."

"Is that what you did?" Billy walked toward her, his ghost looking more solid the closer he came. "The other times I've felt you close, and I followed you, if that makes sense."

"Not really, but I'm not a ghost." Robin kept the sketchbook open. She had no idea what would happen if she closed it. Would he disappear? She had a few questions she wanted to ask. "So this time what happened? What was different?"

"I felt a pull. You weren't just a bright, warm spot in the fog—being here is kind of like living in the fog—but I felt a tug in my mind. Like that feeling when you know you're forgetting something, so you go to the last place you were? It felt kind of like that."

"Huh." Robin wondered how far it worked. Did geography matter? Or did ghosts not really work like that? "I have some questions for you."

"I'll answer them if I can." Billy picked up some small stones along the lakeside and skipped them across the water.

The ripple wasn't in her mind. She saw the water splash. "You're picking things up again."

"I feel really strong."

"Do you know why all this is happening to me?" Robin asked. "To us? Monica, Val, and I—we all went into the lake. Before that, I hadn't been able to see ghosts. I'd never seen anything like that before."

Billy frowned. "Hadn't you?"

Robin hesitated. "I think I'd remember seeing ghosts, don't you think?" She dismissed her childhood "fairies" as nothing but a vivid imagination.

"I don't know," Billy said. "I forget a lot of things. Like now that I've seen you, how did I not recognize you as Helen's granddaughter? You're the spitting image of her, but I didn't see it before. You just looked familiar."

"Familiar like your resemblance to Uncle Raymond."

"Exactly." He picked up another stone and skipped it. "I'm feeling stronger. Not sure why. More... clear. Clearer than I've been in a long, long time."

Robin shook herself. She'd better ask the questions before she forgot. It was easy to lose track when she was talking with ghosts. "Monica had a vision of us walking in the woods by a cabin," she said. "Do you know what she saw?"

"The cabin?" Billy smiled a little. "It's not far from here. Just an old hunting place my dad maintained. I think it was on Russell land, but it was back in the woods before the lake came."

"Where?"

He nodded to the forest across the road. "You can follow me if you want."

Robin stood and cautiously followed Billy's outline, which was growing slightly more translucent as he walked.

"Helen and me, the cabin was our place. We'd meet there and talk. Meet there to..." His smile was bashful. "Well, you know. We liked to pretend it was our own house. We were young."

"How young?"

"We were the same age. Had known each other all through school. I suppose twenty-one when we started up together? Twenty-two when Helen got pregnant."

"Why did you keep it a secret?"

Billy shrugged. "I knew her family wanted something finer for her. They were good people. Had property once. They knew she was smart and pretty and funny. She'd make someone a real fancy wife."

"They didn't care what she wanted?" Robin had seen the sadness on Helen's face. She'd loved Billy. Wanted Billy.

"They didn't see it that way," Billy said. "To them, security would mean happiness. It was a different time."

He was leading her on an animal trail through the trees

and along a creek bed. The creek was dry because the rains hadn't come yet, but they would. Soon, the shallow channel up the hill would be full of water, only to be covered with snow and ice when winter came.

"It's not far now." Billy stopped at the rise of a small hill to let Robin catch up.

Her knee was aching, but she pushed herself. It was hard hiking through the woods with a ghost who didn't have to breathe.

"Where... is it?" Robin panted. "I don't see." She felt her phone buzz in her pocket, but she ignored it. Billy's outline was starting to fade.

"There." He pointed to the east. "See?"

Robin squinted and peered through the trees along the creek. Her phone went still in her pocket, only to start buzzing again almost immediately. She could see a deep green sweep of moss in a fold of the hillside, just under a granite outcropping.

"Is that it?" She reached for her phone.

Billy was walking up the creek and toward the granite rocks.

"Hello?" Robin tried to keep her eyes on him as she answered her phone. She didn't want to lose him.

"Robin?" Mark's voice was low and worried. She could hear someone crying in the background. "Robin, honey, you need to go to Russell House right now."

She froze, watching Billy walk away from her into the shadows. "What is it?"

"It's Helen."

Emma's voice was in the background. She was the one crying. Robin spun and started walking down the hill.

"Helen?" Robin's voice caught. "No, she can't have—"

"She's alive, but she fell, Robin. Your mom found her this afternoon. She's been in and out of consciousness since then."

"Did they call an ambulance?"

"They did, and the EMTs called her doctor and home-health aide."

"Are they at the hospital?"

"No."

"What?" Robin started walking faster.

"They did not take her in."

"Why not?" Robin started jogging. Damn her knee.

"She has a living will or something. She doesn't want any extraordinary measures. Doesn't want a hospital. The doctor's with her and Grace right now at the house with a nurse. Just get over there. Emma and I will meet you."

CHAPTER 21

*R*obin sat at her grandmother's bedside, listening to the low voices of her mother and her husband in the background. They were discussing Grandma Helen's wishes and her current status. She'd been in and out for the past few hours. She'd woken up when Robin got there, squeezed her hand, smiled, and then fallen back to sleep. She'd spoken to Grace a few times and smiled when she saw Mark.

Emma was sitting next to Robin, holding her great-grandmother's hand, as Robin stared at the painting over her grandmother's bed.

It was one of Helen's own pieces, but the subject of the painting wasn't the lake Helen had grown to love, it was the valley as it had once been. At the bottom of the painting, the twisting blue and white of the river snaked through a steep mountain canyon, threading through hills dotted by cattle and rolling through dense forest.

In the foreground, a cluster of cabins peeked through the

trees, smoke rising from stone chimneys. There were wagons and a water tower. There were tiny trucks and horses.

It was Grimmer. How had Robin never noticed before? In her own bedroom, near the place she slept every night, Helen kept a crystal clear portrait of the town where she'd been born. The memory of it had been so crisp, she'd painted it in vivid oils. It must have hung on the wall for years, but Robin had never noticed it.

"Don't you think she should go to the hospital?" Emma asked. Normally her daughter was confident and mature, but in that moment she sounded like the girl she still was.

"No, baby." Robin stroked Helen's hand. "Grandma wasn't too happy when she had to go to the hospital last year. She made it clear with her lawyer and Dr. Cramer that she didn't want that again."

"But what if there's bleeding or something?" Emma leaned on the foot of Helen's bed. "Like, on her brain?"

"What would they do?" Robin said. "She's ninety-five, Emma. She didn't want any more surgeries."

"But she's still here," Emma said. "Doesn't that mean something? Couldn't she get better?"

Robin turned to Emma. "I think it's up to her. But Grandma was pretty clear with the doctor and her home-health aide on this. She didn't want any major medical intervention."

"But—"

"Come here." Robin took Emma's hand and walked out of the side door that led to the rose garden where Helen had been basking in the sun a few days before.

"I know it doesn't seem fair." Robin took Emma into her arms. "Trust me. I don't want to let go of her either, but we have to respect what she wanted. She's really old, Emma. And really frail. Her mind is all there, but she's uncomfortable. She can't do a lot of the things she enjoyed anymore, and she didn't like being limited. She'd never want to be shut-in. She'd never want to live in a bed."

Emma's eyes were red. She bit her lip and nodded. "Did Dad call Austin?"

"Yeah. He's driving down right now. So are Uncle Jack and Grandma's brother, Uncle Raymond."

Robin wanted her boy. Whatever their arguments were, Austin was her boy and she wanted him close. She wanted all her friends and family close. She hugged Emma tight and felt her daughter's arms wrap tight around her body.

They walked back into Helen's bedroom to sit with her. Emma found some of the big band jazz records that Helen loved and put one on the turntable.

Robin was about to text Monica and Val when Mark poked his head through the door. She could tell by his eyes that he was as wrecked as she was.

"Hey, Robin. Can you come out here for a second?"

She nodded and left Emma with her great-grandmother. Her mother was sitting at the kitchen table across from a woman in wine-colored scrubs. They both rose when Robin entered the room.

"Hey, Mom." Robin walked straight to Grace and hugged her tight. "How're you doing?"

Grace's eyes were red, and she looked tired. And sad. But mostly tired.

"The nurse says..." Grace cleared her throat.

The nurse, a smiling woman with light brown hair pulled into a braid, stepped forward and held out her hand to Robin.

"My name is Lily. I'm so sorry to be meeting you all right now, because I know it's hard, but I have to say I admire your grandmother so much." Lily let Robin's hand go. "She is so independent and so sharp. She and Dr. Cramer contacted hospice about five months ago."

"Hospice? Five months ago?" Robin looked at her mom. "Did you know about this? What was going on? Was she sick? Why wouldn't she tell us if she was sick?"

"Hospice isn't only for the dying," Lily said. "It's something Dr. Cramer recommended for Helen because your grandmother sensed that she was nearing the end and she didn't want any extraordinary measures."

Robin was confused. "Mom, did you know about this?"

Grace cleared her throat. "I suspected she'd arranged something. She could be so secretive." Grace took a deep breath and let it out slowly. "She's almost ninety-six and she fell last year. Mother was very realistic about her health."

"As I said," Lily continued, "Dr. Cramer and Helen reached out to us a few months ago and set everything in place for us to take care of her when she got to this point." She smiled kindly. "So I think it's safe to say that she might be feeling ready to go. The important thing right now is for her to feel surrounded by this family who obviously loves her so much."

"We're here." Mark put his arm around Robin's shoulders. "It's Helen. We're here for her no matter what."

Lily smiled. "That's what we like to hear. Just remember, this is a process. For her and for you. I and the other nurses are going to be here with all of you during that process. I've already contacted three of my best people to set up shifts so that someone will be with Helen around the clock from now on."

"So..." Robin felt her throat start to close up. "She's dying? That's what you're telling us."

Lily smiled sadly. "She's ninety-five, Mrs. Brannon. This is up to her now."

Grace sniffed. "Leave it to Mother to make permanent plans without consulting any of us."

Mark laughed. "She knew how to keep a secret."

Oh, you two have no idea...

Robin felt like everything was happening at once. They'd gone from talking about getting Grandma Helen some live-in help to having round-the-clock nursing care in the space of a few hours. Was this how dying happened? Everything all at once?

"What do we do now?" Robin asked the nurse.

She felt adrift. She knew how to schedule her grandmother's doctors' appointments and how to get her in and out of cars comfortably. She knew what food Helen liked and how she liked her coffee prepared.

But Robin had no idea how to help Grandma Helen die. She didn't want Helen to die. As selfish as it might be, she wanted to keep her grandmother forever.

"For now," Lily said, "I want you to relax about any of the practical details. Don't worry about helping her in and out of bed. Don't worry about her medications or pain relief. We are here to take care of that. You need to focus on her."

Robin thought about her last conversation with Grandma Helen.

"Are you happy here?"

"I love this spot. I love the view. The house is too big. I told Gordon that, but he never listened."

"We need to make sure to keep the drapes open," Robin murmured.

"Good idea." Mark squeezed her hand. "She loved the view."

"That's great," Lily said. "Play music she likes. You could read books to her, or letters from family. She might be in and out for a while, but even if she seems asleep, she's still with you. She's still processing all this, just like you are."

"Should we just plan on being here?" Mark asked. "I mean, it's a big house." He looked between Grace and Robin. "Why don't we just bring stuff over and stay with her?"

The wave of gratitude Robin felt almost knocked her over. Some men might balk at disrupting their lives to care for their wife's dying grandmother. Not Mark. Not even for a second.

Robin walked straight into his arms and didn't try to stop the tears. Mark hugged her tightly.

"We'll be here." He rubbed her back. "We'll pack some things and move in."

Robin talked into his shoulder. "It could be days. Or weeks. We don't know—"

"It's not like we're moving across the state." He stroked her hair back from her forehead. "It's just across town. And she needs us. We'll be here until... until she's ready to go."

"Dad and I will do that too," Grace said. "Besides, the holidays are coming. We should all be together."

"We're going to stay here?" Emma's eyes were wide. "At Russell House?"

"Yeah," Robin said. "Your dad suggested it, and Grandma Helen needs us close. There's plenty of space."

"Yeah but..."

They rarely stayed at Russell House. A few times during holidays, or sometimes when the kids had been little. They'd had campouts in the front yard during summers and had spent countless hours at Russell House's private beach.

But living in the grand old mansion, all together?

"Is Austin staying here too?"

"Yes."

Emma stared out the window. "So we're all staying here. Together. In Russell House."

Robin frowned. "Is everything all right?"

"Do we have to stay on the third floor?" Emma was pale. "It's cold."

"No. There are plenty of rooms on the second floor."

Emma nodded and seemed to relax. "Okay. That's okay then."

Whoa. What was going on? "Em, is everything okay?"

"I just had really scary nightmares when I stayed here as a kid. But I know it was my imagination." Emma shook her head. "And it was only on the third floor. I'm not little anymore. I'm sure I'll be fine."

Robin was reminded of the eerie hallway that led to the attic. She let her daughter wander back to the kitchen where Grace was already cooking chili. She walked outside and called Monica.

She picked up after two rings. "Hey. Mark already called

me and Val when he went to the house to get your stuff. What do you need?"

"Company maybe? But I don't want to bother Val. I know she's busy."

"She'll be there when she can. She was finishing homework duty with the boys. I'll bring a breakfast casserole over so you guys have some backup for tomorrow."

"I love you so much." She blinked back tears. Everyone needed best friends like Monica and Val. Everyone.

"Is Emma there? Does she need to go anywhere for school or anything? Do you need help driving?"

"No, she's here. She's okay. But..." What to make of Emma's reaction to staying at Russell House? What to make of her nightmares and reluctance?

"What is it?"

Robin glanced over her shoulder at the hulking mansion overlooking Glimmer Lake. "Monica, I think there's something weird in this house. I don't know what it is, but I want to find out."

"We'll get together and sort it out tomorrow with Val," Monica said. "Right now, focus on your mom and the family."

"Okay." Just as Monica was hanging up, Robin spotted lights turning in to the driveway.

Austin's old Jeep bounced around the circular driveway and came to a stop by the front door. He jumped out of the car, and Robin saw his expression. All the typical arrogance was stripped away. He was her boy again, not a boastful, half-grown man who thought his mom didn't know her ass from her elbow.

A thousand memories flooded her.

Austin in her arms while her mom and Grandma Helen

showed her how to breastfeed. A toddler bumping down the steps at Russell House, too impatient to wait for help down the stairs. Her little boy running across the lawn and down to the lake, bringing Grandma Helen a tiny bouquet of dandelions.

"Mom." He looked like he was about to cry.

Robin opened her arms, and Austin nearly ran into them.

"I'm sorry I didn't come back last summer." He sniffed against her shoulder. "Grandma Helen asked me if I wanted to stay here and—"

"Buddy." She hugged him tight. "She understood. It's fine. You're fine."

"I called her last week."

"Did you?" She kept her arms around him. Austin hadn't hugged her like this since he was eleven. "That's great. I bet she loved that."

"Not really." He sniffed. "She tried to be polite, but she mentioned a couple of times that she'd rather I wrote."

"Well, she is kind of deaf."

Austin let out a watery laugh. "I love you, Mom."

"I love you too."

CHAPTER 22

$\mathcal{I}$t was nearly midnight when Robin had a chance to sit with Helen again. The house was quiet, Mark had set up a temporary office in the old library, Emma and Austin had settled into rooms on the second floor, and Robin's mom and dad were in the old master bedroom.

Robin sat next to Helen, holding her hand and listening to records spin.

"We love you so much," Robin said softly. "So much. Did you know that? I hope we showed you enough. I know Grandfather Russell wasn't a loving man, but I hope your kids and grandkids showed you how much we love you."

The soft sound of a piano recording filled the room, and Robin paged through a box of old photographs Grace had brought to Helen's room.

"Look at you," she said softly. "What a stunner."

Her grandmother's eyes winked out at her from a black-and-white photograph. She was leaning against the hood of an old Packard in a pair of slim black pants and a button-down white shirt, one hand on her hip. "Look at you in those

222

pants, Helen Moore. What a rebel you were." Whose car was it? Would her mom recognize it? Could it have been Billy's? There was no way of knowing.

"Billy Grimmer told me he'd walk through fire to see you smile," Robin murmured. "Did you know that? Did he tell you that?"

Helen's eyes flickered behind closed lids, as if she was dreaming. She'd woken for a few moments and eaten a little broth, but that was all she wanted.

"I guess I don't have to explain that to you anymore," Robin said. "Don't have to worry about you thinking I'm crazy for seeing ghosts.

"Billy showed me your cabin," Robin continued. "I haven't gone in it yet. I'll go back with Monica and Val. See what we can find." She put the box of photographs on the dressing table next to the bed and noticed a cigar box under a pile of magazines.

"You take up smoking in your wild older years, Grandma?" She moved the magazines and books off the cigar box and opened it.

Letters. There were dozens of them. Robin opened one, expecting to see Uncle Raymond's name, but that wasn't the name she found. Her eyes went wide when she saw the signature.

Your man,
  BG

"Holy shit." Robin shuffled through the other letters. There were dozens of them, all written to HM from BG. "Grandma, where did you hide these?"

She must have gotten them out after she and Robin had talked the last time. Despite Grandma Helen saying she didn't want to think about sad things, Billy Grimmer was clearly on her mind.

Robin sorted through the old cigar box, putting all the letters on one side and keepsakes and other miscellany on the other. Billy had written Helen dozens of love letters. There were also two pictures at the bottom of the box, along with a postcard, a dried flower, a ribbon, and two tickets to *Casablanca*.

The pictures were interesting. There was a picture of three boys, one of whom was Billy Grimmer. The other two she didn't recognize, but they might have been his brothers. They were standing next to a giant saw blade in the woods. The second was a picture of Helen leaning against a tree by the river. The postcard was from Reno and only had Billy's initials on the back. There was also a sketch of Billy smiling. From the style of drawing, Robin knew her grandmother had sketched it. The expression was happy. Intimate. Joyful. It was a smile between lovers.

Robin opened a few of the letters and skimmed. Some of them were flowery, but most were light and news filled, talking about what was happening with Billy's family or what was happening at the dam. The cabin was mentioned more than once. It was the place they met on the weekends when Billy could manage to get away.

He called her his "best girl" and spoke often about when the dam was finished and where they would go. Billy was full of plans and promises. He wanted to save enough to buy a little farm "near a river where the light is clear." He talked about Helen teaching painting and drawing classes. Talked about wanting "four or five kids" who looked just like her.

For a moment Robin put herself in her grandmother's shoes and thought about how devastating it must have been. None of these plans had come to pass. Billy and Helen hadn't bought a little farm near a river. They hadn't had children together. Her grandmother had never taught drawing or art. She'd lived her life in the rigid social construction demanded by Gordon Russell, who had found her crying and alone, abandoned and pregnant with Billy Grimmer's child.

What happened, Billy?

The last letter in the box was nearly torn from being open and folded so often. It was smudged with what Robin guessed were tears.

"Best girl, I know you'll meet me at our place on Friday, but this time I want you to be ready. I'm done with this valley, this dam, and this town. We need to leave. Too many of the men here are the wrong sort. Be careful, Helen. Stay home or only go out with your brother this week. Can you do that for me? Some of them have been hanging around town. I don't want to scare my best girl, but be careful. For all of us. Come this Friday, we'll be together. I have a plan."

It was signed *BG* and dated September 1944, the same month the dam was finished and the town of Grimmer was officially abandoned.

"I was going with them. I'm sure of it. But there was some place I needed to be first. And then..."

Billy had needed to meet Helen. He'd needed to meet the

225

woman pregnant with his child so they could leave town, meet his family, and buy their little farm on a river. But he'd never shown up because he'd been kept from her. Chained in an abandoned mine and lost at the bottom of Glimmer Lake.

But by whom? And why? Who were the "wrong sort" Billy had written about? Had one of them been his murderer? And why had it been seventy-five years until the truth of Billy's death had emerged?

ROBIN STRODE INTO THE NIGHT, holding her sketchbook and the cigar box of letters in her arms.

"Billy!" She walked into the trees and sat on a bench near the path, frantically sketching the man who had abandoned her grandmother. "Billy Grimmer, you better show your face," she muttered.

She pictured him in her mind, the ghostly image she'd seen along with the pictures in the library, the sketch her grandmother had made. Every portrait and picture had captured a piece of Billy Grimmer, but she needed to capture the whole.

She opened up her mind and her heart. She sank her feet into the earth and took a deep breath. She felt like the mountain air was expanding her from the inside out. The night filled her, and she could see Billy's image clear as crystal in her mind. Her pencil flew over the page, lines and curves taking shape as she drew Billy's spirit to her.

As the portrait came to life beneath her pencil, she felt him. At first it was just the sense of him. The flicker of his eyes and the line of his jaw. Then she felt him, his confusion and longing. Robin closed her eyes and concentrated. When she looked up again, she caught the outline of his ghost standing at the edge of the forest. Billy was there, staring at the house and looking lost.

"I just want her to know I tried," he said softly. "I tried so hard."

Robin put down the sketchbook and held up the letters. "I found your letters. I know you were trying to leave with her. What stopped you? Who killed you, Billy?"

He looked pained. "I didn't have enemies. Not a single one."

"You talked about the wrong sort in your letters. 'Some of the wrong sort have been hanging around town.' You said that. Who were you talking about?"

Billy shook his head. "I don't know."

"What were they doing?" Robin asked. "Was it illegal? Were they hurting someone? Did you find out something dangerous? What made them the wrong sort?"

"I don't know, dammit!" Billy's eyes burned her. She could feel his anger, and his outline rippled.

"She is in there." Robin pointed at the house. "She's almost gone. She's ready to go, but she's holding on to something. There's something that won't give her peace. What is it? Is it you?"

"I just want to go to her." His outline rippled and wavered. "All I ever wanted was for her to know I tried, but I can't get to her. I can't be near her when she's in there. I know she's in danger, but he won't let me."

Robin's heart beat fast. "Who won't let you?"

"I can only get near her when she's outside. When she's

outside, I can watch over her. But in the house..." His voice started to fade.

"Who is it, Billy?" Robin felt a knot in the pit of her stomach. She knew. It could only be one person. "Billy, who keeps you from the house?"

He was gone. The place where he'd been held no more evidence of Billy Grimmer's ghost than a cool shaft of air. Robin closed her eyes and took deep breaths. In. Out. In. Out.

"Robin?"

She opened her eyes, and Mark was standing on the edge of the grass, staring at her with wide eyes.

"Robin, who the hell are you talking to?"

CHAPTER 23

ark was sipping an herbal tea, and Robin was drinking a large glass of water with two extra-strength pain relievers for her raging headache. They'd taken the tea from the kitchen and into the first-floor library, keeping their distance from the nurses who were tending to Helen in the north wing of the house.

"So..." Mark swallowed hard. "You think you're seeing ghosts."

"I don't *think* I'm seeing them. Trust me, I've already gone up and down with Val and Monica on this. I know exactly how crazy it sounds. But it's not just me."

He blinked. "So you're *all* seeing ghosts?"

"Not exactly."

He narrowed his eyes. "So what *exactly* is happening with you? With them?"

Robin sighed. "Listen, I can tell from your voice you don't believe me—"

"Robin, it's not a matter of believing you." His voice rose. "It's a matter of thinking you probably have more lasting

229

effects from the accident than we realized. It's about getting you help so—"

"This is not a fantasy." She brought out her sketchbook and started flipping through pages. "I'm going to tell you a story, and I want you to listen."

Robin opened her sketch to the first picture she'd drawn of the mystery man. "This is Billy Grimmer. He's the man who rescued us from the car. I've seen him more than once. He's the one I was talking to out in the woods."

She opened Grandma Helen's cigar box and got out the sketch. "And if Grandma Helen were awake, she would tell you this is a picture of Billy Grimmer she sketched back in the forties when they were having a love affair before she married my grandfather." She pointed to the sketch in her book. "This I drew just a week or so after I got out of the hospital." She held up the sketch Helen had done. "This I just found tonight, in this box, which is also full of their love letters."

Mark opened his mouth. Then closed it. "Okay, but—"

"My Uncle Raymond" —she kept her voice low— "is Billy's son. That's why he and my grandfather always fought. That's why he's never been close to the rest of the family." She showed Mark the picture of Raymond just out of high school. "This is Mom and her brother. See how much he looks like Billy?"

Mark said, "Okay, the resemblance is pretty uncanny, but—"

"You can ask Uncle Raymond about his DNA testing kit when he gets here tomorrow. Trust me. It's interesting." Robin showed Mark the photograph in Helen's cigar box. "Billy was a boy from Grimmer. His family founded the old town that was flooded when the dam was built. He and Grandma Helen grew up together. He worked on the dam, and then he was buried by the lake. His bones are the ones that were in the back of my car."

Mark watched her intently. "What?"

"I know *that* because Val can see things sometimes when she touches objects, and she touched the chains attached to the body and she saw him. Trust me, she was not happy about that." Robin flipped back to the picture she'd sketched of the mine. "Like this. She saw this image, and she described it to me. Someone chained him up and let him drown in the bottom of this mine shaft. Only according to Sully, they got impatient and cut Billy's throat first. I guess they really didn't want Billy escaping."

She handed Mark the last letter from Billy. "In this letter, Billy Grimmer mentions a cabin. It was his and Helen's secret place, and it's not very far from where my car went into the lake. Monica saw that in a vision. Saw me and Billy walking by it. Billy's ghost led me to it just before you called to tell me Grandma had fallen. I still need to go back with Val and Monica though, because I didn't really get much information and I think the cabin is important." She shoved her sketchbook toward him. "So there you go. There's all the evidence that your wife is completely nuts."

Mark stared at her. He folded his hands and pressed his thumbs to his lips. Then he looked down at the sketchbook, the photographs, and the letters.

"Well," he said slowly, "this would definitely explain why you've been so distracted lately."

Robin blinked. "You don't think I'm crazy?"

He frowned. "Robin..." He bit his lip. Looked away, then

looked her straight in the eye. "If you had told me anyone else was seeing ghosts—Monica or Val or Emma or anyone—I would think they were in need of serious mental help." He spread out his hands. "But this is... an investigation. This is evidence. Combine that with your telling me that *you*—the most practical person I know—have seen this... person." He held out his hands in a helpless gesture. "I can't ignore that. Even though it kinda fries my brain. It's you."

She felt a tight knot in her chest begin to unravel. "Thank you."

Mark sorted through the pictures and flipped through the sketchbook. "Who is this?" He was pointing at the picture of the ghost in the antique shop.

"That's the ghost in the antique shop. Her name's Clara. She died in the house giving birth to her son. You can ask Mom about the story."

"There's a ghost in the shop?" He narrowed his eyes. "Wait, is that why the bell randomly rings sometimes?"

"I think so."

"You said it was a draft."

"I thought it was." She shrugged.

"Have you seen any other... ghosts?" Mark wasn't mocking her, but Robin could tell he was still having a hard time.

"Just Billy and Clara, and there's a little girl I saw once at the edge of the lake. I think she drowned, but I've never spoken to her. And a nurse who was murdered at the hospital."

His eyes were wide. "Wow."

"Oh, and Car Lot Man." Robin nodded. "I forgot about him."

Mark frowned. "There's a ghost at the car lot?"

"Yeah, I'm starting to think sometimes people just stay in places that made them happy. Like Clara? She's happy. She misses not having the children around, but she doesn't seem all that troubled. And the ghost at the car lot was really happy. Big smiley guy with a round face and a droopy nose, wearing the most horrible dated suit, but he was happy as a clam, walking around—"

"Wait, what kind of suit?"

Robin frowned. "Just... dated. Like it was from the seventies, you know, with the big wide collar?" She grabbed a pencil and sketched his face in the margin of her book. "He looked like this. He was happy; he just wandered up and down the rows of cars and—"

"Holy shit!" Mark stood up from the table and started pacing.

"What?" Robin put the pencil down.

Mark pointed to Car Lot Man. "That's the founder of the dealership. The old man. His picture was up in a giant frame inside the building."

"Oh." Robin blinked. "I didn't go in the building. I didn't know."

"I know you didn't go in the building!" His voice was oddly high. "But you just sketched his face."

"Because I saw his ghost at the car lot. I told you."

"I know." He paced. "I know. You told me."

"Wait, so you're just *now* believing me?" Robin rolled her eyes. "Because of Car Lot Man?"

"His name is Jerry O'Donald. O'Donald Motors?"

"I don't know, Mark. I just saw him, I didn't talk to him."

"Oh my God." He was still pacing, looking slightly ill. "You can see ghosts."

"Yep.

"You can see *ghosts?*"

"Yeah, I..." She sighed and just watched him pace. "I just said that."

"You can see ghosts." He stopped and let out a long breath. "Is there a ghost on the third floor of this house?"

Robin's eyes went wide. "Why would you ask that?"

"Because there has always been something about this house and especially that floor that just creeps me out so bad." He rolled his shoulders. "Emma and Austin flat refused to go up to the third floor after that Easter when Emma was ten."

"Is that what that was about? I could never figure out—"

"It was Austin who finally said something. Emma kept crawling in his bed, and he was embarrassed because he was twelve, almost thirteen I think? Anyway, she told him she was having bad dreams about the man in the attic and he got completely creeped out." Mark stopped. "I went up there to check it out because I was worried someone had broken into the house, but it was completely covered in dust so I— Wait." He pointed at her. "Why don't you look surprised?"

Robin felt a knot form in the pit of her stomach. "Let's just say that you're not the first person who might have mentioned it."

THEY WERE LYING in bed after another hour of trying to piece together everything they knew about Grandma Helen,

Billy Grimmer, and the destruction of the town. Mark had offered some insight that Robin wouldn't have thought of, and he'd volunteered to go with her to the cabin the next day.

She was lying in the curve of his arm, feeling more at peace than she had in months. Maybe years. "I think Grandma Helen needs to know what happened. I think that's why she's still here."

Mark twisted a piece of her hair around his finger. "I think whoever killed Billy sent that postcard from Reno. The handwriting is close, but it could have been forged. All that was on there were initials. And it was dated after Helen married your grandfather, so Billy was already dead."

"You think whoever sent it wanted her to think Billy had run off to Reno?"

"Why else? She kept it with her letters and sketches of him. She must have thought he was the one who sent it."

Robin turned to him and burrowed her face into his shoulder. "Thank you for believing me."

"I can't lie—your wife suddenly developing psychic powers is not the change that men are warned to expect when their wife hits the midforties."

She playfully slapped his stomach. "Ha ha. It wasn't exactly in my plan either."

"Hey."

Robin looked up.

Mark winked at her. "Kind of fun though."

She couldn't stop the smile. "You're into this?"

"I mean..." He shrugged. "It's like my wife developed sudden mysterious superpowers. That's pretty cool. You're like one of the X-Men. X-Women. Whatever."

"Don't forget Monica and Val. Visions and telepathy. If

anything, I have the most boring superpower of the three of us."

"Not to me." Mark slowly took her mouth in a kiss that spun out and deepened, heating Robin from her toes to her belly. "You will never be boring to me."

"Good." She hooked her leg over his hips. "I missed you."

"I missed you too."

She bit her lip but decided that she might as well say it. After all, she'd told him she saw ghosts and that had gone over pretty well. "Mark?"

"Yeah?"

"I really, really hate waking up alone."

He locked his eyes with hers. "I didn't know that."

"Communication, right? I'm trying to be better about telling you what I want. Or what I need."

"Right." He nodded. "I'm sorry I didn't react well the last time you tried doing that."

"I'm sorry I didn't say something before."

"A year from now, it's going to be just you and me," he said. "That could be great. Or it could be awful if we're hardly talking to each other."

"Agreed."

"I want to do this right," he whispered. "I *hate* feeling like we're just existing in the same space. I never wanted that for us. My parents are that way, and I get so pissed off with them."

"I miss you." She swallowed hard. "When you leave the bed before I even wake up. I miss you being there. I know you like getting a jump start on work, but you're the senior programmer on your team now and—"

"I'll figure something out."

"I know you want to set a good example for your team, but—"

"Ignoring you isn't good for anyone," he said. "Not me or the people I work with. Like you said, I'm the senior guy on the team. I'll figure something out."

"Thank you."

"Besides, I need more time in bed with my hot superhero wife."

She smiled. "Yeah?"

"Can I make a request?"

"Does it involve a golden lasso?"

"No. But now you're giving me ideas." The corner of his mouth turned up. "Will you start wearing more spandex?"

Robin couldn't stop her laugh.

"'Cause..." The half smile turned into a full smile. "I'd be into that."

CHAPTER 24

*M*onica and Val were staring at her like she was a crazy person when she pulled up to the lake with Mark in the passenger seat.

"Okay, just stay in the car for a second," Robin said to him. "We didn't exactly agree to tell significant others."

"I'm not a significant other," he said. "I'm your husband."

"Yeah, but I gave Monica shit about telling her daughter, so she's probably pissed at me."

"Sylvia?" Mark scoffed. "That girl isn't going to believe an inch of this. Does Monica know she's not going to Mass anymore?"

"No, and you're not going to tell her."

Mark rolled his eyes. "Okay, whatever."

"Just... give me a minute." She leaned across and kissed him quickly. "Thanks."

The corner of his mouth turned up. "No problem."

Robin left the car and approached her two friends, both of whom looked slightly pissed.

"You told him?" Val asked.

"Yes, but—"

"We didn't agree to that," Monica said.

"You're the one who suggested it in the first place."

"But you said you didn't want to do it, so I thought we were keeping it just between the three of us!"

"He caught me talking to Billy's ghost over at Russell House. What was I supposed to do?"

"Make excuses," Val said. "That's what I've been doing every time Jackson asks why I'm wearing gloves to pick up their laundry."

"I'm not really sure what I could have used to excuse talking to myself in the middle of the night in the forest," Robin said. "But that's probably a very good call with the gloves and the laundry thing."

"Trust me, I learned the hard way." Val closed her eyes and shuddered a little. "Boys are gross. Speaking of which" —she pointed at the car— "Mark is a boy. A grown boy, but a boy. And we did not agree to tell boys."

"Are we twelve?" Robin asked. "He's my husband. And he wants to help, okay?"

Monica softened. "Really? He doesn't think you're making things up?"

"No. He did at first, but no."

"What can Mark do?" Val asked.

"I don't know, help make excuses? Hand us Tylenol when we get headaches from using our superpowers?"

"Superpowers?"

Robin shrugged. "He's kind of taking this as an X-Men thing. Like we suddenly mutated into superheroes."

"It seems like more of a Spider-Man thing, don't you

think?" Val asked. "I mean, we weren't born this way. There was some kind of outside stimulus that—"

"Okay, comic book nerds, can we focus please?" Monica said. "Robin, I accept that if Gil were alive, I would absolutely want to tell him about all this, so... I guess I'm fine with Mark knowing. Val?"

Val shrugged. "I mean, it's Mark—he's Mr. Boy Scout—so okay. It's not like I don't trust him."

"Thank you." Robin turned and waved at Mark. "Come on over, honey."

Mark got out of the car and walked over to Val and Monica, his hands stuffed in his pockets.

"Look at that," Val said. "He does exist outside his office."

"Ha ha," he said. "I'll have you know, I already called work and told them I'm taking family leave to help take care of Helen. So whatever you ladies feel like you need to do, I'm here to help."

Monica smiled. "You're a good man, Mark Brannon."

"Thank you." He turned to Val. "Hmm?"

She crossed her arms. "You're okay, I guess."

"I'm giving you space because I can tell already you're going to have the darkest storyline in the group," Mark said. "So it's fine."

"Darkest storyline...," she muttered. "Whatever."

"The idea is that we're going to go find this cabin, right?" Mark looked around. "The cabin where Helen and Billy used to meet?"

"Yes," Robin said. "Billy was leading me there a couple of days ago, right before you called me about Grandma Helen falling." She pointed across the road to the forest. "It's this way."

"Are you sure you remember?" Val asked.

"Just follow the creek bed," Robin said. "It's isolated, but it's along the creek."

They walked up and over the first hill, and Robin was surprised to realize how far she'd traveled with Billy's ghost without realizing it. They had probably walked nearly a mile before she saw the familiar line of the moss-covered roof.

"There." She pointed. "I see it."

"Wow." Mark huffed a little. "It's back here, huh?" He stopped and looked toward the lake. "This would have been really remote before the lake came. The old town was in the bottom of the canyon."

"They probably rode horses," Robin said. "Grandma Helen told me she rode horses all over the valley when she was a kid, before the dam was built."

The cabin was sitting in a small clearing of sugar pine trees. Pine needles, branches, and other detritus had gathered on the roof and around the structure, but the roof itself was intact, no small feat in a place where winter snowfall could be so heavy it would collapse a house if it wasn't removed.

Dense beds of ferns grew from the creek up to the house. Between two trees was a stacked woodpile that had mostly fallen over, and wood planks were nailed over the windows.

"When do you think the last people were up here?" Val walked around the cabin. "I don't see any cracks. It's well-built."

Monica walked to the door and pushed against it. "It's all boarded up. Did anyone bring a hammer or any tools?"

Mark stepped forward. "See? I'm useful." He reached into his back pocket and withdrew the multi-tool he always carried. "I don't have a pry bar..." He unfolded the pliers. "But this should work, especially on rusted nails."

As Mark and Monica worked on removing the nails from the door and windows, Robin walked over to Val.

"Hey," she said. "How're you doing?"

Val shrugged. "I'm okay. Sorry I flipped the other day. Just... Josh is pissing me off."

"I heard."

"It's going to amount to nothing, but while the kids figure that out, it's letters and emails and phone calls with the county because he's not paying child support again. And I can't say anything or I'm the bad guy." She shook her head. "Add all that to this constant awareness of the things and people around me."

"Sounds exhausting."

"It is." Val's eyes had circles underneath them. "And you know what? I'm half tempted some days to drive Andy and Jackson over to his house and just drop them off and yell 'good luck!' as I drive away. My house would be clean and quiet. I wouldn't have to yell at anyone about homework. I could cook whatever I wanted for dinner."

"Sounds nice."

"Yeah." She glanced at Robin. "I'd hate it, wouldn't I?"

"I can't lie, I start to panic when I think about Emma leaving for college."

Val groaned and pressed her fingers to her forehead. "I don't want to think about what we might find in this place," Val said. "What if it's scary? What if he was taken here?"

"Want to know the horrible and yet comforting thing about this mystery?"

"What?"

242

"Nearly everyone involved is already dead."

Val barked a laugh. "True."

Robin put an arm around Val's shoulders. "I need to find out for Helen," she said. "Thank you for helping."

"You owe me a dozen."

"I so do."

Monica pulled off the last plank from the door and shouted as Mark tossed it across the clearing. "We're in!"

Robin met Val's eyes. "You ready?"

Val nodded and pulled off her gloves. "Let's do this."

The interior of the cabin was dark, so all four of them turned on the flashlights on their phones. Robin started at the floor, but there was very little left inside. There was a cot in one corner. Some ancient provisions. An old woodstove opposite the bed.

"Looks like a hunting cabin," Mark said. "Definitely not a romantic bungalow."

"It might have been cleared out," Robin said.

"Or they might have been fine with snagging a hunting cabin for the afternoon." Val shrugged. "You said they'd planned to run away. This wasn't a house, it was just where they met." She took a deep breath, put her bare hand on the top of the stove, and closed her eyes.

Mark watched with a furrowed brow. "What do you see?"

"Nothing much," she said quietly. "Hunters wearing old clothes. Maybe sixties? Seventies?"

"So it hasn't been abandoned for seventy years," Monica said. "We might not get anything from this."

Val moved to the cot and touched it. "It's new too."

Robin felt her heart sink. She'd been sure something in

the cabin would lead them to Billy's murderer. "Let's look under the bed. There are some drawers over there. Who wants to look in there?" She turned around, only to scream when she came face-to-face with Billy's ghost.

"Robin?" Mark rushed to her, walking straight through Billy in the process. He stopped and a shiver shook his shoulders. "What the—"

"You just walked through Billy." Robin pointed at his chest. "Just straight through him."

Mark looked around. "Uh... sorry?" He frowned. "I don't really know the proper—"

"It's fine," Robin said. "He's probably used to it."

Billy wasn't speaking. He walked around the cabin, running a ghostly hand over the stove and the dresser. He knelt down and peered in the old woodstove.

"Robin?" Val put a hand on her shoulder. "What's he doing?"

"He's just walking around."

Billy stood and walked to the boarded-up window. He stared out it a moment before he turned. "He saw us through the window. I never told her."

"Who saw you?" Robin asked.

"Should I have told her? I think I didn't do right."

Billy was frowning as Val walked out of the cabin. Monica followed a few moments later.

Mark stood at Robin's back. "Is he talking?"

"Kind of." Robin watched Billy's ghost. It wasn't a strong image. He was fractured and wavering. She considered grabbing the small sketchbook she'd been keeping in her purse and drawing him, but she didn't want to interrupt his energy.

"Maybe if she'd known, she wouldn't have, you know?

But then I suppose he took care of her. In a way," Billy mumbled as he paced around the cabin. "I suppose he did. And I couldn't. I don't know if I was right."

"Robin!" Monica's voice rose from outside. "Robin, Val found something."

Billy was pacing in the cabin, walking from the stove to the cot and back again. He was in his own world, barely acknowledging Robin or Mark.

"What's he doing?"

"I don't know." Robin grabbed Mark's hand and walked out of the cabin.

Val was sitting on a fallen log, puking her guts out while Monica rubbed her back.

Monica pointed to something beside her on the log. "It's a watch."

Robin walked over and picked up what remained of a man's wristwatch. "What did you see?"

The strap had mostly rotted away, but the steel case was intact even though the glass was cracked. It wasn't a fancy watch. It was the watch of a workman. A businessman's watch. Robin remembered as a child seeing a similar watch on her grandfather's desk in the library. He'd always worn a watch, and it was eerily similar...

Robin turned to Val, her unspoken suspicion blooming into certainty when she saw her friend's face.

"He watched them," Val said quietly. She swallowed hard. "Robin, I'm sorry."

"I don't care," she said. "I'm done with secrets in my family. Tell me what you saw."

"He was standing outside the window, and it wasn't the first time. He was... excited. Angry, but excited too. He liked to watch them, but he hated..." She covered her mouth and closed her eyes. "He hated Billy so much. And Billy had no idea. Which made him hate Billy even more."

Mark reached for the watch in Robin's hand and looked at it. He flipped it over and wiped away the grime to reveal the words engraved on the back.

"G.R.," Mark said. "*Nitor donec supero.* Anyone speak Latin?"

"It means 'Strive until you overcome,'" Robin said. "It's the Russell family motto."

Mark's eyes went wide. "So the man who hated Billy—"

"Was my grandfather." Robin closed her eyes. "Gordon Russell didn't just find Helen here by accident like she thought."

Val said, "He'd been watching her—watching them—for a long time. I can't tell you how long, but when I touched the watch, I saw him, and I knew it wasn't the first time he'd seen them. The feelings I got were so strong. So... alive. Even now. What he was feeling when he wore that watch was so intense. And so wrong."

Monica's face was pale. "Oh my God. H-he stalked her. He stalked Grandma Helen."

"And then he married her," Robin said.

Mark said, "Do you think he killed Billy?"

Val shook her head. "I can't tell you that. I didn't see or feel anything about that. He was mostly focused on Helen."

"But if Billy was going to take Helen away," Robin said, "that would be a pretty good reason for Gordon to get rid of Billy."

"And then rescue Helen." Mark made air quotes around the word *rescue.*

Robin went to sit next to Val. "Monica's right. He stalked her and maybe he got rid of the man she loved. Then he married her and kept her under his thumb for forty years."

Val leaned on Robin's shoulder. "I'm sorry, Robin."

"Trust me. I have no fond memories of my grandfather. I was eleven when he died, and I don't even remember being sad. He wasn't a nice man." She shook her head. "And Grandma Helen called him kind. She told me he was kind for marrying her."

Mark knelt down next to Robin. "I think there's something else we need to talk about."

"You think we need to tell Grandma about Gordon? We don't know for sure he did it, we just suspect."

Mark shook his head. "I'm talking about now. I'm talking about Helen and the fact that you told me Billy couldn't get near the house because of *him*."

"You think Gordon is still in the house," Monica said. "You think he's still keeping an eye on Helen."

"Think about it," Mark said. "He built that place. It was his monument to himself. And not a single one of us wants to walk up to the third floor."

"You're saying Gordon Russell never left," Robin said. "That he's still in that house. Watching her. Watching all of us."

"He was controlling when he was alive, right? Maybe he's still trying to control things."

Val's expression was grim. "Your grandfather may be gone, but in a way he's still stalking Helen."

CHAPTER 25

*R*obin let Mark drive back to Russell House. Val and Monica followed them. They needed to find out what was going on in the attic, and Robin felt like time wasn't on their side.

Grace opened the front door before they could reach it. "Where have you been?"

"I had an errand I needed to do this morning." Robin embraced her mother. "How are you? How's Grandma?"

Grace looked exhausted as they walked through the front doors. "The same. In and out. She woke up a little a few hours ago and talked with Austin."

"Yeah?" Robin glanced up the stairs and around the formal areas of the house. The dining room had been taken over by the nursing staff, who kept their computers and some of their bags there. The library was Mark's domain. And in the formal living room, shoes, backpacks, and various electronics gave evidence of teenagers claiming territory.

The first floor of Russell House had been taken over by the living, but a cool draft gusted down the staircase.

"Be warned," Grace said. "Mother told Austin that if anyone told him not to pursue his art, they were to be ignored."

Robin rolled her eyes. "I think she told me the same thing at that age, so I can't really say anything."

Grace smiled, but the smile quickly turned to tears. "Robin."

"Oh Mom." She hugged Grace again. "We're not allowed to keep her forever." Robin blinked back tears. "It doesn't work that way."

"I know."

Hear that, Gordon? It doesn't work that way. You're not allowed to keep people if they don't want you around. Robin glanced up the stairs, and it was almost as if the house knew what she was thinking. A chill crept down her back.

"Mom, is Dad here?"

Grace nodded. "He's in the kitchen, cooking that lovely chicken-and-barley soup."

"Oh, that sounds great." Robin patted her mom's back and thought fast. "I had a weird thought yesterday."

"Oh?"

They walked through the dining room and toward the kitchen. "Yeah, I know Dad took all of Grandfather Russell's things up to the attic after he died. Have you ever gone through that stuff? Would there maybe be old pictures Grandma might want?"

"I went through so much of it when he passed," Grace said. "All the clothes. His books are still in the library. Most of the things in the attic are keepsakes. Some of his weapons collection. His hunting trophies. Things like that." She waved a hand. "I don't think Mother would want any of those things."

"Huh."

"Though..." She looked thoughtful. "I do think there were albums or scrapbooks. Things of that nature. Let's ask your father." She walked through the kitchen door. "Phil?"

Robin and Mark followed Grace with Monica and Val right behind them.

"Do you feel how cold the entryway is?" Monica asked quietly.

"Yeah. It's a pretty huge difference," Val said, "between the entryway by the stairs and the rest of the house."

"Philip?" Grace called again.

"Yes, dear?" Robin's adorably scruffy father turned around.

"Hey, Phil." Mark walked over and gave his father-in-law a hug. "How're you doing?"

Her father smiled sadly. "I'm okay. It's great to see the kids. I'm sad that we're not getting together for another reason. Austin is so excited about his new direction at school."

"I know." Mark glanced at Robin, who couldn't stop her eye roll. "Hey, we were thinking about getting some of Gordon's things down from the attic. Things Helen might enjoy looking at. Grace thought there were some scrapbooks or albums maybe?"

Phil furrowed his brow. "Well, I can't remember. There was so much happening after the old man passed, and Helen was so insistent that all those hunting trophies and weapons be put away. She hated those things, and she was always terrified the kids would get into them. Not that Jack was ever much interested in hunting. Gordon did his best, but the boy kept getting distracted by birds."

Bless her brother. "Speaking of Jack," Robin said, "When is he coming down?"

"He should be here in a few hours," Phil said. "He had to organize a few things at work, and then he was picking up your Uncle Raymond in Sacramento on his way down."

"But there might be some things up in the attic?" Mark asked. "Nothing is locked, is it?"

Phil shook his head. "I haven't been up there in years. I worried a little when Austin and Emma were young that they might go wandering, but they always seemed a little afraid of it, so I didn't worry much."

Gee, I wonder why they would be worried about an attic full of hunting trophies, old weapons, and possibly the ghost of a dead murderer?

"I'm going to check on Grandma real quick," Robin said. "Then why don't we go check it out? Monica and Val offered to help."

"Oh, that's a nice idea." Phil stirred the soup. "I'll keep everyone fed. Grace?" He walked over and kissed Grace's forehead. "How does that sound?"

She leaned against him and sighed. "That sounds fine."

"Good."

As her dad rubbed her mother's shoulders, Robin slipped into Grandma Helen's room, where Austin and Emma were playing cards. They'd dealt their great-grandmother in and were taking turns playing her hands.

Austin looked up. "Can you believe she's winning?"

Robin smiled. "She was always the smartest one." She

bent over and brushed a kiss over Helen's warm cheek. "Hey, Grandma."

Helen took a deep breath and let it out slowly, as if sighing in relief.

"Has she said anything while I was gone?" Robin brushed her silver-grey hair back from her forehead. "Did she wake up at all?"

"Not much. She's mostly sleeping." Emma leaned over and pressed her cheek to her great-grandmother's arm. "We're just keeping her company."

"Great." Robin glanced at Mark, who was standing in the bedroom door. "Dad and I are gonna take care of some stuff upstairs, okay?"

Emma put her hands over her ears. "Lalalalala. If that's a euphemism for having sex, I don't want to know."

"Dude!" Austin threw a card at his sister. "So unnecessary."

Mark stared at their offspring. "How much longer do we have to keep feeding them?"

"Legally?" Robin asked.

"Yeah. Just eighteen, right? That was in the rulebook they gave us at the hospital."

"I believe so." Robin slid her arm around Mark's waist.

"Ha ha," Emma muttered, looking at her cards. "You love us."

Robin smiled and tugged on her braid. "We'll see you later. Stay here with Grandma Helen. Uncle Jack and Grandma's brother are on the way."

"'Kay," Austin said.

"Sure."

Robin took one more look at Grandma Helen.

We're going to find out what happened, Grandma. I promise.

VAL, Monica, Mark, and Robin stood at the foot of the attic stairs. All four had flashlights in hand, and Mark held a set of work lights he'd grabbed from the boathouse.

"Okay," he said. "I'll go first."

Robin stepped forward. "If there's a ghost up there, I should go first. I might be able to see him, and I'm his grand-daughter."

"Do you think that makes a difference?" Monica asked.

"Maybe?" Robin shrugged. "I have no idea, but I'm going."

Mark called her name, but she was already on the stairs. She felt the chill run down her spine like a long, cold finger.

You don't scare me.

If you're up there, you're a ghost.

You can't hurt me.

The only problem with that theory was that Robin knew firsthand that ghosts *could* move things in the living world if they wanted it enough. Billy had broken the window. Nurse Hawkins had taken her blood pressure. If her grandfather's spirit was in the attic, how angry might he be?

She clutched her flashlight in one hand and her sketch-book in the other. It felt like precious little defense against an angry ghost. Mark was behind her, shining his flashlight into the darkness as Robin opened the door.

The air in the attic smelled of must and earth. Robin stepped inside, and everything was immediately muffled. Her footsteps fell flat on the hardwood planks of the floor. It was as if the darkness in the room absorbed sound, light, and warmth. There was one window in the room, but the light was fading, and the room was drenched in shadows.

As she stepped farther into the room, a pull chain hit her forehead, startling a gasp from her.

"Robin?" Mark was right behind her.

"I'm okay. There's a light." She pulled on the chain, but nothing happened. "Never mind." She swept her flashlight around the room.

"Let me..." Mark pushed past her and searched the baseboards for an electrical socket. "We need light," he muttered as Robin walked farther into the room.

She could hear Monica and Val behind her, but every sound was muffled. The energy wasn't warm or cold.

"Robin?" Monica called. "Are you getting anything?"

Boxes lined the walls, and furniture was covered in white sheets. "I don't feel anything. It's like a vacuum."

"This feels weird." Val held her hands out and pulled off her gloves, but she was careful not to touch anything. "Agreed. It feels like there's some kind of barrier."

The feel of the room reminded Robin of the hearing loss after a concert. You could hear, but everything was muffled. Only in the attic, it wasn't only her hearing; *all* her senses were muffled. Shadows and light blended together. The air smelled of old musty corners and also the earth and the outside. Sound was swallowed by the corners of the room.

"Mark, do you have the light?"

"Just found an outlet," he said. "Let's hope it's connected to something."

Robin heard a clicking sound, and suddenly the dark room was flooded with light.

Monica gasped.

Robin spun around. "What it is?"

She was staring above the window and pointing. "There. It's the stained glass window I saw in my dream."

"I'd forgotten that was even here," Robin said.

There was a single odd dormer built onto the back of the house that looked away from the lake and into the woods. At the top of the window was a spreading shell of Tiffany-style stained glass, the colors dull in the fading light.

Mark stood from plugging in the work lights. The bright yellow lights reflected off the sloped ceiling, illuminating the attic. "That's better." He put his hands on his hips. "What window?"

"That one." Monica pointed again. "I saw it in a dream, along with a bloody knife." She spun around. "But I don't see a knife. In my dream, there was a bloody knife."

"But in your other dream, you saw me and Billy walking by the cabin in the woods," Robin said. "And we didn't actually do that. So I think the knife is here. We just need to find it."

Mark said, "Didn't your dad say there was hunting stuff?"

"Yeah." Robin scanned the large attic. It was larger than the master bedroom, and boxes were stacked along every wall. "I don't see much labeled, so I think we're doing this the hard way."

Val walked to the other wall. "Four walls. Four of us. Let's start or we'll never finish."

Box after box lined the walls. The furniture was evident from each tented outline. There was a draped table. A dresser. An armoire. Several chairs were stacked in the corner with a plastic tarp thrown over them.

"I don't get the smell." Val walked around the room. "It smells like fresh dirt. But there's no dirt in here. There's not even much dust."

It was the truth. Though there was a fine layer of dust over the surfaces, there were no cobwebs. No dust bunnies. The dirt smell was a mystery.

The creeping sense of dread that Robin felt when she first entered the attic hadn't left, but she focused on each box as she opened it. "This looks like holiday decorations." She moved to the next. "School records."

Monica was across the room. "This looks like business stuff related to the lumber company."

"Skip," Mark said. "Jack told me all that stuff is electronic now."

Val said, "This looks more promising. Maybe scrapbooks from when your mom and her brother were little?" Val grabbed a heavy book and brought it to a table covered in a sheet. "This looks like your mom."

Robin walked over and looked at the album. "We should bring that down. Mom and Grandma might actually enjoy that one. Val, you keeping your gloves on?"

"While we do this? Definitely." She looked tired. "If and when we find something incriminating, I'll take them off."

Robin walked over and hugged her. "Thank you."

"You owe me a bottle of my favorite whiskey," Val said, hugging her back. "Maybe two."

"I'll do you one better. I'll come over and help you fold laundry while we drink the whiskey."

Mark said, "I could probably help fold laundry if you

gave me whiskey."

Val smiled. "If only I could offer whiskey as bribes to my boys. Maybe then they'd clean their rooms."

"Guys!" Monica's voice cut through the laughter. "I think I found something." She was digging through a box filled with dingy clothes.

"What is it?" Robin walked closer and realized the clothes weren't dingy, they were camouflage pattern. "That's Grandfather Russell's hunting gear."

Val said, "Didn't your dad say that he had a knife collection with all his hunting stuff?"

"Yeah," Robin said. "I remember it. He had a bunch of knives, all spread out on the wall above the mantel in the living room."

Mark frowned. "Not gonna lie, I like sharp, pointy things as much as the next guy, but that's kind of creepy. Maybe in your office, but the living room?"

"Yeah." Robin walked over and opened the box next to the one Monica was going through. "Christmas Day and we'd have stockings hanging on the mantel. Right under the massive knife collection."

"What kind of knives?" Monica asked.

"Hunting knives mostly. He had some historic pieces." Robin searched her memory, trying to put herself back into childhood. "They weren't collectors' pieces. They looked used. There were some really old ones. I remember a buffalo-skinning knife with a horn handle. One little short one that he said went in your sock? I don't remember them all."

"No knives in here," Mark set another box to the side. "Let's concentrate on this section though."

"The knives were the first thing Grandma wanted packed

up," Robin said. "I do remember that. I remember her talking to Dad. I don't know why that memory is so clear, but it is. She said, 'Philip, I've been living with those things in my face for forty years. Put them away, won't you?'"

A chill swept down Robin's back and she turned. Was she seeing things? There was a shadow just behind the work lamps in the corner of the room. She walked toward it.

Val shouted, "I think I found something."

Robin turned for a moment and the shadow was gone.

"Robin, come here," Mark said. "Is this the collection?" He, Val, and Robin were standing around a box on the sheet-covered table. He held up a familiar bowie knife.

"Yes," Robin said. "That's it."

They started unwrapping each blade. Five weapons in, Monica dropped a knife, which fell to the table with a hard thud.

"Monica?"

She pointed to the weapon. "That one. That's the knife I saw. It's not covered in blood, but that's the one in my dream."

The knife she was pointing to didn't look particularly ominous. Like so many of the others, it was an old-fashioned hunting knife with a fixed blade about six or seven inches long. The handle was wrapped in leather, and the hilt was detailed in brass. It was secured in a thick leather sheath.

Mark reached for it and slid it out of the sheath. "It's clean."

Val took a deep breath and took off her gloves. "Monica, are you sure?"

Monica looked like she was going to cry. She slid the knife across the table. "Yeah. I'm sorry."

"Don't be." Val looked around the attic. "There's something up here. You guys feel it?"

"Yes," Robin said.

"Yeah." Mark crossed his arms. "I don't even have superpowers and I can feel it."

Val stared at the knife in front of her. "Grandma Helen fed me cookies and rubbed sunscreen on my back when I was a little kid. She braided my hair for me. She gave me money for a prom dress when my parents told me they didn't have enough."

Robin looked at her. "You never told me that."

"Me either," Monica said.

Val blinked hard. "She told me it was between us. That ladies needed to look out for each and take care of each other." She looked around the attic. "She's been living with this... whatever it is... for how long? Thirty years? Longer?" Val looked at Robin. "We need to get rid of it. We need to keep it away from her. Once and for all."

Val wrapped her fingers around the handle of the knife and closed her eyes.

A spark snapped beneath her hand, then she gasped and fell to the ground, still clutching the knife. She arched her back and her whole body shuddered.

"Get the knife!" Mark yelled. "Monica, hold her arm still." He knelt down and grabbed Val's wrist, tearing the knife from her rigid grasp. He stood and put it on the table, sliding the knife back in the sheath.

"Val!" Robin knelt next to her friend and held her head. "Val, we're here."

"She's gonna throw up," Monica said. "Mark, is there a bag? A bucket? Anything!"

He ran to the corner and grabbed an old brass wastebasket. "Got it."

Val opened her eyes, and Robin helped her up to her knees and then pulled her hair back while Monica held the wastebasket in front of Val's face.

There wasn't too much in her stomach, but she dry heaved for what felt like five minutes straight. Robin and Monica rubbed her back, and Mark ran down to the third floor to look for tissues and some water.

"It was him," Val said quietly. "Gordon waited for the dark. Billy was trying so hard to get out of the chains that he didn't even hear him. He snuck up on Billy and cut his throat, just as Billy worked his foot free. He was bloody all over his leg, but Gordon..."

"Shhh." Monica brushed her hair back. "It's okay. We get the picture."

Robin stood and walked to the table. She stared at the plain hunting knife her grandfather had used to murder her grandmother's first love. Gordon Russell had stalked Helen Moore, killed the man she loved, and then married her, all the while making Helen believe he'd been her rescuer.

Robin had known her grandfather as a hard man, but what Gordon had done was evil. Flat-out evil. Even in death, his presence was everywhere, driving wedges between his descendants, stoking conflict, and haunting his wife.

She turned in a circle, feeling the malevolent energy of the dark and dusty attic, the coldness of the house. Gordon Russell had left a legacy of darkness, secrets, and fear.

Enough.

Russell House had seen enough evil. It was time for Robin Brannon to clean house.

CHAPTER 26

Robin, Val, and Monica sat in Grandma Helen's bedroom, watching over the sleeping woman. They had taken everything they could find that belonged to Gordon and loaded it in the back of Mark's truck. He was driving it to their house. He'd put it in the garage until they could rent a storage unit somewhere.

"My knee is killing me," Robin whispered.

"Same," Monica said. "The stairs in this house are ridiculous."

"Remember when we thought stairs were cool?" Val asked. "I did. When I was a kid, I thought houses with stairs were so fancy."

"This house *is* fancy," Robin said. "It's kind of ridiculous for one family."

She looked around the room, realizing that Helen had chosen to spend her later years in the maid's quarters rather than the ridiculous and fancy house her husband had built her. Robin had always assumed it was because Helen didn't want to deal with all the stairs, but Helen could have turned the downstairs library into a bedroom. She could have made her bedroom in the cozy den behind the formal living room.

But those were all rooms where Gordon had once lived. Only this room and the kitchen felt free of her grandfather. The kitchen, the breakfast nook, and the maid's room.

"She loved being outside," Robin said. "I can't even count how many signs there were that something in this house was wrong. I just thought she liked the outdoors."

"Do you think she's why Billy stayed?" Val picked up a comb and smoothed Helen's hair back. "Do you think he protected her?"

"Billy's ghost said he couldn't come in the house," Robin said. "But that tells me he could be near her when she was outside. So maybe."

"She spent as much time in the garden as she possibly could," Monica said. "And the woods and the beach."

"She used to tell me houses were for being sick and sleeping. But you lived outdoors."

No one had told Grace, Phil, or the kids what they were doing. The rest of the family had been busy welcoming Jack and Uncle Raymond into the house and updating them on Grandma Helen's condition. No one noticed the boxes or the many trips up and down the stairs. There had been too many things going on. Grandma Helen woke up and talked to both Jack and Raymond for a while. Then she'd had a short conversation with Grace and Raymond, after which they'd gone to the den on their own to talk.

"There are so many people in this house," Robin said. "My mom and dad. The kids. My uncles. How are we supposed to banish Grandpa Russell's murderous ghost without anyone knowing? Because I do *not* want to have to explain this to the whole family."

"You don't want to tell Raymond?" Monica said. "That his father—"

"He already knows Gordon wasn't his father," Val said. "I'm with Robin. It's not like anyone liked the man. They're not singing songs about him. Telling the whole story will only bring up too many questions. They'd probably never believe us in the first place."

"I guess you're right."

Robin held Grandma Helen's hand. "She would have believed us."

"Do you think she knew?"

"No." Robin shook her head. "She told me over and over he was kind to Uncle Raymond."

"Leave it then," Monica said. "But we need to get rid of him. He's been hanging over her for decades. Once he's out of this house..."

"I think that's what she's waiting for." Robin stared at Helen's profile in the low light. "I think on some level, she's always known he's still here. Still keeping her under his thumb."

Val shuddered. "I just had the mental image of a ghost following her. If you died while a ghost was following you, would they get attached?"

"The more important question is, how do we banish a ghost? Do any of you have any idea?"

Val and Monica both looked as clueless as Robin felt.

"I just barely learned how call one," she said. "And now I need to figure out how to send one away?"

"What do you do to call one?" Monica said. "The drawing thing?"

"Yeah."

"I don't suppose you saw Gordon up there?" Val asked. "That might be helpful."

"I saw... something. A shadow. I could *feel* him up there, especially when we had his things spread out. But I didn't see him. Not like I've seen Billy."

"What if you drew him?"

"That would call him, but we want to get rid of him."

"Right." Val bit her lip. "I have no idea."

"Well." Monica pulled out her phone. "Pretty sure you can find anything on the internet."

Two days later, Robin, Val, and Monica were still batting theories around. Grandma Helen had seemed to perk up with Raymond's arrival, and there was a happy hum in the house. Helen was still in and out of consciousness, but between the nurses, the company, and the music and movies the kids had on, she seemed comfortable, even if she was sleeping most of the time.

Robin had nearly convinced herself that taking all of Grandfather Russell's things out of the attic had done the trick. That was until she visited the attic again. The earthy smell still lingered, and the cold was even more pervasive.

"Sage." Val put down a book she'd picked up from the library. "I'm pretty sure we need sage."

"Are we going to *cook* his spirit out of the house?"

"No, for burning." Val turned the book around. "It's

called smudging. I've read about it in a couple of different places now. I think we definitely need sage."

Monica said, "I read about the sage thing too."

"Is it the same sage you use for cooking?" Robin asked.

"If it is," Monica said, "I've got a whole bunch of that. I dried it from the garden this summer."

"I think it's different." Val looked at the book again. "I'll keep reading."

"I feel like salt keeps coming up too." Robin stood and stretched her back. "Is anyone else reading a lot about salt?"

"Yes," Monica said. "Salt in doorways and windows. But that's supposed to keep ghosts out I think, and we already have one in."

"Josh got Andy one of those salt guns last summer," Val said. "Maybe that would work. We could shoot the ghost out."

"Salt gun?" Monica frowned. "What—?"

"It's for bugs. The boys think it's hilarious. They shoot mosquitoes, flies—"

"With salt?"

Val shrugged. "I mean, is it any worse than those electric zappers?"

"Look at this." Robin held out her phone. "Apparently, amethyst will dispel negative energy. Do you guys have any amethyst jewelry?"

"Do we really believe in crystals now?" Val asked. "Are we those people? Are we going to start putting crystal eggs in our vaginas next?"

"Good Lord!" Robin stared at Val. "Do people do that? Why?"

"I have no idea, but it seems like the same people who put

crystal eggs in their hoo-has might be the same people who wear amethysts to dispel negative energy."

"So we're judging folk wisdom about gemstones now?" Monica just looked at her. "How's your headache from the last telepathic vision, Val? You need any more aspirin?"

"Fine, point taken. Apparently we *are* the people who believe in crystals." Val muttered, "I'm not putting anything in my vagina though."

Robin said, "Considering how tense you've been, I'd say that's pretty obvious."

Monica snorted.

Val looked up with a smile. "Yeah, but you and Mark seemed to have made up, so I can't say the same to you."

"Thank God," Monica said. "You are so much more relaxed."

"No comment." Robin glanced at Val, then at Monica. "You know who I've been thinking we should bring in on this?"

"Who?" Monica asked.

"Sully." Robin didn't miss the look of alarm on Val's face. "Don't you think he'd be helpful?"

Monica immediately picked up what Robin was doing. "You know, maybe. I don't think he'd be as skeptical as he seems."

"Both of you shut the fuck up. I know what you're trying to pull," Val muttered. "Just stop."

"What we're trying to pull?" Monica batted her eyes at Val. "What would that be?"

Val slammed her book down. "Okay, we had one... thing. A few months ago."

"I knew it!" Monica said.

"And you didn't tell us?" Robin asked. "What the heck, Val?"

"It didn't go well, and we're just trying to forget about it, okay?"

"I don't sense things being forgotten." Robin's eyes went wide. "Monica, you're Catholic!"

"Uh, yeah. Have been for years. What does that have to do with Val and Sully?"

"Nothing, but that means you know priests!"

"I know *a* priest. Father Frank."

Val narrowed her eyes. "Neither Sully nor I are Catholic. What does that have to do—"

"I'm not talking about your love life anymore," Robin said. "I'm thinking about *priests*."

Neither Monica nor Val said anything.

"You know, priests who can do *exorcisms*."

"Uh, Robin, I don't really think Father Frank is trained in exorcism or anything. I mean, he doesn't even teach the catechism all that well. Gil was the one who had to help the boys with—"

"But maybe he knows other priests who do exorcisms."

Monica rolled her eyes. "Dude, do you think exorcism is covered in Being a Priest 101? I don't think they really deal with that much. Also, that's for people who are possessed, not weird, murdery grandparent ghosts." She winced. "No offense."

"I'm over it."

Val said, "You know what I think?"

"That you need to bone Sully?"

"Are you twelve, Robin?" Val glared at her. "Just forget I said anything!"

Monica was biting her lip, clearly trying not to laugh.

Robin cleared her throat. "You were saying?"

"I think" —Val shot her a dirty look— "there are two people in this house who've probably run into more spirits and ghosts and all sorts of weird things than any of us ever have."

Monica frowned. "The... kids?"

"Teenagers are hormonal, not possessed," Robin said. "Not that it doesn't feel like the same thing sometimes."

"The nurses," Val said. "Think about it."

"Oh, that makes sense. They're hospice nurses." Monica kept her voice low. "People die around them all the time."

Val cringed. "Wow, that sounds so bad."

"You know what I mean! If there are people who have been around spirits—"

"I'd be willing to bet every single nurse you've ever met has a story or two," Val said. "Didn't they have one in the hospital in Bridger City with that ghost Robin saw there?"

Monica asked, "Robin, what do you think?"

"I don't know." She thought about sensible, kind, and thorough Lily. The last thing she wanted was to make her grandmother's caretaker think she was nuts. Then again, they weren't likely to spend that much time with her after Grandma Helen passed.

"Sure," she said. "Let's ask Lily first." Robin glanced at the clock. "It's two now, she usually comes in at three."

"Okay." Val nodded. "And I'm getting some sage."

"Grab the salt gun too," Monica said. "Just in case."

CHAPTER 27

*L*ily frowned. "Are you asking me if there are ghosts in the house?" She looked between Val, Monica, and Robin. "I mean... I'm your grandmother's nurse. I don't—"

"I know it sounds completely bizarre," Robin said. "Just... I'm so sorry. Forget we asked."

Lily kept her voice soft. "I was going to say I don't usually encounter spirits of the deceased until after they are, in fact, deceased. Your grandmother is not."

The library was dead silent for a few awkward minutes.

"So you don't think we're nuts?" Val asked.

"Not at all," Lily said. "I think anyone who's worked in palliative care has at least one or two stories about spirits of the recently deceased doing strange or unexpected things. It's not uncommon. I had a patient a few months ago who showed up in her sister's room shortly after she passed; then her prized flock of chickens all went insane for about a half an hour, squawking and making a horrible racket even though it was the middle of the night." Lily shrugged. "There's a lot about the world we don't really understand. I accept that."

Monica put her head on her folded hands. "We thought for sure you were going to think we were the crazy grand-daughters."

Lily frowned. "Are you all granddaughters to Helen?"

"Not technically," Robin said. "But she was a big part of all our lives. And thank you for not thinking we're crazy. I guess you could say that we recently went through some fairly big life changes that we weren't expecting."

Lily nodded. "Menopause can surprise anyone. I know when I was going through the change—"

"Not exactly menopause," Robin said. "Though I'm defi-nitely sweating more at night, so that's probably coming too."

"Don't forget the chin hairs."

"I found three yesterday!" Val huffed out a breath. "What is that about?"

"No one understands chin hairs," Monica said. "I feel like I'm always finding new ones." She turned back to Lily. "But we're not talking about hormones. We're talking about being a little bit psychic for the past couple of months."

"A little bit" —Lily's eyebrows rose sky-high— "sorry, did you say *psychic?*"

"Just for the past couple of months," Robin said. "And regarding what you were saying before, it's not Grandma's spirit we're worried about. It's my grandfather's."

Lily looked even more confused. "Did he pass recently?"

"No, it was about thirty-five years ago."

"Wow, okay." Lily cocked her head. "Um... I guess I did notice that she has no pictures of him in her room. No mementos that look like they belong to a man. She doesn't even wear a wedding band."

"She told us years ago that she lost it," Robin said. "We never questioned her. It wasn't a happy marriage."

"But you think he's still..." Lily's gaze moved around the room. "...hanging around?"

Val took a deep breath. "Gordon Russell was known to be kind of controlling."

Understatement of the decade. Robin said, "We've removed most of his things from the house and they're in storage now, but the third floor and the attic are still kind of... cold."

Monica said simply, "There's something not right."

"Uh-huh." Lily nodded. "And you think it's his ghost?"

"Is that" —Val narrowed her eyes— "too weird?"

Lily opened her mouth. Closed it. "I don't know. I guess not. Something other than biology animates us, I know that. I've seen too many cases where even when a person is still living, I can touch them and know that they're already gone. Many people in comas or vegetative states are like that. But others aren't. And I don't know how to explain the difference, but I can always tell."

Robin asked, "Is Helen—?"

"She's still here." Lily's smile was sweet. "She became much more content when all the children and grandchildren arrived. She loves your father especially. She's tired. I can feel that. But she's working through things in her mind. That's why she's in and out so much."

Monica raised an eyebrow. "Sounds like you might have a little bit of the slight psychic-ness we're talking about."

Lily shrugged. "I'd call it intuition. I don't really look much past that. I'm sensitive to my patients. It's part of what allows me to help them and their families during this transition."

"Okay," Val said. "So I guess what we're asking is, what would you do if you felt like someone's spirit... wasn't very excited about moving on?"

"You want my advice on how to banish a ghost?"

"Yes," Robin said. "I know it doesn't exactly fall within your job description, but that is exactly what we're asking for help with."

Lily looked thoughtful. "You know... I actually do have an idea."

"Do you really think this is going to work?" Mark asked under his breath.

"I have no idea, but Lily said it's worked for her in the past, so who knows?"

Mark nodded and closed the door to the attic, pouring the salt in a thick line at the baseboard. "Okay, so Monica and Val are already up here?"

Robin shivered. "Yeah. Sheesh, it's cold."

Monica peeked her head over the railing as they climbed the steps. "That's because we opened the window. It's not just the ghost." She looked at Mark. "You brought it?"

Mark took the knife Gordon had used to kill Billy Grimmer from his jacket pocket. "Yeah. I'm not gonna lie, I felt weird stuffing a knife I know was used to kill someone under the seat of my truck."

Val said, "It's not exactly like you're hiding evidence of a crime or anything. Everyone involved in it has been dead for decades; it's barely even a cold case."

They reached the top of the stairs, and Robin wrapped her sweater around herself. It was midnight and the attic was freezing. Freezing and dark. Everyone in the house—save for the nursing staff and Uncle Raymond, who was sitting with Grandma Helen—was sleeping.

Val and Monica had uncovered the table and placed four chairs around it. They'd lit white candles and placed them around the room. The air smelled like frost and pine. The earthy smell had dissipated, but it wasn't entirely gone.

"You know what I was thinking about the other day?" Monica asked. "Gordon killed Billy Grimmer and nothing happened to him. Seriously. Not legally. Not personally. Not even karma caught up with him. It's kind of depressing. He killed a man and married the woman that guy loved. He got to have a successful business and a family and everything."

"He died young," Mark said. "I guess there's that."

"Sixty-five isn't *that* young," Val said.

"It's not that old either," Robin said. "Think about it. That's only twenty years from now."

Val made a face. "Good point. Sixty-five is very young."

"Did he have any friends?" Monica asked. "There's all sorts of stuff in town named for the Russells."

"No, he just gave people lots of money," Robin said.

"Maybe it was penance," Mark said. "Maybe deep down he knew he was living another man's life and it was a life he'd killed for." His eyes lit on the yellow plastic gun on the table. "Ooh, is that a salt gun?"

Robin felt something move in the room, but she couldn't

tell if it was supernatural or a gust of wind from the open window.

"Yeah, I brought it from the house," Val said. "And I think I bought out the boxes of kosher salt at the market."

"I brought some holy water from the church." Monica held up a water bottle. "Just in case."

Mark looked around the room. "Okay, so I salted the door, and you got the corners of the room, right? But not the window?"

"No, we want to give him some place to leave," Val said. "So we're hoping that Lily's advice and then the sage will do the trick."

"Okay." Robin grabbed her sketchbook and sat at the table. "Are we ready to try this?"

Monica, Val, and Mark all nodded. They sat around the table. Mark placed the knife on the table; Val had the salt gun. Monica had her holy water, a rosary, and was lighting the white candles in the center of the table. They'd gathered a few pictures of Gordon Russell from the newspaper and found a few lying around the house. They were sitting in the center of the table with the candles.

Robin began to draw. She'd refreshed her memory with the pictures, but she tried to draw more than that. She started out with a rough outline of the hard man she'd known, but that gradually morphed as she filled in the drawing. The eyes were unlined. The hair was dark and parted in a severe style.

A twisting feeling turned in her belly as she sketched. The image on the page became clearer, and she concentrated on the memory of a young girl wandering into the library long past her bedtime.

"You should be in bed, Robin Marie."

Robin looked up. She blinked. Her memory of the old man in the library overlapped with the image of the man standing near the window.

"You should be in bed." Gordon Russell's ghost turned toward her, arms crossed over his chest, a severe frown set between his eyes. "Just what do you think you're doing in the library?"

"You're not supposed to be here," Robin said quietly. Her heart raced, and she felt the darkness swallow her voice. She forced the words past her frozen lips. "It's not the library. I'm not ten anymore. And you're not supposed to be here, Grandfather Russell."

He towered over her, glowering. "I think you forget who you're speaking to, young lady."

"Robin." Mark put his hand on her shoulder. "What are you seeing?"

"He's here." Something pressed against her chest. He didn't want her to speak.

Children should be seen and not heard.

"Back to bed, young lady." The scowl on his face never wavered.

Robin felt like she was a child again, punished for sneaking down to the library past her bedtime to look for the next Narnia book. She didn't have the books at home, but Grandma Russell had them. She'd even painted a picture of Aslan for Robin's room.

"Robin?" Mark squeezed her shoulder. "Talk to me."

"She can see him." Val was speaking. "Robin, remember what you're supposed to do."

Grandfather Russell never wavered, not even for a minute. "Do I need to get your mother?"

No, not her mother. Mom didn't have any patience for Robin, and she'd do exactly as her father wanted. Robin always knew that. If it was a question of taking Grandfather Russell's side or Robin's, her mom would always stand with her grandfather.

"Robin, he's dead." Monica's hand was in hers. "Remember that. He's dead. He is not here. He cannot hurt you."

"Don't be ridiculous," Grandfather Russell scoffed. "I'm too busy for this nonsense." He started to walk back to the corner, into the shadows.

"NO." Robin gripped her pencil in one hand and cleared her eyes. "You are the one who doesn't belong here."

Her grandfather turned. "Mind your manners, Robin Marie."

Robin stood and walked to her grandfather. He wasn't as tall as she remembered. To a child, the domineering man had seemed like a giant.

"You don't belong here," she said again. "You need to leave."

Gordon lifted his chin defiantly. "This is my house."

"Not anymore." The weight on her chest lifted, and the choked feeling left her throat. "This is Helen's house. You need to go away."

Robin felt Val and Monica flank her on either side. Mark stood behind her.

"Go away," Robin repeated. "Leave Helen alone. You are not welcome here."

The ghost morphed from her memory of an older man to

the haughty visage of a young and angry one. "This is my house. I built this house, and every inch of it belongs to me." The corner of his cruel mouth inched up. "I don't know what you think you're going to do, Robin Marie, but it won't work. I built this house. I built this family. And you're never going to get rid of me."

CHAPTER 28

"Wrong," Robin said. "You're dead. You aren't welcome here." She stepped closer, Val and Monica on either side, herding the ghost toward the open window. "Leave, Gordon Russell. You are not welcome here."

He sneered. "This is my home." The handsome visage turned ugly and angry. "*My* home! I built it!"

"You built it from the blood of an innocent man and the life of a woman you didn't deserve." Robin blinked a tear from her eye. "You stalked Helen Moore. You murdered the man she loved. You lied to her and you tormented her son."

He lifted his chin. "This is my home. I'll *never* leave."

Be firm, Lily had said. *Remind them that they're dead. They don't belong with the living. Be firm.*

"Go away." Robin spoke forcefully and took another step forward. "You are dead. You are not welcome here. Leave Helen alone."

He smiled again. "She's almost mine."

The last shred of her patience snapped. The arrogance of

him! Even dead, they hadn't been able to escape him. "She will *never* be yours!"

The shadow wavered, and a light switched on in Robin's mind.

"Helen was *never* yours," she said quietly. "That's why you're so angry, isn't it? That's why you've never left her alone. You know she was never really yours."

The ghost flickered, just for a moment, and Robin knew she'd hurt him.

"She was never yours, Gordon Russell. She never loved you. Not like she loved Billy. The most she would *ever* give you was gratitude. Gratitude for saving her from a future that you ruined. And gratitude isn't love."

A wind whipped through the room, knocking over a candle in the corner.

"I'm on it," Mark said. "Keep doing your thing, Robin."

Robin kept her eyes on Gordon's ghost. "She loved Billy. She never stopped loving him. You could follow her. Spy on her. You could even kill Billy and marry her. But she never loved you. Not for a minute."

"You stupid, silly little girl," he said. "Shut your mouth. Children should be seen and not—"

"Seen and not heard, yeah, yeah, yeah." The outline of the ghost wavered, and Robin said, "Someone give me the sketch. He's trying to get away. What are you doing, Gordon? You running away from a little girl?"

Val shoved a paper in her hand and Robin clutched it. The outline grew clear again.

"Time to face your sins, Grandfather Russell. You didn't just kill Billy. You sent a postcard after he was dead so

Grandma would think the man she'd loved had abandoned her. And even after that, she still didn't love you."

"Get out!" the ghost shouted, and wind whipped through the attic. "Get out of my house!"

"Nope." Robin raised her chin. "Gordon Russell, you're dead. This is not your house. This is our house now."

"Is he leaving?" Monica said. "Lily said if you spoke firmly and clearly, he should leave."

"Yeah," Val said. "But I have a feeling that Grandpa Murderer isn't too keen on letting Helen go after he's been stalking her for over half a century. I have an idea."

Robin kept her eyes on Gordon's ghost, never looking away. She barely even blinked. "Val, if you have an idea—"

"Salt." Val raised the salt gun and fired toward the window. "Am I getting anywhere close?"

"A foot to the left."

"Fuck, this is so weird," Val muttered. She shot three rapid bursts of salt straight through the ghost's body. "Anything?"

"He's scowling at me and he winced a little," Robin said. "He doesn't like it. He moved another foot to the left."

Which put him right in front of the open window.

Monica raised her rosary and threw a handful of holy water toward the window. "Anything?"

"No, the salt seems to work better than the holy water."

The wind was picking up. It wasn't in gusts now; it was a steady breeze that was growing in strength.

"Monica, hand me that box of salt. I want to try something. Val, keep firing the gun. He really doesn't like it."

"Right!" A blue cardboard box was shoved in her hand.

Keeping her eyes on Gordon's ghost, Robin knelt down. "Mark, hand me the knife."

Gordon's eyes lit up. "Did you bring me one of my knives?"

"You're a pretty sick puppy," Robin said. "I remember where you kept this knife collection. Did you enjoy displaying the weapon you'd used to kill Billy Grimmer over the living room mantel?" Robin asked. "You hung a murder weapon on the wall over the mantel where you kept your wedding picture, you sick bastard."

Gordon's lip curled. "Language, Robin Marie."

Robin poured a circle of salt on the ground and set Gordon's sketch in it. "I bet you loved thinking about it, didn't you? I bet it killed you not to brag."

The ghost's face was transforming from something recognizable into something dark, shadowed, and twisted in rage. "What are you doing?"

"I asked you politely." Robin grabbed the knife in her right hand. "And you didn't leave. Aren't you the one who always stressed manners?"

"*What are you doing, Robin Marie?*"

Robin placed her hand firmly on the sketch in the middle of the salt circle, keeping it from blowing away in the whipping wind that filled the room. With the sketch firmly in the circle of salt, Gordon's ghost solidified. He stopped pacing.

"He's not moving anymore," Robin said. "The salt works on the picture too."

He might not have been able to move, but he could definitely move things. More and more candles tipped over. Mark hurried to each one, blowing them out before they could catch fire.

"You'd burn it all down, wouldn't you?" Robin asked, staring at the man who had haunted her grandmother, her mother, even herself, for so many years. "I spent forty-five years walking on eggshells because of you. Taking up as little room as I could because you raised a woman who feared you. And she raised her daughter the same way." Robin turned the knife in her hand. "No more."

She sliced a fine line through the sketch, across Gordon's neck, and the ghost grabbed his neck. "Just like Billy Grimmer," she murmured, watching the blood seep between Gordon's fingers. "I can't kill you like you killed him."

"Robin Marie," he hissed. "Get to bed. Children should be see— Ggrhg." The blood poured faster when Robin sliced again.

"Get out of this house, Gordon." Robin spoke clearly. "Leave Helen alone. Leave Grace alone. Leave all of us alone. We don't belong to you, and we never did."

Gordon's feet couldn't move, but he twisted and shuddered in agony.

"Leave, Gordon Russell." Robin picked up a candle and lit the corner of her sketch. "This is not your home."

He screamed in rage, but as the thick sketch paper burned, Robin saw smoke rising from his feet. Then his legs. His torso and his arms were enveloped in smoke.

"Robin Marie, don't you—" His mouth turned to ash, and the last thing Robin saw was a pair of angry black eyes staring at her through a veil of smoke; then the shadow twisted through the open window and it was gone.

Robin held her hand out. "Monica, you still have some water? I really don't want to burn the house down, and these candles are making me really nervous."

"Yep!" Monica tossed a water bottle at Robin.

"Is he gone?" Val asked.

"I think so."

Mark sprang toward the window, slamming it down. He grabbed the salt and ran a line along the windowpane. "Val, maybe that sage stuff?"

"On it." Val grabbed a bunch of sage and put it in a small bowl they'd borrowed from the kitchen. "I have no idea what I'm doing right now."

Robin poured water on the black, curling scraps of the sketch, soaking it.

"Don't blow on the sage," Monica said. "I watched some traditional healers on YouTube. Light it and let it smolder in the bowl. Let the smoke build, then move it over you, almost like you're washing with it."

"Okay?" Val scooped up smoke with her hands and waved it over her head. "Robin?"

She rose and used her hands to wash the pungent smoke over her body, scooping it and trying to picture the smoke pouring over her like water. "Monica?"

"I got it." Monica looked far more practiced. She'd obviously studied what to do. She murmured soft prayers as she smudged over her body. Then she picked up the bowl and walked to Mark. "Our faithful sidekick." She grinned and wafted the sage smoke over Mark.

"Let's get the room." Robin could already feel the difference in the attic. The earthen, moldy smell was gone, both from the fresh air from the window and the smell of the burning sage.

Monica walked around the entire attic, waving and spreading smoke in the corners and along the edges. By the time Monica returned to the center of the room, Robin was looking out the window, staring at the starry night sky.

"Did it work?" She glanced at Mark. "What do you think?"

"I mean... I'm not gonna lie, that was weird as hell." Mark nodded. "But whatever was in here—and there was definitely something in here—seems like it's gone."

"Let's clean up," Val said. "I want to go visit Helen."

WALKING DOWN to the third floor, they noticed the change immediately. Though the house was dark, the smell of baking wafted up the stairs and the air felt warm and cozy. Robin poked her head in the old nursery and saw the darkened room full of old toys and small beds. For the first time ever, she felt warmth and remembered laughter.

"He's gone." She reached for Mark's hand. "I think he's really gone."

When the four of them entered the kitchen, the only one awake was Lily.

The nurse turned wide eyes toward them. "Something happened upstairs."

Robin nodded. "I think the ghost is gone."

"Is it?" Lily looked around. "I felt something. Your grand-mother's room is warmer. I had to turn down her space heater."

"Did she wake up?" Robin harbored a faint hope that Grandma Helen's wavering consciousness was a byproduct of Gordon's interference. Maybe with Gordon gone...

"No." Lily smiled sadly. "In fact, according to the last

nurse's notes, she hasn't opened her eyes in about twelve hours now."

Robin bit her lip to keep from crying. She nodded. Mark put his arm around her shoulders, and she leaned into his embrace.

"I'm sorry," Lily said. "But remember, she's very tired. And she's been surrounded by love for days now."

"Can we go in?" Val asked.

"Raymond is in there, but I think he's sleeping in the recliner." Lily put a finger to her lips. "So just be quiet."

Robin and Mark, Val and Monica, entered Grandma Helen's bedroom, where a dim lamp cast a golden glow around the room. Raymond was sleeping in the corner, his grey head peeking out from under a yellow blanket. Helen was sleeping, and it was the most peaceful Robin had ever seen her.

The hospital bed they'd moved her to was partly raised, and Helen's mouth was curved into a slight smile. Her hands were lying on either side of her body, fingers relaxed. The wrinkles lining her face seemed to fade in the soft gold light.

Something flickered in the corner of her vision, and Robin turned her head.

Billy was leaning against a wall, watching Helen sleep. The look on his face was adoring and tender. "Isn't she the most beautiful thing you ever saw?"

Robin smiled. "She's pretty special."

"I know," Mark said, his voice just over a whisper. "She was the first person who welcomed me into the family. Do remember that? Your mom and dad were kind of suspicious, but she was the best. She was so confused about my job though." He smiled. "I think she still is."

Val and Monica dragged chairs from the sitting area so Robin and Mark could be close to Helen. Monica reached for the book on the bedside table and opened it. Val moved to the turntable to change the record.

Robin clasped Helen's hand and laid her cheek next to her grandmother's on the crisp cotton sheet. "Billy never left you, Grandma. I know you don't want to talk about sad things, but I want you to know that. He tried so hard to get to you and the baby." She looked over her shoulder at Raymond, who was still sleeping like a stone. "He loved you so much," she whispered. "He still does. He watched over you the best he could. I just wanted you to know that."

Grandma Helen took a deep breath and let it out, her mouth still curved in a smile.

Mark looked at Monica. "What was she reading?"

"A romance." Monica wriggled her eyebrows. "Looks like a pretty racy one too."

Mark shook his head. "She was always full of surprises."

Val leaned against the far wall, not far from Billy's ghost. "I think I want to be Grandma Helen when I'm old. Only I'm going to embarrass my children by having torrid affairs with much younger men."

"Embarrassing your children is the reward for raising them," Monica said. "Gil and I tried to embarrass ours regularly."

"I miss Gil," Mark said. "So damn much. Can you imagine how much better this would be if Gil were here?"

"I know," Monica said. "It pretty much sucks."

"Yeah," Val said. "Robin, have you ever—"

"I have never felt Gil anywhere." She looked at Monica. "And I never want to."

Monica frowned. "If he was hanging around here, I'd be pissed. I can take care of myself. The kids and I will be all right."

Billy's ghost moved from the corner to walk next to Helen's bed. "She's ready."

Robin bit her lip and fought back tears. She reached for Helen's hand as Billy stood over her and held out his.

Helen blinked her eyes open, sat up, and looked into his eyes. "You're here."

Her spirit rose and appeared in an instant, standing next to the bed, looking down at her frail body.

Her spirit, as Robin had always suspected, was in the vibrant prime of life.

"I've been waiting," Billy said.

"I know." Helen looked over at Raymond. She walked over and passed a ghostly hand over his forehead. "Do you see him, Billy?" Her voice was young and clear, brighter than Robin had never heard in life. "Isn't he beautiful?"

Billy was at her side, his own hand passing over Raymond's forehead. "He's wonderful, Helen. You raised a fine man."

"And my girl Grace." She turned to Billy with a brilliant smile. "She's so smart and funny. She's just the picture of my mama. I love her so much. You'd love her too."

"Of course I would," Billy said. "But I've been watching a long time, best girl. I'm pretty tired. You ready to go?"

Helen looked around and locked eyes with Robin, who was staring straight at her. "Look at you. And you thought you were ordinary."

Robin smiled and swallowed hard. "Goodbye, Helen. I love you so much."

"Extraordinary." Helen's face was glowing. "Simply... extraordinary."

Helen's and Billy's ghosts grew brighter and brighter. Robin closed her eyes, and when she opened them, they were gone.

CHAPTER 29

Six months later

April sunshine poured over the gardens at Russell House, casting shadows beneath the trees and flashing like diamonds on the wind-whipped surface of Glimmer Lake. The deep blue water was warming up, and Robin saw boats dragging water-skiers in the distance.

Mark shuddered. "Too cold."

"They're young and senseless," Robin said. "Hand me the hammer?"

"You got it."

They were building a gazebo in a far corner of the front lawn that backed up to the manicured forests that surrounded Russell House. In the distance, Jake Velasquez was painting the bright red trim on the boathouse that would finish the face-lift he'd given the entire dock.

When Monica had first approached Robin's mother with the idea of turning Russell House into a bed-and-breakfast,

Grace had been reluctant. She'd hesitated at the idea of partnering in a brand-new business when she was already retired.

But Monica's enthusiasm had convinced her. Russell House would be a bed-and-breakfast, an event venue, and the old house would uphold the tradition of the Russell family by adding something grand to the community of Glimmer Lake.

Plus, Robin added, Grandma Helen always wanted more people around.

"I think Grandma would have loved this." Robin squinted as a delivery truck rolled into the driveway, carrying yet another shipment of furniture. Grace and Robin were slowly sorting through the enormous house, picking out pieces they wanted to keep, antiques they would sell, and things that would be repurposed in the new inn. If everything went according to plan, the inn would be finished in time for Christmas.

When it was finished, Russell House Inn would have seven richly appointed master suites and seven smaller and more economical bedrooms with shared baths on the third floor. It would have a library and game room, a dining room with catering potential, and a formal room where guests could mingle, dance, or enjoy a cocktail after a day on the lake or the ski slopes.

The inn would be the perfect place for a destination wedding or a romantic getaway. The gardens could host lavish parties in the summer and sumptuous holiday gatherings in the winter. Russell Lumber's employee Christmas party had been their very first booking.

"You know," Robin said, "I never thought my mom and one of my best friends would go into business together, but they're kind of perfect."

"It probably helps that Monica has the uncanny ability to predict which things are going to work perfectly and which things would be a disaster." Mark winked. "That definitely helps."

Robin grinned. "True."

In the months since Grandma Helen's death, no sign of Gordon Russell's spirit had been detected in the house, but none of their powers had seemed to fade. Robin still saw the occasional ghost wandering around town, though none of them seemed particularly eager to talk to her and she could mostly ignore them.

Monica still had flashes of insight and the uncanny ability to predict exactly when a rain jacket was needed, even on seemingly sunny afternoons. She'd also bloomed with a new project on her hands. Jake had moved into Grandma Helen's old room and was the live-in handyman on the property, which gave him a steady job and allowed him to still keep in close touch with his mom. It was exactly the level of space Monica needed.

Val struggled with her abilities and had taken to wearing gloves pretty much all the time. Robin worried about her the most, but until they could figure out some way for her to tamp down or control what she was seeing, gloves were the only thing that helped. People asked, but Val had come up with all sorts of imaginative excuses for the unusual wardrobe accessory.

I've developed a circulation problem.

I'm filthy rich.

Have you heard about superbugs?

And pretty regularly: *I've developed psychic powers and*

can read the mind of anyone I touch. She always offered to shake people's hands after that. No one took her up on it.

But all in all, life for Robin had settled back into a seminormal pattern. She had exciting work with fun new challenges like helping to decorate a brand-new inn. She was painting again. She had friends who continued to be the best. And the worst. And the best. Her son was discovering his passion for art and finally finding purpose. And her marriage got better and better as each month passed.

Robin was even thinking she'd be okay when Emma left for Oregon State in the fall.

"Hey, honey?" Mark was scratching his forehead. "Didn't we measure this twice?"

"Nope." The little girl who lived in the forest sat on the edge of the gazebo, swinging her legs. "You told him to measure it again, but he didn't."

Robin glanced at her and winked. "I'm not sure. Is there a problem?"

"I think I cut it about an inch too short." He tugged on his baseball cap. "Man, I could have sworn I measured it twice."

"No big deal." She walked over and kissed his cheek. "It's just a two-by-four. We have a whole load of them. We can use the short one on the roof."

"Right."

The little girl skipped across the lawn in her billowing white nightgown, golden hair flowing behind her.

"Hey, honey?"

Robin looked up. "What?"

Mark looked at her, then followed her eyes; a smile touched the edge of his mouth. "Everything okay?"

Robin smiled. "Just the usual."

Mark gave her a grin. "Well, you can't say it's boring."

Is this my life?

Really? This? Every day until I die?

The sun flashing on the deep blue water of Glimmer Lake. Her husband working next to her. Ghosts dancing across the lawn.

"Nope." Robin smiled. "It's extraordinary."

Continue reading for a preview of Semi-Psychic Life,
Val's story and the next book in the Glimmer Lake series

FIRST LOOK: SEMI-PSYCHIC LIFE

*V*al was battling a headache that had been brewing since she'd woken up that morning. It was just her luck that Americano Asshole handed her a refillable coffee cup. One that he hadn't rinsed out. Of course.

"The usual," he said brusquely.

"Got it," Val said under her breath. "Anything else?"

There were baskets of fresh lemon scones on the counter, homemade energy bars, and decadent blueberry muffins that her baker, Honey, had made fresh that morning, but he ignored them all.

He was staring at his phone and fingering the zipper pull on his Patagonia vest. "Nothing. Just my usual."

The usual for Americano Asshole was a café Americano diluted with so much milk and sugar that it would be impossible to detect the subtleties of flavor between espresso and the regular brewed coffee Val had sitting on the counter.

There was a valued place in the coffee world for the café Americano, but not when you drank it like Americano Asshole. That's why he had his name.

"Café Americano, heavy cream, three sugars," Val said, ringing up the customer. He had a name, it was Allan Anderson, but nobody at Misfit Mountain Coffee Shop used it. He was Americano Asshole or AA for a reason.

Val reached for the silver coffee mug on the counter. She hadn't even noticed the hole in her glove until the flashing image of a woman pouring coffee into the mug filled her mind. The woman was wearing nothing but Americano Asshole's button-down shirt. The woman was also *not* AA's wife. Val knew that because he was married to a genuinely lovely woman named Savannah who came into Misfit every other Tuesday night with her book club.

The image was fast and graphic. It was as if Val had been plopped in the room with AA and his side piece for a split second, then yanked out.

"Shit." She sucked in a breath and AA looked up.

"Problem?"

Val plastered on a smile and swallowed the ream of curses she wanted to throw at him. "It's fine. Let me just rinse this out."

She turned and adjusted her glove to turn the hole to the back of her finger before she slipped up again. Then she went to rinse out AA's coffee mug so she could get back to the growing line at Misfit that morning.

It had been over a year since she'd experienced the car crash that had triggered her weird telepathic abilities, and most days she was able to live pretty normally. She only reacted to objects, not people. She didn't hear random voices or see ghosts like her friend Robin. She didn't have scary premonitions or graphic dreams like her friend Monica. All in all, she wore gloves at work and while doing chores around the house, and she lived pretty normally.

Most of the time.

She handed the rinsed cup to her barista Eve and turned back to the register to get AA's money for his Americano.

"Two seventy-five," Val said, worrying the hole in her glove. Touching money without gloves could be a nightmare.

AA noticed her glove and smirked. "You'd think with what you charge for coffee you could afford new gloves."

Eve sucked in an audible breath, and behind AA, the next customer's eyes went wide.

Val wasn't bothered. They called him Americano Asshole for a reason. "I try to coast on my wealth from twenty-five-cent tips like yours, but the struggle is real."

Ramon, her cook, barked a laugh from the kitchen behind her, and AA's eyes went cold.

"I'd give anything for a decent coffee shop in this shithole town."

Eve handed her the Americano and Val passed it over with a smile, along with the quarter AA usually left in the tip jar.

"But instead you're stuck with us. Bite me! And have a nice day."

He turned without dropping the quarter in the jar and Val flipped off his back before she turned to the next customer.

"Hey, Mom."

Marie Costa pursed her lips. "Honey, you really shouldn't treat customers that way."

"You worry too much. That guy's always in a bad mood." She handed her mom a coffee cup. "Dad coming in?"

"He's parking the car."

Val handed over another and pointed to the counter. "The counter is yours. Grab stools and Ramon will make up your usual."

"Thank you, Valerie." She pulled out her wallet and took out twenty dollars even though Val never took her money. She wasn't going to make her parents pay for their weekly coffee shop breakfast when they'd been the ones to loan her the start-up money to begin with.

Marie, knowing Val wouldn't take her money, put it in the tip jar, just like she did every week.

"And this is why my employees love you more than they love me." Val grinned.

"They're the ones cooking for me," Marie said. "Not you."

"And be grateful for that."

"Thanks, Mama Marie!" Ramon shouted. "You better grab one of those lemon scones Honey made."

"Oh, that sounds good." Marie's eyes lit up. "I do love Honey's scones."

"She's trying to make me fat, Marie."

Val and Eve both laughed at that. Ramon was thin and wiry, the kind of guy who ran marathons and couldn't put weight on to save his life. He was married to Honey, who was as sweet as her name and carried all the curves in the family.

Val grabbed three more coffee orders and passed them to Eve before there was a break in the line. Two more tables had seated themselves, and Max was already getting them set up with coffee.

Long before she'd been a mom or a telepath, Valerie Costa had dreamed of having a place like Misfit Mountain

Coffee Shop. She'd never gone to college, though she'd done administration courses at the community college in Bridger City. Instead, she'd married her high school sweetheart and spent her twenties partying up and down California with Josh, living for the next concert or road trip. Josh fixed cars and Val got jobs at whatever office was hiring and didn't mind someone with multicolored hair and tattoos.

Val tried lots of things. She worked in restaurant kitchens and accountants' offices. She worked as a landscaper for a while, then at a big coffee chain in her late twenties just to get medical benefits. Around that time, she started to realize that while punk rock life was fun, having a house and a retirement account might be kind of necessary.

It was during her coffee stint that she got pregnant with her oldest son, Jackson. Val was thrilled, and at first Josh was too. He made all the right noises and dressed their newborn son in punk rock onesies, combing his fine baby hair into a Mohawk.

Things got tense when kid number two rolled around. Though Josh liked the fun stuff about being a dad, he didn't do well with changing diapers, balancing work and parenthood, and losing his nights to crying babies. Punk rock parenthood wasn't punk rock life, and Josh started to stay out later and later. He didn't show up for school meetings, and more and more of his paycheck started going missing.

By the time Jackson was seven and Andy was three, Val knew he was fooling around. She confronted him. He denied it, then he walked out.

And that was that.

Val was a single mother of two with no college degree, no steady job, and no resources except great friends and family.

She decided she could work with that.

Her mother and father loaned her the money to start Misfit Mountain Coffee Stand. She brought her kids to work in the tiny coffee outpost while she figured out how to make better coffee than the chain she'd worked at. She stumbled and messed up a lot along the way, but she had a few things working in her favor.

Everyone in Glimmer Lake liked Val, even if they didn't get her. She was weird, but she had cute kids and she was Marie and Vincent's daughter. She made great coffee and always made you laugh.

A drive-through coffee stand turned into a café. Then Val met Ramon and Honey. Ramon was a kick-ass cook, and Honey was a baker. They'd grown up in Glimmer Lake but moved to the East Bay to work in the restaurant business, where they'd been happy. Then Honey's mom got sick and there was no one else to take care of her.

Ramon and Honey had been the spark that started the coffee shop. They weren't a full restaurant, and the menu was limited to what Ramon could get delivered and what he felt like cooking that day. Honey's baked goods became legendary. Along with Val's personality and coffee skills, they'd been making it work for about three years, but they weren't out of the woods yet.

Of course, it was Glimmer Lake. They'd never really be out of the woods.

And Josh?

He was around, but he wasn't. He flitted in and out of her boys' lives like a punk rock fairy godfather, missing for months, only to show up with brand-new iPads for everyone or professing his eternal love for Val after he'd broken up with yet another girlfriend.

Val ignored him. She had her two kick-ass kids, amazing parents, and the two best friends anyone could ask for. She had her coffee shop, a good tattoo artist, and was paying her own bills. Just barely, but she was making it.

Okay, and now she had weird telepathic abilities that were kind of complicating her life, but she could handle that. Probably.

JUST AFTER TEN O'CLOCK, Val's two favorite people walked into Misfit.

Robin, Monica, and Val were as different as three best friends could be. If they hadn't all been put in Mrs. Cowell's advanced reader group in fourth grade, they might never have been friends. But that reading group had turned into a lifeline in junior high school, then a united and unbreakable front in high school.

Val was the crazy and slightly dangerous one. Monica was the nurturing big sister of the group, and Robin was the planner with the heart of an artist. All three had married early, and Monica and Robin had both had their kids before Val. They'd seen each other through marriage, pregnancy and miscarriage, crying babies, hormonal teenagers, divorce, and death.

Monica waved Val over. She reluctantly handed the register over to Eve and walked to the corner table where Robin already had some notebooks spread out.

"I have fifteen minutes," Val said. "That's it."

"That works." Robin spread her hands on the notebooks as if she was bracing herself. "What do you think about opening a mini version of Misfit at Russell House?"

Val blinked. "That's sudden."

Russell House was Robin's family home that they'd de-ghosted the year before. Robin's grandfather had been haunting her grandmother and there was another ghost involved from a man her grandfather had murdered, and it was a whole thing.

But then they got rid of Grandpa Murderer Ghost, Grandma Helen passed peacefully, and Robin's mom and uncle were left with a giant house that neither knew what to do with, so Robin's mom and Monica had gone into business to turn the grand old house into a boutique hotel and event venue.

The first events had been hosted, but they were still working out the kinks on having real hotel guests.

"We've already nailed down baked goods from Honey," Monica said. "She'll be doing an exclusive Russell House scone for the room bakery boxes every morning. But then we were thinking, do we want to have coffee makers in all the rooms? Or would it be better to have an espresso bar in the lobby and do in-room deliveries?"

Robin tapped her fingers. "It would basically be a coffee stand like you started out with. The hotel would just pay you instead of the public. And you could make extra money during events."

Val perched on a chair. "Let me think about it. I like the idea, but I just went through that whole expansion drama last year that didn't work out, so I'm feeling a little wary, and also

—no offense—but I want to make sure I don't cannibalize my business here, you know?"

"Makes total sense." Robin slid a folder across the table. "I put a couple of ideas together for you to look at. Just some thoughts about how you could make it work *if* you wanted to." She shrugged. "I had time."

Monica and Val exchanged a look. "How's life without Emma?"

Robin's youngest had shipped off to university in Washington State the previous fall, leaving Robin and her husband Mark official empty-nesters.

"It's good. It was nice to see her and Austin over the holidays but..." Robin smiled. "It's also nice to have the house back to ourselves again, you know?"

Monica whispered loudly, "They're having freaky sex in whatever room they want now."

Val whispered back. "That's what I figured too."

Robin rolled her eyes. "Listen, weirdos, this is me and Mark, not..." Robin's eyes lifted when the bell over the door rang. "Oh hey, speaking of freaky sex."

Val whipped her head around, only to see Sullivan Wescott, sheriff of Glimmer Lake and the source of Val's headache, walking into the coffee shop.

She immediately spun around. "Shut up, Robin."

"I didn't say anything!"

"You were thinking it."

Monica raised her hand. "No, that was me, actually. I was the one suspecting you and Sully of having freaky sex."

Val hissed, "In what universe do I have the time to have freaky sex with anyone?"

"That wasn't a denial," Robin said. She held her fist out to Monica, who bumped her knuckles. "We were right."

"You're both ridiculous." Val glanced at her watch. "And your time is up."

Monica leaned over to Robin. "She's leaving us so she can get his order."

"Of course she is," Robin said quietly. "I mean, who else is going to make flirty eyes at Sully? She can't have Eve doing it. She's young enough to be his daughter."

Val turned, flipped both of her best friends off, then walked back to the register.

***The next Glimmer Lake book
is coming April 2020!*** *Please sign up for my newsletter
for more information about Glimmer Lake and my other
works of fiction.*

MORE PARANORMAL WOMEN'S FICTION

I hope you're enjoying this new genre as much as I am! And I really hope you're excited for Val's story, which is up next in the Glimmer Lake series. There will be more awkwardly psychic moments, more minivan shenanigans, and as always, more fun and friendship with Robin, Val, and Monica.

Looking for more paranormal fiction featuring women at midlife and later who are ready for adventure? Check out the amazing authors in the paranormal women's fiction genre at:

www.ParanormalWomensFiction.net

Books included:

Robyn Peterman, It's a Wonderful Midlife Crisis

Shannon Mayer, Grave Magic Bounty
Michelle M. Pillow, Second Chance Magic
Mandy M. Roth, Cloudy With a Chance of Witchcraft
Darynda Jones, Betwixt
Denise Grover Swank, Let It All Burn
K.F. Breene, Magical Midlife Madness
Eve Langlais, Halfway There
Jana DeLeon, Wrong Side of Forty
Deanna Chase, Witching For Grace
Kristen Painter, Sucks to be Me
Christine Gael Bell, Writing Wrongs

ACKNOWLEDGMENTS

First of all, to the ladies of the Fab13,

I appreciate and admire you all so much. Working on these books and promoting this genre with you has been an absolute blast.

To all the paranormal women's fiction readers, this book is dedicated to you. I hear you, I see you, and I'm one of you. The first forty-two years have been full of surprises, and I can't wait to see what the next forty bring.

A giant thank you to Gen and Jenn, my super twin assistants! You are both the best. Thank you for making my work possible. Thank you to Emily Kidman at Social Butterfly, who makes me look fancy and PR Ready. Many thanks to the Hunters' Haven team, Hannah, Meg, Tiffany, Danielle, and Fiona. You all do an amazing job and I am so grateful for the love and dedication you offer so generously.

To my independent publishing team, I want to offer even more thanks. **Amy Cissell** at Cissell Ink is my developmental editor extraordinaire. **Anne Victory** at Victory Editing is my line editor and (along with **Linda**, my proofreader) makes me look like a pro and not an amateur. Any typos you find in this have probably been added by my tinkering with things after they've tried to slap my hands. The cover artists at Damonza.com are responsible for the beautiful cover for Suddenly Psychic, and I could not be more thrilled with their work.

In the end, with all the ghosts and supernatural elements, this book is really about friendship. It's about how we deal with the unexpected things in life and who we turn to when things get weird. For that reason, I want to send a special shoutout to my real-life besties, sisters of the heart and blood, the ones I can always depend on, who have been there through life and death and work and marriage and kids and divorce and sickness and falling in love and starting over.

Genevieve, Kelli, and Marianne. I call you in the best times. I call you in the worst times. Thanks for always picking up the phone. I love you so much.

ABOUT THE AUTHOR

ELIZABETH HUNTER is a *USA Today* and international best-selling author of romance, contemporary fantasy, and paranormal mystery. Based in Central California, she travels extensively to write fantasy fiction exploring world mythologies, history, and the universal bonds of love, friendship, and family. She has published over thirty works of fiction and sold over a million books worldwide. She is the author of Love Stories on 7th and Main, the Elemental Legacy series, the Irin Chronicles, the Cambio Springs Mysteries, and other works of fiction.

ElizabethHunterWrites.com

The Elemental Mysteries

A Hidden Fire

This Same Earth

The Force of Wind

A Fall of Water

The Stars Afire

The Elemental World

Building From Ashes

Waterlocked

Blood and Sand

The Bronze Blade

The Scarlet Deep

A Very Proper Monster

A Stone-Kissed Sea

Valley of the Shadow

The Elemental Legacy

Shadows and Gold

Imitation and Alchemy

Omens and Artifacts

Obsidian's Edge

(novella anthology)

Midnight Labyrinth

Blood Apprentice

The Devil and the Dancer

Night's Reckoning

Dawn Caravan

(Spring 2020)

The Irin Chronicles

The Scribe

The Singer

The Secret

The Staff and the Blade

The Silent

The Storm

The Seeker

The Cambio Springs Series

Long Ride Home

Shifting Dreams

Five Mornings

Desert Bound

Waking Hearts

Dust Born

(Newsletter Serial)

Contemporary Romance

The Genius and the Muse

7th and Main

INK

HOOKED

GRIT

Linx & Bogie Mysteries

A Ghost in the Glamour

A Bogie in the Boat

Printed in Great Britain
by Amazon